Sarah's heart p
unnatural rhy

Even though she'd
moment was inevi
to scoop her daughter in her
door…before Reese realised she was his…before
Sarah saw that being a father didn't matter to
him, that he didn't care.

Sarah's gaze met his. His eyes flamed with the
fires of hell…shock…anger. It was all there, then
swiftly doused and gone, leaving behind only a
chilling emptiness.

He stood for an eternity, and Sarah waited. Then,
without saying a word, Reese turned his back on
her and walked directly out the door.

The slam of the door echoed the slamming of a
chamber in Sarah's heart, one she hadn't realised
was still open.

Dear Reader,

Welcome to this month's selection of Intrigues, and what an exciting month we have for you!

First, rising star Gayle Wilson returns with another of her ever-popular SECRET WARRIORS novels; *Midnight Remembered* is the last in the current series about former agents with new identities.

There's more mystery and suspense in our latest mini-series SECRET IDENTITY, where Debbi Rawlins gives us *Her Mysterious Stranger*—a sexy lawyer who is not what he appears to be meets his match with feisty Taryn Scott!

This month's LAWMAN LOVER is protective, sexy Sheriff Reese Walker from Carla Cassidy's *Fugitive Father*; he's discovered he's a father, and that his daughter and her mother are in danger—and he isn't going to lose them again!

Finally, Dani Sinclair returns with *My Baby, My Love*. Sydney Edwards woke up in hospital pregnant, a widow, the only witness to a murder and with a handsome man gazing down at her, vowing to protect her at all costs...

Enjoy!

The Editors

Fugitive Father

CARLA CASSIDY

SILHOUETTE
INTRIGUE™

First published in Great Britain 2001
Silhouette Books, Eton House, 18-24 Paradise Road,
Richmond, Surrey TW9 1SR

© Carla Bracale 1994

ISBN 0 373 07604 5

46-0801

Printed and bound in Spain
by Litografía Rosés S.A., Barcelona

CARLA CASSIDY

is the author of ten young-adult novels, as well as her many contemporary romances. She's been a cheerleader for the Kansas City Chiefs football team and has travelled the East Coast as a singer and dancer in a band, but the greatest pleasure she's had is in creating romance and happiness for readers.

To the members of MARA—
thanks for the support

Chapter 1

The shrill ringing of the phone rent the stillness of the night. Sarah Calhoun jerked upward, fumbling in the dark for the receiver, the pleasant dreams falling away as full awakeness abruptly claimed her.

"Hello?" she breathed sleepily into the receiver.

"Sarah?" The voice was faint but instantly recognizable. "Sarah, it's me."

Sarah gripped the receiver more tightly against her ear, her heart pounding an unsteady rhythm of dread as she heard the voice of her younger sister. She wouldn't be calling in the middle of the night unless something was horribly wrong. "Lindy, what's the matter? What's happened?" Sarah reached over and turned on the lamp on her bedside table.

"Mama's dead." The words, so simple, so stark, were followed by low sobs of despair.

For a moment there was a loud roar in Sarah's ears. She squeezed her eyes tightly closed, wishing she could hang up and crawl back into the peaceful oblivion of her sleep.

Mama dead? It wasn't possible, her brain protested. It *couldn't* be possible. It was the middle of the night. Lindy must be having a nightmare. Yes, that was it. *Lindy is having a nightmare...or perhaps I am,* she thought irrationally.

What Lindy had said couldn't be true. Sarah had spoken with her mother only the day before and she'd sounded fine. "Lindy, what happened?" she finally managed to breathe into the receiver.

"I don't know...she fell...she fell down the stairs...." A torrent of weeping made her words nearly unintelligible.

"Lindy? Lindy, talk to me." Frustration whipped through Sarah as her sister continued crying so hard it made conversation impossible.

Maybe she's mixed up, Sarah thought hopefully, still refusing to believe that her mother might be dead. Margaret Calhoun was spry, almost athletic. She wouldn't have fallen down a flight of stairs.

"Sarah?" This was a new voice, older but strong. "Sarah, it's Gladys Prather."

"Yes, Mrs. Prather?" Sarah gripped the phone cord more tightly, her hope suddenly fragile as she recognized the voice of the neighbor who lived on the place next to the Calhoun farmhouse. She wouldn't be at the Calhouns' at this time of night unless what Lindy said was true.

"I'm afraid, dear, that there's been a terrible accident. I came over this evening to check on your mother and Lindy. I often stop by when Ben is out of town." The woman hesitated a moment, then continued. "When I came in, I found your mother at the foot of the staircase.

She'd apparently fallen. She was dead, Sarah. Lindy was holding her, in a state of shock. I'm sorry for the lateness of this call, but until a moment ago I couldn't get Lindy to dial your number. Here's Lindy. She wants to talk with you again.''

"Sarah, please come home. I need you," Lindy cried, sounding much younger than her twenty-two years.

"Of course," Sarah replied numbly. "Of course I'll be there as soon as I can." She rubbed her forehead, trying to think, trying to get past the shock that made rational thought nearly impossible. "Where's Ben?"

"He's not here. He's got a case in Kansas City."

Sarah twisted the phone cord around her hand. "Lindy, are you all right? Have you taken your medicine?"

"I'm okay. I just need you here. The sheriff was here asking questions and I need somebody to help me with everything."

"Don't worry, Lindy. Everything will be fine. I'll get there as soon as I can."

It wasn't until she hung up that Sarah wondered if she hadn't spoken far too optimistically. My God, how could everything be all right with Mama dead? The horrible word whirled around and around in her head and she stared at the phone for a long time, grief mingling with regret and sweeping over her.

She fell back against her pillow, trying to absorb the fact that her mother was dead, gone forever. She felt the press of tears but willed them away. She had to be strong.

She pulled herself out of bed, knowing further sleep would be impossible. There would be time for her grief later. At the moment, there were a million other things to worry about. Lindy needed her. Her heart ached as she thought of her younger sister trying to handle all this alone.

Sarah padded into the kitchen and placed a teakettle of water on the stove. A cup of tea would help her think…help her prepare for the fact that she was going home.

Going home. How many times had she dreamed of her homecoming? Fantasized a joyous reunion with her mother and her sister? In the past six years they had often talked of Lindy and Margaret flying to New York, but somehow the plans never worked out. Lack of money, lack of time, illnesses—it seemed as if everything conspired to keep the reunion from happening. And now that reunion would never be possible.

Never had she thought that the event that would finally take her back home would be the death of her mother.

Her head ached as she realized that returning to Clay Creek brought with it a whole bundle of concerns. As she waited for the water to boil, she drifted out of the kitchen to the smaller bedroom next to hers.

Standing in the doorway, she looked at the little girl sleeping peacefully beneath the colorful rainbow motif blanket. Jackie—her daughter, her life…her secret.

Sarah walked quietly into the bedroom, smelling the lingering sweet scent of Jackie's strawberry bubble bath. She stood at the foot of the bed, her heart swelling with love as she gazed at the silky, dark hair splayed across the pillow, the spiky, dark lashes that shadowed childish cheeks and the full bottom lip that puckered slightly with each breath.

How could she go back to Clay Creek, Kansas, and keep Jackie's existence a secret? There were only three people in her hometown who knew about Jackie, and now one of them was dead.

She sighed, knowing the answer to her question. She couldn't return home and keep Jackie a secret. She pulled the blanket up more firmly around the little girl's neck, kissed her lightly on the forehead, then went into the living room and stared out the window of her sixth-floor apartment.

The streets below were lighted by the pinkish illumination of anticrime lamps. Beyond the faint glow was the dark silhouette of trees and bushes of the small neighborhood park.

She'd rented this apartment a year earlier because of the park. The rent was exorbitant but worth every penny to someone who longed for a touch of the countryside she'd left far behind. Besides, she'd wanted Jackie to know the feel of grass beneath her feet, the scent of nature in the air, the tactile pleasure of digging in a mound of mud.

Surely he's not in Clay Creek anymore, she thought. After all, it had been six years since she'd left. A lot of things happened in six years.

All he'd ever wanted to do was get out of that town, make a life someplace else. Most likely by now he would have achieved his dream of blowing the Kansas dust off his shoes.

Strange, there were times she had to really concentrate to bring her mother's features into focus, but his were always there, just under the surface of her consciousness, waiting to haunt her, mock her. And with each passing day, Jackie looked more and more like him.

No, there was no way to keep Jackie a secret. The minute anyone from Clay Creek got a good look at her, they would realize who her father was and the reason Sarah had left town so long ago.

The teakettle whistled shrilly, shoving thoughts of him away. The last thing she needed to do was worry about seeing the man who was Jackie's biological father. Yes, she was certain he would have left Clay Creek long ago.

Besides, she had bags to pack, airline tickets to purchase, arrangements that had to be made. Fixing herself a cup of tea, Sarah sat down at the table, her thoughts drifting back to her mother.

Gone…gone forever. There was still a sense of unreality in the words. Jackie would never get to meet her maternal grandmother. She would never know the quiet sense of humor, the loving hands, the gentle heart of Sarah's mother. The reunion that Sarah had put off, waiting for the right moment, the right circumstances, would never take place now. It was too late. She covered her face with her hands and finally allowed her grief to overtake her.

Reese Walker stood in front of the Good Morning Café on Main Street, the busiest place in Clay Creek following rainy weather that made it impossible for the farmers to work in their fields.

For a moment his gaze lingered on his reflection in the large plate glass window of the café. He grinned ruefully, still not accustomed to the respectable image that was reflected back.

His long legs were encased in a pair of khaki slacks and his broad shoulders were covered by a matching crisply ironed shirt. It was a far cry from the jeans and leather jacket that had been his "uniform" while growing up. Who would have thought…?

Reese pushed open the door of the café and was immediately greeted by the scents of freshly brewed coffee, homemade biscuits and frying bacon. The place was noisy with the sounds of people at ease with one another, clinking silverware, friendly chatter and raucous laughter.

Behind the counter that stretched the length of the café an attractive blonde poured a cup of coffee for a customer and a little old woman stood behind the cash register.

"'Morning, Reese." It was the old woman who greeted him and gestured to the leather stool opposite where she stood.

"'Morning, Anna." He smiled gratefully as she poured him a cup of the steaming coffee.

"Got a fresh, homemade doughnut that's got your name written all over it," Anna announced, setting a plate with the sweet before him.

"Ah, Anna, you spoil me," Reese said with a grin.

"Nah, they're bribes," Anna returned, her blue eyes twinkling brightly. "I figure if you ever have to write me a ticket for breaking the law, you'll remember all the mornings I saved you a little something special."

"I can't imagine what law you'd ever break. You don't drive a car, and most days you're here working twenty hours at least. The only thing I could possibly write you up for is being drunk and disorderly on Harvest Day." He grinned, remembering the town holiday two weeks earlier, when Anna had gotten her nose into old Doc Burwell's homemade punch. She'd entertained everyone with songs and naughty stories for the remainder of the evening.

Anna cackled with amusement, the skin around her eyes crinkling so deeply her eyes nearly disappeared. "I think Doc fed me that potent punch on purpose." She leaned forward across the countertop. ''I think the old fool was trying to get me drunk so he could take advantage of me.'' She sniffed indignantly, her eyes not losing a bit of their good-natured sparkle.

''The whole town has been buzzing, everyone wondering if Doc's ploy worked,'' Reese said with a laugh.

''Humph, let them just keep right on wondering,'' she snorted derisively. ''If the folks in this town didn't have somebody to gossip about, they'd all curl up and die.'' She grinned, then sobered slightly. ''Besides, from what I've heard in here this morning, everyone has found a new topic to chew on.''

''What's that?'' Reese asked curiously.

''Margaret Calhoun.'' Anna clucked sympathetically. ''That woman had more than her share of troubles in her lifetime, what with her husband taking off years ago, then Lindy's fits. Imagine, falling down a flight of stairs in your own home and dying.'' She shook her head slowly. ''Sad...so sad.''

Reese nodded. He didn't want to talk about the Calhouns. He didn't even want to think about them, especially one in particular. It had been difficult enough going out to the Calhoun farm yesterday for the first time in years, back where the memories were so palpable they had been physically painful.

Suzanna Wilcox, the blond waitress, joined them at the counter, shooting a flirtatious smile at Reese.

''Poor Lindy,'' Anna continued, shaking her head sadly. ''How's she ever going to get along without Margaret? Ben was in here day before yesterday, said he was on his way to Kansas City to handle a sticky divorce case. Has anyone been able to get hold of him?''

Reese shook his head. ''By the time I got around to talking to Lindy, she was so upset I couldn't get any answers out of her. She couldn't remember the name or the number where Ben was staying.''

"We still on for Friday night?" Suzanna asked, abruptly changing the subject.

Reese smiled lazily. "Nothing's changed in my plans.''

"Then you'll pick me up at my place around seven?" Suzanna leaned over the counter, the buttons of her white uniform open to expose the rounded tops of her ample breasts.

"I see several people with empty coffee cups," Anna observed. "Are you working for me or filling your social calendar?"

"Both." Suzanna laughed, grabbed the coffee server and left the counter.

"She looks at you like you're her favorite piece of pie and she's starving to death," Anna said in disgust.

Reese laughed, his gaze shooting to the buxom blonde. "Suzanna's all right. She and I are two of a kind. We understand each other.''

Anna snorted. "You aren't anything like her, and the sooner you know that, the better off you'll be." She poured him another cup of coffee, then paused and looked at him in speculation. "You know, Sarah will probably come back for the funeral.''

Her name was like a punch in the stomach and Reese drew in a deep breath against the unexpected sharp, jabbing pain. The sweet taste of the doughnut transformed to bitterness in his mouth. "I suppose she probably will," he finally said. "Although she didn't come back for Ben and Lindy's wedding last year." He shrugged. "Besides, whether she comes back or not doesn't have anything to do with me. Sarah and I...that's ancient history.'' He stood up suddenly. ''And I'd better get to work.''

''That's right. We can't have criminal characters running amok in Clay Creek. You'll be back later?''

''I always am.'' With a wave to Suzanna, Reese left the café and stepped outside into the cool autumn air. Criminal characters running amok. A grin of ironic amusement curled his lips as he climbed behind the wheel of his patrol car. Five years ago, he'd been the worst of the criminal characters in town.

For most of his life, he'd been on a collision course with self-destruction. It had taken a bullet in the gut and facing his own mortality to force him to take an objective look at his life and the anger that had eaten away at him for years.

He pushed these thoughts aside. Like Sarah Calhoun, it was all ancient history. He'd worked hard in the last five years to get his life together, earn the respect of the people in the town, overcome the reputation he'd once fought so hard to maintain.

He tightened his grip on the steering wheel, turning onto the gravel road that led to the Calhoun farm. He had questions that still needed to be answered concerning Margaret's death.

He hoped Anna was wrong. He hoped Sarah didn't come back here. She had no place here anymore.

How ironic it was that he'd always been the one who'd wanted out of this town, and he was the one who'd stayed and finally found peace. She'd loved Clay Creek, had never spoken of any desire to be anywhere else, yet one day without warning she had left and never returned.

Yes, it was ironic, and there were times when he thought he might hate her, first for having the guts to leave Clay Creek, but most for being able to leave him and never look back.

"Jackie, honey, don't put your feet up on the dash," Sarah instructed her daughter, who'd grown more and more antsy with each passing mile.

"When are we gonna be there?" Jackie asked, her voice holding the distinctive whine of overtiredness.

"Not too much longer now," Sarah replied.

"I'm thirsty. Can't we stop and get a drink?"

"It's only been a little while since the last time we stopped," Sarah said, trying to hold on to her patience. "Why don't you jump in the back seat and read your book?"

"Okay," Jackie agreed, although she sounded less than enthusiastic.

Within ten minutes, Sarah released a pent-up sigh of relief as she realized Jackie had finally fallen asleep. It was just after noon and already it had been a long day. They had caught an early morning flight out of New York and had landed at the Kansas City, Missouri International Airport by ten. Once there, they had rented the car for the three-hour drive across the Missouri state line into Kansas and to the farmhouse in Clay Creek.

It had been a difficult day for a five-year-old who thrived on routine. Jackie had been full of questions about the relatives she'd never met, the grandmother who had died. At least Jackie and her grandma had managed to talk on the phone to each other several times a month, Sarah consoled herself.

Sarah rolled down the window and allowed the cool autumn air to fill the car with its crisp, clean scent. She could smell the trees that lined the country road, the rich farmland that lay beyond, and the familiar smells caused a bittersweet ache to rise in her chest. With each mile that brought her closer to Clay Creek, the ache intensified.

Home. Oh God, how she'd missed it. The smells of the country, the sight of the rolling farmland, the small community where she had grown up. For six long years it had called to her in the night, beckoning her to return.

But she'd been afraid—afraid of what people would say, afraid of what they might think of her, of Jackie. She'd heard that you couldn't go home again, and she'd believed it.

Now it suddenly didn't seem to matter any longer. She didn't care what people would think. She didn't care what gossip might circulate. She was going home, and that's all that mattered.

She pulled the car off to the side of the gravel road, her attention focused on the large billboard that loomed out of what had once been the Johnson family's cornfield. She got out of the car and approached the sign: Future Site Of The Boswell Power Plant.

She squinted her eyes, searching out the spot where the Johnsons' house had once stood. In its place was a variety of heavy earth-moving machinery, all parked and waiting only the touch of a human hand to put them into motion.

The mark of progress, she thought with a scowl, kicking a beer can that lay discarded at the foot of the massive sign. She looked northward, able to see in the distance the two-story house that had been her home.

Maybe it's a blessing that Mama won't be around to see this, she thought, easily imagining how the steel-and-concrete power plant would mar the beauty of the fields. *It will make great scenery from the kitchen window,* she thought dryly, once again gazing at the farmhouse in the distance.

From this vantage point, the dwelling looked dark and foreboding. Not even the brilliant autumn leaves of the trees surrounding the house could brighten the aura of darkness that clung to it.

For a moment Sarah studied the structure where she had grown up, wondering if it really looked as forbidding as she thought, or if it was merely the fact that she knew her mother was gone that made her perceive the house as such.

It wasn't until moments later when she pulled up in front of the farmhouse that she realized it wasn't just the absence of her mother that colored her perceptions. Neglect would be apparent to a stranger. She stared at the house in dismay, shocked at its obvious state of disrepair. The once white paint was weathered gray and peeling. The screen door hung crookedly from one hinge, and one of the steps leading up to the front porch was broken in half.

It had always been difficult for the three female Calhouns to maintain the farmhouse. There had been too little money, too few hands and too much hard work. Sarah had hoped some of that would change last year when Lindy married Ben Watters. She'd been grateful there would be a man around the house to take care of the place, ease the burden on her mother. Things had changed all right. In the six years she'd been gone, they appeared to have gotten worse.

"Jackie, wake up. Honey, we're here." Sarah got out of the car and opened the back door. She smiled as Jackie mumbled incoherently but didn't wake up. Oh, to be a child and sleep that deeply, with no adult worries or concerns to interrupt, she thought. She scooped the sleeping child up in her arms and started for the house.

The steps leading to the front porch creaked and groaned beneath their weight, and she grabbed the wobbly handrail for support. The place looked deserted.

As she opened the front door, Sarah bit back the automatic impulse to yell for her mother. "Hello? Anyone home?" she called. "Lindy? Are you here?"

She walked in, wrinkling her nose as she smelled the familiar scent of old wood, lemon polish and an underlying mustiness. She made her way into the living room, squinting against the darkness of the room. She frowned as she saw that all the heavy draperies were pulled tightly closed so that not a single ray of sunshine could peek through. Shifting Jackie's weight from one side to the other, she opened the curtains. Where was everyone?

She placed Jackie on the sofa, where the little girl curled up, still in the deep throes of slumber. It was her habit to nap for a couple of hours each afternoon.

Knowing she probably wouldn't awaken for a while longer, Sarah left the living room. She went from room to room, opening curtains and calling Lindy's name. Everywhere she saw the remnants of her mother's life, frozen in time as if awaiting her imminent return—needlework in a basket, the floral apron on a hook by the oven, the bottle of rose-scented hand lotion she would rub on after doing the dishes. Sarah's heart ached with emptiness.

Sadness welled up inside her, but she knew her mother was gone and it was Lindy she was now worried about. Where was she? She'd sounded like a total basket case the night before.

Sarah's concern increased as she searched the rest of

the house and still found no sign of her sister. "Where can she be?" she asked aloud, staring out the front door.

Of course. The dogs, she thought suddenly. Her mother had told Sarah often about Lindy's dogs. Whenever Lindy was upset or worried, she always sought out the companionship of her animals. After checking to make sure Jackie was still soundly sleeping, Sarah headed for the dog pen beyond the back door of the house.

Lindy was there, in the middle of the large pen, surrounded by the animals with whom she'd always felt most at peace. It was an incongruous picture, the dark-haired, small-boned, frail-looking woman surrounded by three of the largest, strongest of dogs. At Sarah's approach, the dogs barked and jumped at the high fence that enclosed them.

"Sarah?" Lindy's blue eyes widened, then filled with tears. "Oh, Sarah!" She quickly let herself out of the dog pen and moved into Sarah's embrace.

Sarah wrapped her arms around her sister and hugged her tight, tears burning in her eyes. Too long…it had been far too long. She should never have allowed her pride and her fear to keep her away from home.

She released Lindy and stepped back to look at her. When Sarah had left Clay Creek, she had been seventeen and Lindy had been fifteen and just beginning to show the symptoms of her disease.

Margaret Calhoun had kept Sarah informed about the battle with Lindy's manic-depression and Sarah had been under the impression that it was being controlled by medication. However, as she gazed at her sister, clad in a wrinkled nightgown, her hair looking as if it hadn't even been combed that morning, Sarah knew that her sister wasn't in terrific shape. Was it her illness or was it the horrible events of the night before? She hoped it was the latter.

"You okay?" she asked, wrapping an arm around Lindy's shoulders as she guided her back toward the house.

Lindy nodded, even the small action seeming to take enormous effort. "I'm fine now that you're here. Everything is all mixed up. I just can't think. I couldn't handle everything…" Tears once again welled up in Lindy's eyes. "And I can't seem to stop crying.…"

"I'm here now, and we'll handle everything together." Sarah gave Lindy's shoulders a squeeze. Maybe it was just the shock of Mama's death and not the disease, she thought hopefully. But as she remembered the drawn curtains in the house, she knew it was more than a reactive depression—Lindy was on the verge of going under.

"Did you bring Jackie with you?" Lindy asked.

Sarah nodded. "But she's sleeping right now. You two will have plenty of time to get acquainted later. Right now we need to talk."

They walked in the back door and Lindy immediately slid into a chair at the kitchen table, as if she'd expended too much energy walking the short distance from the dog pen to the house. She ran a hand down the front of her nightgown. "I—I meant to shower and get dressed earlier."

"It's all right," Sarah said gently. "Have you eaten anything today?" Lindy shook her head. "Why don't I make us some lunch, maybe some soup and sandwiches. By that time Jackie should be awake."

"Where is she? Can I just see her? I promise I won't wake her up." For the first time since she arrived, Sarah detected a spark of life in Lindy's eyes.

"Sure," she agreed. Together the two women left the kitchen and went into the living room, where Jackie was still curled up on the sofa.

"Oh, she's beautiful," Lindy whispered, tears once again filling her eyes. She reached out a hand as if to stroke Jackie's hair, then froze suddenly, and Sarah saw that her gaze was now focused out the window where a patrol car was winding down the lane toward them.

Lindy turned to Sarah, the tears coursing faster down her cheeks. "Please...please don't make me talk to him. Not now. I can't. I can't talk to anyone. I just can't." Without waiting for a reply, Lindy turned and ran for the stairs, leaving Sarah to face whoever had pulled up out front.

Chapter 2

Even if a hundred years had passed, Reese would have recognized her anywhere…on any street, in any city of the world. He would have known that lustrous dark hair, the attractive heart-shaped face and those Calhoun eyes, so hauntingly blue they almost shimmered violet. He would have known the curve of her jawline, the swell of her breasts, the shapeliness of her legs no matter how many years had gone by.

At the sight of her, anger and resentment swept through him so swiftly, so suddenly, it nearly buckled his knees. Damn her. She was every bit as beautiful as she had been the last time he'd held her in his arms, the last time he'd made love to her. Damn her for coming back here and making him remember things better left alone.

"Sarah," he said in greeting, grateful that his voice was cool and didn't betray any of his tumultuous emotions. He approached where she stood on the porch.

"Anna wondered if this tragedy would finally bring you back."

She nodded curtly. "But only long enough to take care of things and settle the estate." She smoothed her skirt with one hand, then reached up to pull an errant dark curl away from her large blue eyes. "When I saw the car pull up, I expected Sheriff Taylor. I certainly didn't expect to see you."

"You've been gone a long time. Things change. Jim retired last year and I'm now the man in charge." He couldn't help the small touch of pride that deepened his tone.

"I'm surprised to see you here at all. I'd have thought you would have left Clay Creek long ago."

Reese shrugged and cast her a bitter smile. She looked so cool, so calm. If any memories of what they'd once shared lingered, they didn't faze her. Maybe he'd never been important enough to remember. Again anger swept through him and he swallowed hard to keep his composure. "I guess some of us just dream of leaving Clay Creek, and others actually do it."

She opened her mouth as if to say something, then seemed to change her mind and clamped it shut. She looked back at the house, her body radiating an inexplicable tension. She gazed at him once again, her eyes slightly narrowed. "What do you want, Reese? Why are you here?"

"I need to talk to Lindy. I've got a few questions I need to ask her. Paperwork…" He saw her slender shoulders stiffen.

"I'm afraid that's impossible at the moment. She's really confused and upset by all this. Can't it wait a day or two?"

Reese hesitated. He knew of Lindy's mental instabil-

ity. Over the last several years the whole town had wit-
nessed Lindy's bouts of manic-depression. He knew
there was no point in trying to talk to Lindy when she
was in a manic phase or deep in a depression. "What
about tomorrow? I can come back out here."

"No." She said it sharply, firmly. "I'll bring her into
town in the next day or two."

The questions he'd wanted to ask for years whirled
around inside him, but he refused to give them voice.
He didn't want to hear Sarah's reasons or explanations.
She'd disappeared out of his life as cleanly as a dream,
and perhaps that's all she'd ever been. In any case, it no
longer mattered. She was ancient history.

"Fine." Again she looked back at the front door. "I'd
better get back inside. As I said, Lindy isn't handling all
this very well."

Reese nodded and turned to walk away, then, as a new
thought struck him, he looked back at her once again.
"About your mother. She's been released to Walt Deca-
ter over at the funeral home. He's waiting for somebody
to make arrangements with him."

Her expression didn't change, and if not for the momentary flicker of pain in her eyes, he would have sworn
the thought of her mother's body lying unattended in a
mortuary hadn't fazed her. But he had seen the shaft of
raw pain and he fought a crazy impulse to gather her
into his arms.

Reese got back into his patrol car and slammed the
door more forcefully than necessary. Damn her hide.
He'd thought he'd gotten over her, thought his heart had
healed from the hurt she'd left behind when she'd disappeared from his life with no warning.

And maybe his heart was healed, but his body still
remembered the satiny feel of her skin, the scalding heat

of her caresses, the sweet nectar of her kisses. His body remembered every single time they'd made love…and he wanted to again. And that made him angry, so angry he trembled with the effort of suppressing the emotion.

As he drove back toward town, he wondered how it was possible to hate a woman so deeply, and yet want her so desperately at the same time.

Sarah sagged in relief, watching until the last dust particle from his tires had dispersed in the air. She closed her eyes and drew in a deep breath, trying to regain her composure.

She'd almost fainted when he'd gotten out of that patrol car. It had taken every ounce of her willpower not to show her shock—first at seeing him again, then at seeing him in that uniform.

Reese Walker was the sheriff of Clay Creek. She couldn't believe it. It simply wouldn't compute.

Thank God Jackie hadn't awakened and wandered outside while he'd been there. She didn't want Reese to know about her. He didn't deserve to know.

What was he doing still here in town? she wondered. She'd been so sure he would have been gone by now. He'd vented his hatred of Clay Creek and everyone in it so often. And what in hell was he doing in a sheriff's uniform?

When she'd first seen him getting out of the car, for just a single moment reality had seemed to fade away and it wasn't the patrol car parked before the house but Reese's souped-up, rusted-out Chevy. In her memory she could see him bounding up the stairs, clad in obscenely tight worn jeans, a white T-shirt and a leather bomber jacket. He'd smell like hot oil and lube grease and cold beer. And his eyes would burn with the fervor of repressed anger, shattered dreams and the passionate wildness that drew her to him with a force she couldn't fight.

He'd been like an angry bee, and Clay Creek the bonnet that held him tight. She'd known that he would eventually sting her, but she hadn't been able to resist his fiery appeal.

She shook her head, dispelling yesteryear's images, not wanting to remember the exquisite pleasure and the torturous pain that those memories always evoked.

As he'd approached, she'd noticed the changes that had occurred in him in the past six years. Although his hair was still the black of midnight, it was much shorter, neater now. His was a face chiseled by trouble, sculptured by anger's heavy hand, and time had only deepened those lines. Unfortunately, the deepening of lines simply added to his overall attractiveness.

The biggest change of all had been in his eyes. Those charcoal eyes had always held the glow of smoldering fire, but the eyes of the sheriff had been cool, with no hint of the old, wild tempest within. Still, it was a handsome face…dangerously so.

Some of us just dream of leaving…and others actually do it. A bitter smile curved her lips as she thought of his words. She hadn't just left. She'd been forced to leave.

She'd been seventeen years old and pregnant. Afraid of the town's censure, fearing Reese's anger, his rejection, she'd been forced to leave her family, her home. She'd had no other choice. She'd heard his opinions on marriage and children a hundred times and knew there was no way she could stay. So she had left the place she loved, and for that alone she would never forgive him. And she would never give him the opportunity to reject Jackie.

Jackie. Thoughts of her daughter drew Sarah back into the house. She was surprised to see Lindy sitting on a chair in the living room. She was dressed in a pair of jeans and a blouse, and her hair, although still lank, looked as if it had just been brushed. *She'll be all right,* Sarah thought hopefully. *Jackie and I can pull her up before she descends all the way down.*

"Is he gone?"

Sarah nodded, still shaken by the shock of seeing Reese again. "Why didn't somebody tell me he was still here?" she asked softly, hoping her voice didn't betray the tumultuous emotions that swirled inside her.

Lindy shrugged. "You never asked about him. Mama always told me not to mention him to you unless you specifically asked."

Of course she'd never asked. It hurt too much to think of him, let alone speak his name. "Is he married?" The words fell stiffly from her lips. She was instantly sorry she'd asked. What difference did it make?

"No. He dates Suzanna Wilcox quite a bit, but that's been going on for years and I don't think it's really serious."

The answer didn't surprise Sarah. He could put on a uniform, but that didn't change who he was. No commitments, no strings, that had always been Reese's way.

Lindy gazed at Sarah sadly. "You aren't going to stay, are you?"

Sarah knew immediately what Lindy was talking about. There had been moments on the trip back when Sarah had thought she might come back to Clay Creek to stay. She'd envisioned settling back here, resuming the life she'd had before her pregnancy. She'd missed it so desperately and would have loved to raise Jackie in the small-town atmosphere. But now that she knew Reese was still in town, there was no way she would make her home here.

"I'll stay as long as you need me…long enough to get everything settled."

Lindy sighed. "I'd hoped you'd be home for good." She leaned her head back against the chair, looking scarcely older than she had at fifteen. "I used to stay awake at night, plotting ways to get you to come back home. I missed you so much, and felt so lost without you. I would have done anything to get you back here." She looked down at her hands, then up at Sarah. "Especially lately I've needed you here. Mama and I hadn't been getting along very well and Ben is having an affair."

Sarah gasped in surprise. Although she had never met her sister's husband in person, she'd spoken to him by phone many times. Margaret had always told Sarah what a wonderful man he was, so patient and so obviously in love with Lindy. "You must be mistaken," Sarah protested. "What makes you think he's having an affair?"

Lindy shrugged her shoulders helplessly. "I just know." Her eyes filled with tears. "I don't know who with…but I know he doesn't love me anymore. He's tired of me, of my craziness."

"You aren't crazy," Sarah scoffed. However, she wondered if what Lindy said about Ben was true, or if it was merely her sister's depression talking. "When do you expect Ben home?" she asked.

"I'm not sure. He's handling some big divorce case in Kansas City."

"Does he know about Mama?" Sarah asked.

"I had the phone number where he's staying and I

looked everywhere for it last night, but I couldn't find it." Lindy sighed. "He'll probably call tonight. You'll tell him, won't you? I can't." Lindy stood up. "In fact, I think I'll go up and take a nap. I'm tired...really tired."

Sarah wanted to protest. She knew Lindy was on a downward plunge, descending into the blackness of one of her depressions. But she didn't know what to do to stop the progression, and Lindy did look exhausted. "Okay. While you nap, I think I'll head into town and take care of things for the funeral."

"I'm glad you're here," Lindy said, then moving like an old woman, she went up the stairs and disappeared into her bedroom.

When she was gone, Sarah got up and walked over to the living room window. She'd always loved the view from here. There was nothing but nature as far as the eye could see. Huge oak and maple trees dotted the landscape, reaching out their massive limbs, their colorful autumn leaves whispering into the wind.

She squinted her eyes, spying the tree—her tree—that had provided hours of solitude when she needed to think. It was an ancient oak with gnarled limbs that created a cradle of sorts in the center.

She'd have to show Jackie the tree tomorrow. She'd love it. After several trips to the neighborhood park, Sarah had discovered that her daughter was a natural-born tree climber. She was long-legged and agile as a monkey.

Sarah turned and looked at her daughter. She needed to go into town and make the arrangements with the funeral home, but she didn't know what to do with Jackie.

What difference would it make if Reese saw her or not? a caustic inner voice asked. He'd know at first sight she was his—she was a feminine replica of him. But it wouldn't make any difference. She and Jackie wouldn't be in town long enough for Jackie to know that Reese was her father and didn't want anything to do with her. And that was why there was now absolutely no way in hell she could ever come home again. She wouldn't let Jackie feel the pain of Reese's rejection.

But she wasn't willing to spend the next couple of days hiding Jackie away like some horrible, embarrassing secret.

Initially, with Reese's baby inside her, she'd been scared to death with thoughts of responsibility and the future. She'd considered all the options to the pregnancy but couldn't follow through on any of them. In truth, she'd wanted the baby…Reese's baby.

Finally, early on a Wednesday morning after fifteen hours of labor Jackie had been born. The doctor had placed the baby at Sarah's breast, and as those new eyes had gazed into hers, she'd felt the bond, the eternal connection that would make her walk through fire, face any obstacle to keep her daughter safe and loved.

Yes, she loved Jackie, wanted her to see her roots, the town where her mother had grown up. And because of her love for Jackie, she would make certain the child never had anything to do with her father.

''Mommy, are we there?'' Jackie sat up and rubbed her eyes as if pulled from her sleep by her mother's reverie.

''Yes, honey, we're here.'' Sarah sat down next to her daughter.

''Where's Aunt Lindy and Uncle Ben?'' For so long, all of Jackie's contact with family had been by phone. Sarah wasn't surprised that she was anxious to actually meet the only family she had.

"Uncle Ben is out of town for a little while and Aunt Lindy is taking a nap," Sarah explained.

Jackie's eyes widened. "Aunt Lindy takes a nap just like me?" she asked incredulously.

"Just like you." Sarah laughed and touched the end of Jackie's nose. "How would you like to go into town and eat lunch at the café?"

"Can I get a grilled cheese?" Grilled cheese was one of Jackie's favorite foods and she ate it whenever possible.

"I'm sure they can handle that," Sarah assured her.

Fifteen minutes later, Sarah and Jackie were back on the road again, heading the five miles into the small town of Clay Creek. As they traveled, Sarah pointed out different places of interest to Jackie—the barn where she and her friends had played in the hayloft as kids, the creek where she caught her first fish, the pasture where they often played impromptu games of baseball. She didn't point to the blackberry bushes where her mother used to take Lindy and Sarah to pick berries for jelly, and she didn't point out Miller's pond, where she and Reese had parked so often…where Jackie had probably been conceived. At the moment, those places brought with them too much pain.

As they entered the town and drove down Main Street, Sarah felt a sense of satisfaction that it was all almost exactly as she remembered it. As she pulled into a parking space in front of the Good Morning Café, for the first time since arriving in Clay Creek, she felt a welcomed warmth seep through her. She'd spent many happy hours here in the café.

As she and Jackie entered the restaurant, she was instantly assailed by sounds and scents that evoked bittersweet nostalgia.

"Well, bless my soul," a familiar voice cracked with emotion. "If it's not my girl finally come home."

Before Sarah could respond, she found herself in Anna's embrace. The old woman smelled of cinnamon and fried potatoes...and love. "I'm sorry about your mama, honey."

Sarah nodded and clung to her, her heart swelling with love for the woman who'd been like a second mother to her. For a moment, regret stirred inside Sarah. She should have stayed in touch with Anna over the years. Sarah had been so heartbroken, first in leaving Clay Creek, then so caught up in the mere act of surviving as a single parent in New York City. She'd also instinctively known that thoughts of Anna would always bring with them painful memories of Reese, and ultimately that's what had made Sarah not stay in touch with the old woman.

"Let me take a good look at you." Anna held her at arm's length and Sarah saw that the old woman's gaze was as keen as ever. "Ah, Sarah, you were always a looker, but you've only managed to get prettier."

Sarah blushed and Anna smothered her in another hug. "Anna, there's somebody with me I'd like you to meet." Sarah turned around and placed her hands on Jackie's shoulders, pulling the little girl from behind her. "Anna, this is my daughter, Jackie."

Sarah saw the shock that swept over Anna's face— shock followed by instantaneous recognition. "Well, blow me over," she whispered softly. She dabbed at her eyes, then crouched down to look at Jackie. "Hi, sweetie. I'll bet you're a chocolate milk drinker."

"It's my favorite," Jackie agreed shyly.

"Let's get you two a booth and see if we can't rustle up some chocolate milk for this little sugarplum." As

Anna led them to a booth in the back, Sarah could feel the questions bubbling inside the old woman, questions she knew sooner or later she would have to answer. But at the moment all she wanted to do was enjoy some of Anna's home cooking and eat a pleasant lunch in the familiar surroundings.

They placed their orders, then Anna slid into the seat next to Jackie and grabbed Sarah's hands across the table. "So tell me, how are you getting along in that god-forsaken city of New York?"

"Okay. We get by."

"I suppose you've got some fancy dancy city man who keeps you jumping."

Sarah laughed. "No, no man. Just Jackie and me."

"Mommy and me are best buddies," Jackie quipped.

"I'll bet you are, sweetie." Anna gave the girl a quick hug. "You know, your mama used to come in here all the time, and she loved chocolate milk, too."

"She did?" Jackie looked at her mother as if trying to imagine her young. She giggled.

"She even worked for me when she was in high school. She was the best waitress I ever had."

"That's what Mommy does in New York," Jackie said. "Sometimes she lets me come to work with her and I get to eat anything I want."

"Yes, but waitressing here and in New York City are two very different experiences." Sarah smiled, remembering those days and nights of working in the café. She'd hurry here directly from school, eager for the tips that would line her pocket. She wasn't sure what she was saving for, but she had a nice nest egg started and knew eventually she'd be able to buy something wonderful.

Around nine o'clock Reese would come in to pick her

up after work. He always showed up early and would sit at a booth in the back, his gaze hot and hungry as it followed her. And she would try to hurry out the last of the customers, anxious to be in his arms. God, it had been the one period in her life when she'd suffered a severe case of temporary insanity. She'd thought she could be enough for Reese, thought she could make him whole. God, she'd been a foolish child living in a world of dreams.

"There's your orders. I'll be right back." Anna jumped up and went to the counter.

"I like her. She's nice," Jackie observed as Anna left.

Sarah smiled. "Yes, she's very nice."

Anna returned moments later with Jackie's grilled cheese and milk and Sarah's meat loaf special and iced tea.

"Oh, Anna, nobody cooks like you. I think I missed your meat loaf as much as anything," Sarah said a moment later as she tasted her meal.

"If you moved back here you could have my meat loaf every day."

Wistfulness welled up in Sarah's chest, pressing hard against her heart. "No, I can't come back here. The price is much too high." Her gaze lingered on her daughter, who'd quickly polished off most of her sandwich and milk and now had a frothy chocolate mustache on her upper lip. "Use your napkin, honey. You have a mustache."

"I do?" Jackie peered into the shiny chrome surface of the napkin holder and giggled at her distorted reflection. "Can I have a quarter?" she asked, gazing longingly at the jukebox in the corner.

"Okay, just one." Sarah dug into her purse and handed her daughter the coin, then watched as Jackie scampered to the jukebox, where she couldn't read many of the song titles but knew her favorites on sight.

"She's the spittin' image of—"

"I know." Sarah cut Anna off before she could say his name. She didn't want his name mentioned aloud.

"Well, she sure explains why you hightailed it out of here years ago without a word to anyone."

Sarah shrugged. "At the time it seemed the only answer. I knew I couldn't stay here and see him every day. I knew he'd somehow feel like he had to marry me and he'd grow to hate me. Mama made the arrangements and I lived with my Aunt Karen for a couple years, then finally got a place of my own."

"Have you seen him yet?" Anna asked.

Sarah nodded, knowing immediately who she meant. "He came out to the farm earlier. He wanted to talk with Lindy, but she's in no shape to talk to anyone."

"Then you know he's the sheriff now."

Sarah laughed, a harsh sound that rang hollowly in her own ears. "What a surprise. The boy everyone thought most likely to end up in the state pen is now protecting the good folks of Clay Creek."

"He's good at his job."

Sarah laughed again. "He would be. Who else knows the mind of a criminal better than a man who spent most of his life as a juvenile delinquent?"

"He's changed, Sarah," Anna said softly.

Sarah held up a hand. "Please, spare me the details. I'm not interested. I don't need him and neither does Jackie."

"Did you ever stop to think that maybe he might need you two?" Anna's eyebrows danced upward.

"That'll be a cold day in hell," Sarah exclaimed. She shoved her plate away, the topic of conversation effectively killing her appetite. "The day that man needs any-one is the day I need two heads."

"Has he seen Jackie yet?"

"No, she was napping when he stopped by earlier."

"Well, grab a head and pull up a couple of hats—you're about to be part of a family reunion of the first kind." Anna gestured toward the door, where Reese had just walked in.

He smiled at Anna, nodded curtly to Sarah, then slid onto a stool at the counter.

He seemed to fill the entire place with his presence.

Sarah looked over to where Jackie still stood at the jukebox. Her heart suddenly felt too big for her chest. Her head pounded with an unnatural rhythm. Even though she'd known instinctively when he'd stepped out of the patrol car earlier in the day that this moment was inevitable, she had a sudden desire to scoop Jackie up in her arms and run for the door...before he realized she was his...before she saw that it didn't matter to him, that he didn't care.

Everything had gone into slow motion. Each and every sound in the café was magnified as Sarah waited for her own personal moment of reckoning.

She heard the clink of silverware from a nearby table, the distant sizzling sound of meat hitting a hot grill, the squeak of Reese's stool as he swiveled around at the same moment that Jackie turned away from the jukebox.

"Mommy, they've got lots of good songs. Can I have another quarter?" Her voice seemed to echo as she came running back to the table, her eyes—the same shade as her father's—glittering with excitement.

"Okay," Sarah said, digging into the bottom of her purse, studiously keeping her gaze away from Reese. She gave Jackie another quarter, then watched as the little girl ran back to the jukebox. Only then did Sarah slowly turn to Reese.

Her gaze met his and she realized the tempest was back. His eyes flamed with the fires of hell. Shock. Anger. It was all there, then swiftly doused and gone, leaving behind only a chilling emptiness.

He stood, his gaze never leaving hers, and for a moment Sarah felt as if the entire café had vanished around them, leaving the two of them completely alone, isolated from the rest of the world.

He stood for an eternity and Sarah waited, knowing somehow this was a moment she'd dreaded for a very long time. Then, without saying a word, he turned his back on her and walked directly out the door.

The slam of the door echoed the slamming of a chamber in Sarah's heart, one she hadn't even realized was still open.

"You okay?" Anna asked softly, her eyes bright with sympathy.

Sarah nodded. Even though she had expected his reaction, the hurt still surprised her. Knowing she'd been right all those years ago didn't stifle the sudden sob that choked at the back of her throat. She raised her hand to her throat. She wouldn't cry. Not in front of Anna, not in front of Jackie. She drew in a deep breath, trying to control her emotions.

Making the painful decision to leave town and never return six years ago had definitely been the right choice. She wouldn't raise Jackie in a town where her father lived, where she would eventually grow old enough to realize he didn't want her.

As music filled the air and Jackie ran back toward the table, Sarah was grateful that the little girl would never know that her father had just turned his back on her and walked away.

And that's exactly what Sarah had expected. What she hadn't expected was that, after all this time, it would still hurt so much.

Chapter 3

It was too nice a day for a funeral, Sarah thought as she stood at her mother's grave site. Somehow it would have felt more appropriate if the sky had wept rain or the wind had blown with death's cold breath.

However, the sun was brilliant, using the last of its fall rays to warm the mourners gathered at the Clay Creek Cemetery. Overhead in the boughs of a huge oak, a bird chirped a cheery song, as if unaware of the human drama being played out beneath the tree.

A huge crowd of people had gathered to say their last goodbyes to Margaret Calhoun. Sarah wasn't surprised. Margaret had been well liked, and besides, funerals were always social events in the small town. It was an opportunity for neighbors to visit, offer comfort and be grateful it wasn't one of their own being buried.

As Reverend Creighton droned on, Sarah looked around her, desperately seeking any diversion from the grief that swelled oppressively inside her. She noted the changes that had occurred in the people from her youth. The young had matured with the passing of years, and the old had become ancient.

Mrs. Wilton, the woman who'd manned the post office for as long as Sarah could remember, was now in a wheelchair, her left side paralyzed by a recent stroke. Mike Johnson, the little boy she had occasionally baby-sat, stood tall and proud, wearing a high school letter jacket bedecked with football medals.

She also recognized Suzanna Wilcox. She'd gone to school with the buxom blonde, although Suzanna had been two years ahead of Sarah. And if she remembered correctly, Suzanna had once had an enormous crush on Reese—as had most of the girls in town. She frowned as she remembered Lindy telling her that Suzanna and Reese were dating. She wondered if Suzanna knew that getting a commitment from Reese was like wringing water from the desert. Impossible.

Reese…he'd arrived in the patrol car moments before and had taken a position at the back of the crowd opposite where Sarah stood. She shook her head, not wanting to look at him, not even wanting to think about him. She hadn't seen him since the day before, when he'd stomped out of the café without a backward glance. Bitterness welled up inside her as she thought of him and the way he had run out the door, as if running away from her and the reality of his daughter.

She swallowed hard and looked over to where Lindy leaned weakly against her husband, her eyes red and swollen with the tears that seemed to come from a bottomless well.

Ben was a tall, lean man with hair already thinning and eyes the color of a muddy stream. Sarah had finally managed to contact him at his hotel in Kansas City. He'd arrived at the farm late last evening and he and Sarah had spent most of the night getting acquainted and talking about Lindy.

She knew little about Ben Watters, only that he was thirty-three years old and had moved to Clay Creek two years before. He'd met Lindy during a time when she'd been fairly stabilized on medication. Even though Sarah didn't know him well, she found it difficult to believe he might be having an affair. She couldn't doubt his concern, his obvious love for Lindy. Surely the affair was just a figment of Lindy's imagination, a symptom of her mental state.

"Let us pray…" Reverend Creighton intoned, obviously winding down. Sarah bent her head and squeezed her eyes tightly closed. She still couldn't believe her mother was gone. She knew sooner or later the reality would hit and she would grieve long and hard. But for the moment there was a sense of unreality about the whole thing, and the knowledge that she had to remain strong for Lindy.

She looked back at her sister, worry deepening. There was no doubt that Lindy was settling into a dark depression. They'd had to physically pull her out of bed this morning and help her dress to attend the funeral. She was noncommunicative, without energy.

Despite Sarah's own misgivings and her desire to leave as soon as possible, she had offered to stay with Lindy until Ben finished up his trial in Kansas City. Ben had protested, telling her he could get somebody to take his place for the remainder of the trial, but Sarah had insisted, knowing she couldn't leave Lindy in her present condition. And she had to stay until whatever estate there was had been settled. Besides, she wanted to spend time with the sister she'd left behind. She needed to make a connection with Lindy. She wanted to help if she could.

As Lindy's sobs increased, Sarah was grateful that Gladys Prather had offered to baby-sit Jackie so the little girl wouldn't have to attend the funeral. Gladys often baby-sat her six-year-old granddaughter and insisted the two girls would get along famously.

Against her will, Sarah looked up at Reese. She breathed inward sharply as her gaze met his. He didn't look like a man who'd come to pay his last respects. His shoulders were set, his jaw taut, and his eyes burned with the same fire that had once been so magnetic, so dangerously appealing. He looked like a man who'd come spoiling for a fight. He held his hat in his hands, working the rim with his blunt fingertips as if imagining it was her slender throat instead.

Sarah once again averted her gaze from him, a chill of apprehension sweeping through her. One of the things that had always intrigued her about Reese was his unpredictability. Now it didn't intrigue her. It frightened her. Of all the emotions she'd expected from him, she hadn't expected his hard, cold anger.

He probably thinks he has a right to be angry, she thought bitterly. *He probably sees Jackie as an embarrassment, an unwanted remnant of his past wild life.* There was nothing like an illegitimate child to darken the sterling character he'd obviously been trying to build for himself.

Without willing it, she looked at him again, his gaze still hot and angry as it remained fixed on her. Suzanna said something to him, but he appeared not to hear her. He didn't move, he didn't answer. He simply continued to glare at Sarah.

She breathed a sigh of relief as the ceremony came to

an end and people began milling about. She was anxious to get back to the farm, anxious to be with Jackie and away from Reese's accusing stare.

"Sarah, I'm so sorry about your mother," Suzanna Wilcox said, coming to stand next to Sarah and bringing with her the cloying, sweet scent of her perfume.

"Thanks, Suzanna."

"It's a shame it's something like this that finally brought you back here."

Sarah nodded, deep regret forming a lump in her throat too big to speak around.

"I heard you have a daughter." Suzanna was unable to mask the open curiosity in her tone.

Sarah forced a small smile. "I had a feeling it wouldn't take long for that fact to circulate."

Suzanna laughed. "You should know there are very few secrets around here."

"You okay, honey?" Anna came up on the other side of Sarah and put an arm around her shoulder.

"Fine," Sarah answered. She nodded goodbye to Suzanna as the blonde moved away. "Are you coming out to the house?"

"You know most everyone will," Anna replied with a nod. "Besides, I baked a big ham to bring out. That and a tub of potato salad should be enough to feed everyone who shows up."

Sarah kissed the old woman on the cheek. "Thanks, Anna."

"It's the least I can do for the very best waitress I ever had." Anna hugged her.

Sarah released the old woman and scanned the crowd. Reese had disappeared. Good, she thought, breathing a sigh of relief. "Mama had a lot of friends."

"Your mama was a wonderful woman, a strong

woman," Anna observed. "She had more than her share of troubles, but she always had a helping hand for others in need. She'll be sorely missed around here."

Sarah smiled, the smile dropping into a frown as she saw her brother-in-law talking to an older, distinguished-looking man she didn't recognize. "Who's that with Ben?" she asked.

Anna looked over at the two men, her eyes narrowed in displeasure. "That's Raymond Boswell, the owner of the power plant operation."

Sarah watched as Ben and Raymond shook hands, then Ben approached Sarah. "The car's ready to leave," he said, his brow seemingly permanently wrinkled with worry. "We need to get Lindy home."

She nodded, told the others goodbye, then followed him to the car, where Lindy immediately wrapped her arms around her. As Sarah held her sobbing sister and remembered the arctic anger in Reese's eyes, her own grief for her mother buried someplace deep within her, she suddenly felt overwhelmed. She had a dead mother, a mentally unstable sister, a brother-in-law she hardly knew and an old lover whose eyes had promised something unpleasant. Things were flooding out of control. It was as if she'd been caught in a fast-running stream that was carrying her toward a deadly waterfall. As she rode the turbulent waters of fate, she knew there was no way she'd avoid the devastating plunge. In fact, she felt as if she were already on the verge of drowning.

Reese stood near the back door of the Calhoun kitchen, wondering why in hell he'd decided to come here. The place was packed with people—friends and neighbors bringing food and platitudes of sympathy, all the town gossips looking for a new morsel to chew on. Today they'd hit the jackpot.

He could feel the furtive glances, cast first at him, then at the little girl who stood at Sarah's side. He saw them whispering, felt their speculation. He stiffened his shoulders, again wondering why in the hell he had decided to come here.

He kept his own gaze averted from the child. To look at her was to give her substance, and he wasn't prepared to do that until he could pick through the assorted emotions that railed inside him. At the moment he couldn't seem to get beyond anger. It ripped at his insides, tore at his guts, keeping all other emotions at a distance.

For the first time in years he longed for a beer—a dozen beers, enough to anesthetize himself against the burning rage inside him. It was this rage that had made it impossible for him to speak to anyone at the cemetery.

He'd liked Margaret Calhoun, had respected her, and it was that respect that had brought him to the funeral. But he'd been unable to focus on anything except Sarah and his incredible anger. How could she? How could she keep a secret like the child to herself for so long? How *dare* she!

His thirst fled as quickly as it had appeared, gone with the knowledge that a dozen beers wouldn't straighten out his rage, only give him a hangover as a partner to his anger.

"You look like you've got a burr in your britches."

Reese turned at the sound of the familiar deep voice, offering a tight smile to Jim Taylor, the former sheriff and the man who, over the past several years, had become his mentor and friend.

"Funerals always put me in a foul mood," Reese replied.

Jim grinned knowingly, his wrinkled face furrowed with seventy-two years of living, fifty in law enforcement. "That's an acorn that didn't fall far from the tree." His grin widened as he looked at Jackie. "Funny how the past has ways of jumping up and biting you in the butt."

"Only if you let it," Reese replied. Again he felt his anger bubbling within him, stirring him to depths of emotion he'd forgotten he was capable of. "I'm going to get some air." Without waiting for a reply from Jim, Reese opened the kitchen door and walked onto the back porch, then to the browning grass, needing to be away from the crowd, away from the secretive glances and speculation.

When he'd left the cemetery, he should have gone back to his office and tackled the mountain of endless paperwork. He shouldn't have come here where he felt unwelcome, knew he didn't belong.

He walked a short distance to a large woodpile and sat down, his gaze traveling across the expanse of overgrown lawn and thick brush, back to where the gnarled posts of a grape arbor were just barely visible.

It had been their favorite trysting place. He could still remember the scent of overripe grapes mingling with the sweet fragrance of her skin. They usually met there in the early morning or at twilight, and the pale gold light would sneak through the clusters of grapes and leaves to paint her features with gentle fingers of predawn or dusk.

His memories of her were deeply ingrained, etched in his mind in vivid detail. He needed to be here with her, needed to spend time with her again. He knew this was what had brought him here...the need to get her out of his system once and for all. He had been on hold for the past six years, unable to get on with his life until he managed to forgive and forget Sarah Calhoun.

Forgive. Yes, that was a big part of what he needed to

do. He needed to forgive her for leaving him so long ago. Forgive her for running out on him and not telling him about the baby, taking away any choice he might have had in the matter. Unfortunately, he couldn't seem to crawl past his anger to even begin to contemplate forgiveness.

"Hi. Are you a policeman? You have a police car." She pointed at his patrol car in the distance.

He felt the blood leave his face at the sound of the child's voice. He looked into gray eyes, eyes that mirrored his own. Panic rose in him and he turned away.

He didn't want to look at her. He didn't want to talk to her. He wasn't ready for this...didn't know how to handle it. He took a couple of deep breaths, fighting down the sensation of panic that clawed upward from his stomach.

She sat down next to him, bringing with her the sweet scent of strawberries and bubble gum. He could feel her eyes on him, expectant and curious.

He cleared his throat. "I'm a sheriff. It's like a policeman."

She was silent for a moment, seemingly at ease with him. "My grandma died."

"I know. I'm sorry." He wanted to look at her, but he was afraid to. By looking at her, studying her features so like his own, he would have to acknowledge emotions other than anger, and at the moment he needed his anger.

"I'm trying to feel bad...about my grandma. But I didn't know her." Again she looked at him expectantly.

Anger reared up inside Reese. She should have known her grandma. Damn Sarah. "It's hard to feel bad about somebody you didn't even know." He was acutely aware of her in his peripheral vision.

She scratched her stomach unselfconsciously. "I hate dresses. Mommy made me wear this one, but it itches."

It was a pretty dress, bright yellow with little white polka dots and a white sash around the waist. Before he realized what he was doing, he found himself studying her, feature by feature. Her hair was all Calhoun. Dark and rich, it fell to her shoulders in gentle waves. The roundness of her eyes was also from her mother, but the shape of her face, the color of her eyes and the full bottom lip were all his.

He looked away and sharply drew in a breath. His child. His daughter. Even with the evidence right before him, it didn't seem real. He didn't even know her name.

"I got a scab on my knee." There didn't seem to be any rhyme or reason to her conversation. He marveled at the fact that she just said whatever happened to pop into her mind. Were all kids like this, or was she special?

Reese stood up, uncomfortable with these thoughts. "Uh, how did you skin your knee?"

"Climbing a tree."

Climbing trees. Sarah had always been an ace tree climber. He wondered what talents, what personality quirks, what part of him was hidden inside her.

"Jackie?" Sarah stepped out on the back porch, fear immediately widening her eyes as she saw the child sitting beside him.

"I'm talking to the sheriff, Mama," she answered.

"You need to come back inside." Although Sarah's voice was steady, Reese sensed the panic beneath the surface and he reveled in it.

"Okay." With a sigh, the little girl jumped off the woodpile and started for the house. She got halfway to the porch, then turned back to look at Reese. A smile tilted her lips upward. "Bye, Mr. Sheriff."

He raised a hand, the gesture lost as Sarah hustled the little girl inside the house. Jackie. Her name was Jackie. He had a name, a picture of her face in his mind…and he didn't know what to do with any of it. His brain couldn't take it all in. But one thing was for certain— there weren't enough days left in his life for him to forgive Sarah for what she had done.

Sarah put the last of the dishes away, then sank down in a chair at the kitchen table, enjoying the silence that had finally settled over the house. The last of the guests had gone home a few minutes ago, Ben and Lindy had gone upstairs and Jackie was content sitting on the floor in the living room and coloring in her favorite coloring book.

The house had slipped into a peaceful quiet that would have been comforting if her thoughts hadn't been such a jumble. She rubbed her forehead, not knowing if it was exhaustion or worry that throbbed inside her head.

She'd called her boss at the restaurant back in New York and had explained to him she wouldn't be back as soon as expected. She didn't go into a lot of details, but simply told him there were things she needed to take care of here. Thankfully, he'd been understanding, promising her that her position would remain open and she was welcome back anytime. At least she didn't have to worry about her livelihood when she returned home. However, there were other worries to consider.

A picture of Reese sitting on the woodpile with Jackie next to him exploded in her mind. Father and daughter, sitting next to each other yet unlinked in the most important of ways.

When she'd first noticed them, she'd thought she was going to have a heart attack. Her chest had ached as she saw them so close, yet so distantly apart. It had been like a scene from a fantasy she had absolutely refused to allow herself to entertain.

She'd known from the moment she'd discovered her pregnancy that no one could make a father out of a man who didn't want to be one. Knowing the angry and troubled man Reese had been when she'd left town, she'd never allowed herself to dream of a moment in time when they might ever be a family. It hurt too badly.

When she'd called Jackie back inside, away from Reese, the look on his face had frightened her. It was a look that had promised retribution. He might not want Jackie, but she knew he was the kind of man who liked to be in control. A man who would hate her for giving him no option, no choice in a matter long ago decided.

"Mama, look at my picture." Jackie came into the kitchen, holding on to her latest masterpiece.

Sarah took the picture from her daughter. "Oh, honey, this is lovely." She smiled at Jackie, who seemed to expand upward an inch as she grinned proudly.

"I tried real hard to stay in the lines," Jackie observed.

"I can tell. You did a terrific job," Sarah exclaimed. She leaned over and hugged her daughter to her chest, breathing in the little-girl fragrance that Sarah suspected she would be able to identify even if she was blindfolded and in a room full of kids. "I love you, baby," she whispered into the child's sweet-scented hair.

"I love you, too." Jackie wiggled out of her embrace. "Can we go exploring? You promised me last night you'd show me your favorite tree." Jackie looked at her mother appealingly.

Sarah hesitated. She was really exhausted. However, Jackie had been so good all day and now brimmed with the energy that had been stifled. Besides, Sarah had promised her that if she behaved for Gladys, then she would take her for a walk to explore some of the farm this evening. "Okay. Go change into a pair of jeans and a sweatshirt."

Jackie raced away to change and Sarah pulled herself out of the chair. She spotted a cardigan sweater hanging on a hook by the back door and slipped it on. The sweater smelled like yeasty bread and roses...the scent of her mother. She wrapped the sweater more tightly around her as a hollow ache swept through her. It was the same ache she had taken away with her from Clay Creek six years before, a searing emptiness that never quite went away.

She stroked her fingers down the side of the sweater, wishing her mother was still here to help her cope with everything.

"I'm ready," Jackie announced, coming back into the kitchen clad in jeans and a bright pink sweatshirt.

"I'm ready, too." Sarah smiled, and together they stepped outside into the golden shades of dusk and the chilling evening air.

"Where to first?" Sarah asked, smiling as Jackie automatically reached for her hand.

"To the tree. Show me your favorite tree."

Sarah nodded and headed for the grove that stood in the center of the large side yard. As she breathed in the smell of the farmland, the scent of her home, she felt revitalized. "See that one in the center with the tallest branches?" Jackie nodded. "Last one there is a rotten egg." She dropped Jackie's hand and sprinted ahead, hearing her daughter's delighted giggles erupting from behind her.

They touched the trunk at the same time, Jackie out of breath and Sarah hardly winded. "It's a tie. I guess nobody is a rotten egg," Jackie gasped.

"Or both of us are," Sarah added, laughing as Jackie giggled once again. She sat down on the browned grass beneath the tree, unmindful of any dirt that might cling to her bottom. It felt good to be here with Jackie, sharing a special place and momentarily putting all her concerns, all her emotions, on hold.

She patted the grass and waited until Jackie sat down next to her. "See those branches?" She pointed up into the center of the tree. "I used to sit up there for hours, thinking and dreaming. My mother used to say I was more monkey than girl."

Jackie leaned into Sarah's side. "I like it when you tell me about when you were little." She snuggled closer into Sarah. "Tell me more."

"Sometimes your Aunt Lindy and I would sneak away and climb up there and we'd pretend we were birds and the tree was our home."

Jackie giggled. "Did you eat worms?"

"No, no worms. Usually we each had a handful of cookies that your grandma had baked. She baked the best gingersnaps in the whole wide world."

Jackie stood up suddenly and looked up the tree, her eyes sparking with adventure and challenge. Sarah caught her breath as she saw the child's resemblance to her father, vividly pronounced at the moment. "Can I climb it?" Jackie asked.

"Only to the second group of branches. That's high enough." Sarah stood as Jackie assessed the tree trunk, quickly spotting the natural foot- and handholds in the gnarled wood. It took her no time at all to shinny up the trunk to the limbs overhead.

"Look at me, Mama. I'm a monkey just like you!" Jackie crouched in the tree, her sweatshirt a splash of pink amid the remaining brown leaves that clung tenaciously to the branches.

"That's high enough, Jackie," Sarah admonished as her daughter attempted to climb further.

"Okay," Jackie replied reluctantly. She sat down on a thick limb and began describing to Sarah what she could see from her higher vantage point.

As Jackie chattered, Sarah found herself once again thinking of Reese. She'd been sixteen when they'd started dating. He was three years older than her in age and decades older in experience. He'd been rough-and-tumble. He worked at the gas station and everyone in town knew his mother had left him and his father when Reese was eight, and his father had started to drink heavily after she'd gone.

Reese had been the forbidden, the boy nobody wanted their daughter to date. His mystique among the teenage girls had been one of danger and recklessness. After dating him a couple of times, Sarah had come to recognize the heart within the troubled boy, the wounded child inside the angry man.

She had thought her love would be enough to make him whole. Initially, when she first suspected she was pregnant, a small part of her had been thrilled. Even though she'd heard rumors about Reese and another girl who'd gotten pregnant, even though he'd been quite vocal on his views of parenthood, she was certain this situation was different. After all, this was a child she and Reese had created together in love.

It wasn't until she and Reese attended a wedding of one of his buddies that she realized her dreams of family could never happen with him. He'd ranted and raved after the wedding, telling her his plans to save his money and get the hell out of Clay Creek before some woman trapped him here forever. With each angry word he'd uttered, a piece of Sarah's dreams had shattered. Inch by inch she had died. A week later she left town.

She shoved these thoughts aside, the pain they always brought too intense to deal with at the moment. There was no going back, no changing facts. Reese didn't want to be a father. He didn't think he was father material and nothing was going to change that.

"Jackie, come on down now, honey. It's starting to get dark."

She watched as Jackie began her descent, carefully picking her way down the tree branches. She'd almost reached the bottom when a loud crack resounded and something whined past Sarah's head.

For a moment she couldn't comprehend what had happened. It wasn't until there was another crack and pieces of the tree next to her splintered into the air that she realized what the noise was. Bullets. Somebody was shooting in their direction!

"Hey!" she yelled loudly. "Hey, we're here." There was a moment of silence and Sarah expelled a sigh of relief. Overzealous hunters, she thought. Surely they'd heard her shout and realized their mistake. But then another shot boomed, breaking the stillness and whining as it passed within inches of Sarah's head.

A spurt of adrenaline flooded through her and her blood roared loudly in her ears. "Jump, Jackie," she yelled urgently at the child, who made a perfect target in the lower branches of the tree.

Jackie didn't hesitate. She dropped right into her mother's arms and Sarah immediately shoved her down to the ground. Before Sarah could drop down on top of her, there was another sharp report and a searing pain exploded on the right side of her head.

She covered Jackie's body with hers, unsure if the trembling she felt was her own or her daughter's. The pain in her head made it impossible to think, to assess the situation. She functioned on instinct alone, and her instinct was to remain still and close to the ground.

Minutes passed…minutes of silence. The only sound was the gentle whispering of the leaves in the night breeze.

"Mama?" Jackie's voice was a terrified whisper.

"Shh." Sarah listened, waiting to hear the sound of footsteps, the pop of another gunshot. There was nothing. It was as if she'd imagined the whole thing. But she wasn't imagining the nauseating pain that rocketed through the side of her head. It wasn't until several torturous minutes had passed that Sarah ventured to sit up.

The last golden light of dusk had been shoved away by the deepening purple shadows of night. She looked around, her heart still pounding.

Jackie struggled to a sitting position next to her. "Mama?"

Sarah looked at her daughter, fear once again racing through her. "Jackie, are you all right?" She ran her hands down the little girl's arms, over the top of her head. "You aren't hurt, are you?" She could hear the hysteria edging her voice and knew she was on the verge of losing control.

"Mama, you're bleeding! Your head is bleeding!" Jackie's voice echoed the hysteria in Sarah's. Jackie reached up and gently touched her hand to the side of Sarah's head, and when she drew her hand away, the fingertips were covered with blood. Jackie's eyes widened in horror. Somewhere nearby a bird called out, the sound immediately usurped by Jackie's scream.

Chapter 4

"You were damned lucky. It's just a flesh wound," Doc Burwell said as he washed the blood off the side of Sarah's head. "I'm going to have to cut some of your hair, but you've got more than enough here for two heads."

Sarah closed her eyes as the scissors snipped close to her scalp and she felt pieces of her hair falling to her shoulders. "There we go." Doc finished the impromptu haircut. "It's bleeding pretty good and you'll probably have a headache for a couple of days, but no permanent harm seems to have been done."

She winced as he applied antiseptic to the wound. The headache had already made its appearance, pounding with a nauseating intensity.

She looked over to where Jackie sat on a chair. She was glancing through a picture book and twirling a grape sucker in her mouth, obviously anxious to get to the chocolate center. Amazing, the resilience of children, she thought.

After she and Jackie had made their way from the grove of trees to the house, Sarah had grabbed her car keys and taken off for Doc Burwell's. She'd functioned on instinct, without much thought or logic. She'd had no idea how bad the wound was, but she had comforted Jackie with assurances during the short car ride.

Jackie had been a trouper. She'd sat next to Sarah, pressing a towel to the bleeding area and patting Sarah on the shoulder. Thankfully it hadn't been a long drive to Doc Burwell's office.

All three of them jumped as the door to the office suddenly flew open and Reese filled the space. "What the hell happened?" he demanded.

"What are you doing here?" Sarah exclaimed irritably. She already had a headache. She didn't need his presence to escalate the pain.

"I called him," Doc replied, giving the wound a final swab. "I have to call the sheriff on any gunshot wounds." He carefully applied a bandage, then stood and went to the wooden cabinet in the corner of the tiny examining room. Unlocking the glass door, he rummaged through the bottles and withdrew one. He handed it to Sarah. "This is for the pain. They're pretty strong, so I wouldn't take one then get on the tractor to plow a field."

"I'll keep that in mind," Sarah said dryly. She put the pills in her purse then got up off the examining table, a wave of dizziness causing her to stumble backward and lean heavily against the table.

"Are you going to tell me what happened?" Reese's voice boomed, reverberating at the base of Sarah's skull.

"Would you please not yell," she retorted, closing

her eyes for a moment and taking a few deep breaths. "It's really not a big deal."

"I'd say it's a very big deal. If anyone is going to shoot you, it's going to be me." Reese glared at her, those angry eyes of his making her swallow convulsively.

"If you hurt my mama, you'll be sorry." Jackie jumped off her chair. With her sucker in one hand, she doubled up her other hand into a fist and waved it at him. "If you hurt her, I'll give you a knuckle sandwich."

"I prefer ham and cheese on rye." Reese's quick reply successfully diffused some of the tension in the room. Jackie giggled and Sarah felt a strange bittersweet ache rush through her. She'd forgotten his sense of humor. He'd always been able to make her laugh…when he wasn't breaking her heart.

"Come on, I'll take you home." Reese reached out and took her arm, his grip firm yet gentle. "You can tell me all the details on the way."

"Don't be silly, I can drive myself home." Sarah jerked her arm away from him. Even his most insignificant touch sent an ache of memory through her that caused her heart to hurt. She began to walk, appalled to realize her legs trembled, barely holding her up.

"Honey, I recommend you let Reese take you home," Doc said softly. "You shouldn't have driven yourself here to begin with. You've been through quite a shock. I don't think driving is such a good idea at the moment."

"You drove yourself here?" Reese sounded appalled at the very idea. "Why didn't you get Ben or Lindy to bring you in?"

"I didn't want to bother them. Lindy has been so upset. She would have completely lost it. Besides, everything happened so fast, I just got in the car and drove."

"Well, that does it. I'm definitely taking you home," Reese replied firmly.

Sarah hesitated. She didn't want to go with Reese, but she knew she wasn't in any condition to drive home and she had Jackie's safety to consider. The adrenaline flood that had allowed her to drive herself to the doctor was gone, leaving her shaking and exhausted.

Besides, if Reese took her home, he could talk to her on the way, then leave when they got there. If he followed her, he'd have to come in and discuss the details with her and she didn't want him in the house. She didn't want his scent lingering after he'd gone, his presence remaining when he left.

"I can get you in the morning and bring you back into town to pick up your car," Reese said, as if this might be what caused her hesitation.

"You won't have to do that. Ben can bring me in on his way out of town in the morning."

"I don't care the whys or hows," Doc Burwell interjected. "I'm an old man and it's getting late and I think you all should get the hell out of here." He gave Sarah an awkward pat on her shoulder and led them all to the door. He pointed at Sarah. "I want to see you again tomorrow."

She nodded vaguely, wanting only to get home, take a pain pill and escape from the throbbing ache in the side of her head.

"Are we gonna ride in a police car?" Jackie asked as they stepped outside into the chilly night air.

"You sure are." Reese opened the back door so Jackie could scramble inside. Sarah slid into the passenger seat, closed her eyes and leaned her head back. The interior of the car smelled like Reese, a tantalizing scent that conjured up unwanted memories from the past. She shoved the memories away and focused instead on the pain in her head. It was much more manageable than the ache in her heart.

"Mr. Sheriff, will you turn on the siren?" Jackie asked, talking around her sucker as Reese got in the car.

"It's a little late for the siren," Reese replied. He started the engine and pulled away from the curb. "But when we get out of town, I'll turn on the lights. And before we do anything, all little girls have to have their seat belts on."

Jackie immediately complied, sitting back on the seat and buckling the belt around her.

"You ready to tell me what happened?" Even with her eyes closed, Sarah could feel his gaze on her.

She sighed, opened her eyes and stared out the window, where the blackness of night seemed as dense as the events that had unfolded over the past hour.

"Jackie and I were out by the grove of trees at the side of the house," she began.

"I was climbing Mom's favorite tree," Jackie added.

"Jackie was up in the tree when somebody started shooting. After the second shot, I shouted to tell whoever it was that we were there. The shooting stopped for a minute but then started again. It had to have been some crazy mistake—a hunter or a drunk or something." This is what she had told herself on the drive to Doc Burwell's. It was a mistake, an accident. To consider any other scenario was too frightening.

"Could you tell where the shots came from?"

Sarah frowned and rubbed two fingers across her forehead. "I don't know...it all happened so fast." She swallowed convulsively. "They seemed to have come from someplace near the house, but I could be mistaken.'' She rubbed her forehead once again, trying to still the throbbing ache.

''Where were Ben and Lindy?''

''After everyone left the house, they went upstairs to their room. Lindy isn't handling any of this very well. They have a VCR and a TV in the bedroom. Ben was going to pick out a couple of Lindy's favorite movies and watch them with her.'' She knew she was rambling, giving him useless information. She stopped rubbing her forehead and gazed at him, noting the tautness of his features in the dim light from the dashboard. ''I'm sure it was just an accident. A careless hunter or stray bullets or something.''

''Or something.'' He looked at her, his gaze lingering on the white bandage. His hands tightened on the steering wheel. ''Whatever happened, I intend to get to the bottom of it. I can't have visitors to Clay Creek getting shot at.''

Visitors to Clay Creek. A feeling of emptiness swept through Sarah, increasing the pounding in her head. She stared back out the window. Yes, that's all she could ever be—a visitor.

She looked over at him again. Everything about him was taut. His jaw was clamped shut and his knuckles were white beneath his tight grip on the steering wheel. The potential fury was there, a potential that frightened Sarah not for herself but for her daughter. Most of the time Reese's anger had produced self-destructive acts, but there had been times in the past when his actions had spilled over to hurt others. She would never allow him to hurt Jackie. She didn't intend to be in Clay Creek long enough to let that happen.

It didn't matter to Sarah that he didn't want to be a

father. Jackie didn't need him. *And neither do I,* Sarah thought. "Maybe I should be questioning you about your whereabouts earlier this evening," she said softly.

He stared at her for a brief moment, his eyes scathing. "Don't be ridiculous," he scoffed dryly. "Hiding and shooting is definitely not my style. If it had been me, I would have made sure you knew it."

She nodded, knowing what he said was true. If and when he decided to hurt her, he'd make certain she knew about it. Once again she closed her eyes against the pain in her head and the sharper ache in her heart.

"Mr. Sheriff, will you turn on the lights now?" Jackie asked.

Reese reached down and punched the button that sent the red lights swirling on top of the car painting the landscape with a red glow. He heard the little girl's gasp of pleasure and smiled as he remembered her clenched fist when she'd thought he was threatening her mother. A brave little thing, he mused.

Again he found himself wondering what pieces of himself might be found in this child. He wondered what Sarah had told her about him. Was Jackie even old enough to wonder about the absence of a father in her life? If she was old enough, what had Sarah told the little girl? That he didn't care? That he was dead? Or had she lied altogether and made up some father image?

He'd been eight when his mother had taken off, leaving behind an angry man and a bewildered boy. Reese could still remember nights of lying awake, wondering what he'd done or hadn't done that had caused his mother to leave them. He could no longer remember her facial features. Over the years, she'd dimmed to a shadowy figure who rarely received more than a passing thought.

Yet Reese still remembered the misery of the little boy he'd once been, and he wondered if Jackie experienced any suffering over the lack of a father in her life. He hoped not.

He looked over at Sarah, the red glow from the lights atop the car washing over her features but unable to cover her unnatural paleness. The bandage was stark against the darkness of her hair and her features were drawn in response to the pain she must be experiencing. Even pale and drained she was beautiful.

Again he realized that his heart had never really gotten free from hers. Six years ago she'd been the very best thing in his god-awful life. When she'd left, she'd taken a piece of him with her, a piece he'd never been able to fully recover.

He shut off the whirling red lights as he turned onto the narrow lane that led to the Calhoun house. He couldn't think of his personal involvement with Sarah right now. At the moment the most important thing he had to do was figure out who, other than himself, might have a reason to want to harm her. Had the shooting merely been an accident or was it something more ominous?

It was more than an hour later that Reese and Sarah finally sat down at the kitchen table, no closer to figuring out who had shot at her than they had been before. Reese had taken a flashlight and examined the area all around the house but had found no spent shells, nothing that would indicate a gun being fired.

He'd talked to Ben and Lindy. Both had said they'd heard the shots and had looked out the window. When they didn't see anyone, they'd assumed it was somebody doing target shooting nearby.

Ben and Lindy had gone back to their room. Sarah had taken a pain pill, made a pot of coffee, then put Jackie to bed. She now wrapped her hands around the mug in front of her, noticing how quiet the house was around them.

It was a comfortable silence, broken only by the noises that belonged—the hum of the refrigerator, the occasional gurgle of the coffeemaker, the audible clicking of the minute hand on the old clock that hung above the stove. They were the sounds of home.

She sighed, aware of Reese's scent, the warmth of his body close to hers at the table. She'd hoped he would question her in the car, then leave. She hadn't counted on the two of them ending up alone in the kitchen, a place where they'd often ended their dates.

"Maybe I was mistaken," she finally said, breaking the silence. "Maybe the shots came from another direction. It all happened so fast, and maybe the sound was distorted or something."

He nodded. "How's your head?"

"Better. The pill took the edge off the pain."

He leaned forward across the table. "Sarah…we need to talk." There was no sign of his anger, though he suddenly looked older than his years. The lines down the sides of his mouth were deeply etched, as was the wrinkle across his forehead.

"Talk about what?" she asked, even though she knew…knew and dreaded the conversation about to happen. She glanced away from him. She'd dreaded it from the moment she'd come back and realized he was still here and would eventually have to be faced.

"About us, about the past…about Jackie." His eyes flared with some indefinable emotion.

Sarah took a sip of her coffee, wishing the warmth

could penetrate through to the sudden chill in her heart. She didn't want to rehash the past. It was over. She'd made her choices and moved on with her life. "Reese, what's done is done. Why go over it all now?"

He seemed to grow, expand in height and width, as his eyes smoked with the fires of suppressed anger. "Because you owe me at least that much. You owe me an explanation—"

"I've never asked you for anything and I don't owe you anything," she retorted, her anger rising to meet his. She didn't look at him, she couldn't.

Despite her anger, despite the deep ache in her heart, she knew all too well the comfort of his arms. Her head pounded and there was a lingering taste of fear in her mouth from having been shot at. She was afraid that if he offered, she'd fall into his arms and lose herself, her sanity, for the second time in her life.

"Damn it, you should have told me. You should have given me some options." His voice was low but filled with bitter anger. "You should have stayed. You should have told me you were pregnant. Maybe we could have worked something out."

This time she did look at him—hard and cold. "Worked something out? Like you worked it out with that other girl who got pregnant?"

He frowned. "What girl?"

"I don't know...somebody named Amy who was a senior when I was a sophomore. I heard you two dated and she got pregnant and you made her get an abortion." She shivered and wrapped her hands once again around her mug.

"Where did you hear a story like that?"

"Girls talk, especially high school girls." Sarah could still remember the conversation she'd overheard in the girls' locker room. At the time it had meant little to her. She wasn't dating Reese, knew him only by sight. It wasn't until she found herself pregnant with his child that the conversation had come back to haunt her.

"Amy Overton was a good friend of mine," he began, his voice tight with tension. "She lived down the street from me and our fathers were both mean drunks. We spent a lot of time together, commiserating with each other, comforting each other. But I never slept with her. As far as I know, she never had an abortion or a baby."

Reese drew a hand through his hair and muttered a curse beneath his breath. "Damn it, Sarah, you know how people are in this town. Somebody locks gazes at the café one night and before morning the stories are circulating that they're having an affair. Gossip is a fact of life in Clay Creek, and it's usually worth every penny that's paid for it."

She stared down into her coffee cup, knowing what he said was true. Still, it didn't matter whether the old rumor was true or not. She'd heard for herself the way Reese felt about having a family. "I almost told you I was pregnant. It was the night we went to Cindy and Bob's wedding. You remember that night?" She looked back at him.

He nodded. "So why didn't you tell me?"

She hesitated and rubbed the side of her head where the sharp pain had dulled to a blunt throb. "We left the reception early because you were so angry that Cindy was pregnant and had trapped Bob into marrying her." Reese opened his mouth as if to protest, but Sarah held up a hand to still him. "You ranted and raved and swore that one way or the other you'd get out of Clay Creek before you got trapped here for the rest of your life. You told me how much you hated your own father and how you'd never give a kid the chance to hate you.''

The memory of his words, each one like a knife cutting into her heart, caused tears to spring unbidden to her eyes. She hurriedly swiped them away and drew in a deep breath. "You didn't want to be a father, so I made sure you didn't have to be one. I let you off the hook. You're free and clear of any responsibility."

She stood, the ache in her head magnified. "It's over, Reese. Over and done. We can't go back." She gestured wearily toward the doorway. "And I really need to call it a night. My head hurts and I want to go to bed."

He hesitated, his eyes still blazing with anger. He drew a deep breath, then nodded, and she walked with him to the front door.

He paused in the doorway, his gaze lingering on her face, his expression inscrutable. He reached up and touched the bandage, his touch achingly gentle. Sarah fought the impulse to lean into him. Despite the hurtful past that was between them, despite her fear for Jackie's emotional well-being, she realized there was still a part of her heart he owned...would always own.

"It may be done, but it's not over," he said softly, his hand moving to capture her chin. "It's not over between you and me, Sarah. We never really finished what we began."

She stepped back, away from his touch. She looked at him without flinching. "Does that mean you're ready to become a full-time father?"

His face blanched and his hand fell to his side. Bitterness welled up inside Sarah. "Good night, Reese." Before he could say anything more, she closed the door and locked it, then leaned wearily against it. The look on his face, his hesitation, had said it all. He might have changed in many ways. He was no longer the hoodlum with the unkempt hair and wild streak, but in the most important way of all, he hadn't changed a bit. You couldn't make a silk purse out of a sow's ear, any more than you could make a father out of a man like Reese Walker.

"Damn it!" The gravel of the driveway crunched beneath his feet as he walked back to his car. Instead of immediately leaving, he leaned against the side of the car and took a couple of deep breaths, fighting against the old demons that reared up inside him.

The whole conversation had disturbed him and still echoed in his head, resounded in the emptiness of his heart. *Does that mean you're ready to become a full-time father?* Her question had thrown him. He hadn't expected it and the unfairness of it railed inside him.

She'd had five years of being a mother—nine months before that to prepare for becoming one. She'd had time to adjust, time to nurture and learn all about their child. He'd had two days to digest his instant fatherhood, two days in which to try to sift through the warring emotions inside him.

He tilted his head up and stared at the stars overhead, each one winking as if it knew the secrets to the entire universe. A father. The word itself was still enough to scare the hell out of him.

Sarah was right about one thing. He'd never wanted kids. He'd never wanted to be a father. The only kind of father Reese knew was the kind that used fists instead of words and hid in the bottom of a bottle of whiskey when the responsibility became too much. With that kind of a role model, what could Reese possibly know about being a good parent?

But she should have given me a choice, a small voice whispered inside, refusing to let go of the anger. *She should have told me, instead of running out on me and taking everything out of my hands.*

"Damn." The word escaped him with a deep sigh. The bottom line was that Sarah hadn't wanted him to know he was a father. If not for her mother's death, he might have never known. She'd made the decision to leave the town she loved, leave her family so that he wouldn't know. And he understood her reason. She'd obviously suspected what he had known all along. He wasn't fit to be a father.

Chapter 5

Sarah awoke groggy from a deep, dreamless sleep. She heard music playing someplace in the house and smelled the hickory scent of bacon frying. She smiled, imagining her mom clad in one of her many flowered housedresses, standing before the stove watching so the bacon got evenly browned and crispy. Margaret always cooked with the transistor radio playing oldies and her foot would tap in rhythm as she went about her morning work.

The vision warmed Sarah, filled her with joy before it shattered and fell away, leaving her aching and empty. She opened her eyes, time and reality jarring firmly into place. Her mother wasn't downstairs cooking breakfast, she was gone forever. Ben must be up, playing the radio as he drank his morning cup of coffee.

She roused herself out of bed, knowing he would be anxious to get her back to town for her car, then continue his three-hour drive to Kansas City. She went into the bathroom and frowned as she stared at her reflection. She looked horrendous.

The bandage on the side of her head caused the events of the night before to replay in her mind. The shooting, the trip to the doctor's office and, finally, the conversation with Reese. That particular conversation was the one thing that stuck in her head.

She'd seen the changes in Reese, subtle changes that spoke of growth and maturity. There was a new confidence in the set of his shoulders, a pride shining from his dark eyes. He looked like a man who'd finally found himself and liked what he'd found. And yet in the most important area of all, there had been no change. She frowned, thinking of her daughter.

Jackie had only asked once about her daddy. It had been after her preschool had invited fathers to class for snack time that Jackie had come home and asked if she had a father. Even though Sarah had known eventually the question would come, that sooner or later she'd have to tell Jackie something about Reese, she had been unprepared. She'd handled it badly, telling Jackie about the frailty of human relationships, the inadequacies of love, the responsibilities that some people couldn't handle, until finally Jackie had said, ''Oh,'' and with a look of bewilderment had wandered off to play.

But Sarah knew sooner or later the questions would come again and the next time Jackie wouldn't be so easy to put off. What was she going to tell her daughter? What could she tell her about the man who was her father?

She shoved these concerns aside. She had enough to worry about without anticipating further complications in her life. She had an appointment at noon with the family lawyer and she wanted to look over her mother's books to see exactly how the farm was doing financially.

She dressed quickly, then worked on brushing her hair, grateful that Doc Burwell had left enough to cover over the unsightly bandage. She checked on Jackie, still sound asleep in the small spare bedroom next to her room, then went downstairs.

"Good morning," Lindy greeted her brightly as she entered the kitchen.

"Good morning," Sarah replied in surprise. She went to the coffee machine and poured herself a cup, trying to assimilate Lindy's unexpected appearance and obvious energy. Lindy not only was cooking breakfast but had apparently been up for some time. She was dressed, her hair clean and shining, and she looked more vital, more alive than she had since Sarah had first arrived. "You must be feeling better," Sarah said.

"I feel wonderful," Lindy exclaimed, moving the skillet of popping bacon from the burner. "I woke up just after five and couldn't stay in bed another minute." She went to the refrigerator and removed a carton of eggs. "As soon as I opened my eyes this morning, I knew I had to strip off this old wallpaper today." As she walked back to the stove she tapped a finger on the faded paper that had adorned the kitchen walls for as long as Sarah could remember. "I've been after Mama for months to redo this room and now, well, I just knew I had to do it today."

Sarah nodded hesitantly, realizing that for the first time she was actually seeing what her mother had related to her by phone—the swift mood shift from depression to mania that marked Lindy's disease.

Lindy sat down on the chair across from Sarah and grabbed her hand. "I know I haven't been much help since you got here and we really haven't had a chance to catch up with each other's lives, but I'm better now and everything is going to be terrific.'' She frowned sympathetically. "How's your head?"

"Okay, just a little sore."

Lindy jumped up and headed back to the stove. "How about some breakfast? I make a terrific cheese omelet."

"No thanks. I'm not much of a breakfast eater. Besides, I'd better get Jackie up so she can go with us to get the car."

"Oh, let her sleep," Lindy protested. "She was up late last night, wasn't she?" Sarah nodded and Lindy continued, "Ben's going to be ready in just a few minutes and you can probably be there and back before she wakes up." She poured the egg mixture into the skillet.

At that moment Ben walked into the kitchen. He nodded a greeting to Sarah, then kissed Lindy on the forehead. "Hmm, smells good."

"Cheese omelet," Lindy replied, smiling up at him. "I wanted to send you off with a good breakfast. I know you don't eat right when you're on a case—fast food and stale coffee. Speaking of coffee, sit down and I'll get you a cup." She paused only a moment for breath, then began describing the wallpaper she wanted to buy for the kitchen.

She kept up a steady stream of chatter as Ben ate his breakfast. Sarah listened, amazed at Lindy's boundless energy, the exuberance she displayed as she washed the dishes and put them away.

"Hard to believe, isn't it?" Ben said later as he and Sarah headed into town to pick up her car. "She becomes a different person when she's up."

"It's pretty unbelievable," Sarah agreed. "Nothing

Mama told me quite prepared me for the reality of it. She was so down last night...and seems so high this morning.''

Ben nodded. ''The doctor explained to us that she's a rapid cycler—her highs and lows sometimes almost collide with each other.''

''Mama told me she's on medication to help with the mood swings. Is she still taking it?''

''Yes, and she'd been doing pretty well until a month or two ago. The medicine doesn't seem to be working as well.'' Ben sighed. ''The last couple of months have really been difficult. She's so unpredictable, at times so irrational.'' He glanced at Sarah for a moment. ''I love her, Sarah, but it's been so hard.'' He looked as if he wanted to say more, but instead closed his mouth and focused on the road ahead.

They rode in silence for a few minutes, then Ben spoke once again. ''It will be good for her to have you around for a couple of days. She's missed you. In the meantime, while I'm in Kansas City I'm going to make an appointment to speak to her doctor. Maybe it's time to try another kind of drug.''

''Why on earth did Mama take her to a doctor in Kansas City to begin with?'' Sarah asked. ''Couldn't she find somebody closer to home?''

Ben shook his head. ''She tried to find a doctor closer to Clay Creek, then she heard about Dr. Manning in Kansas City. He was supposed to be an expert in the treatment of manic-depression.'' He cracked his window open, allowing the sweet-scented morning air to waft in. ''Your mother talked about finding a doctor closer to home, but Lindy seemed to be doing so well with Dr. Manning. She related well to him and until the past couple of months seemed to be thriving.'' Ben frowned.

"Unfortunately, Dr. Manning does a lot of traveling and lecturing and it's sometimes difficult to get an appointment when needed."

"Do you think Lindy would see somebody else if we could find someone?" Sarah asked.

Ben's frown deepened. "I don't know, Sarah, it's difficult to guess what Lindy will do and won't do. There is a new psychiatrist, Dr. Westliner. He just moved outside of town a couple of months ago."

"Maybe I should get Lindy in to see him."

"I don't want her upset. Give me a day or two to see if I can get her in to see Dr. Manning. If I can't, then we'll check out Dr. Westliner."

"I sure would feel better going back to New York knowing that Lindy was more stable than she appears to be at the moment."

"You won't consider staying here in Clay Creek? Moving back here to live?"

She'd told him the night he'd arrived that she was only here for a short visit, that her home was in New York. Sarah looked out the window, her mind immediately filled with a vision of Reese's face when he'd left last night. A mental picture of Jackie superimposed itself over his. Jackie, with her pure heart and giving nature.

If Sarah moved back to Clay Creek, how long would it take for Jackie's pure heart to be tainted by Reese's resentment? How long would it take for her sunny nature to develop clouds of unhappiness as she realized her daddy didn't want to be a daddy? "No, I don't think this will ever be my home again," she finally said. Not as long as Reese was here, and he appeared to have finally dug his feet in and accepted the town he'd once hated. Again the irony of the situation caused a bitter smile to curve her lips.

"I'm hoping to wrap up this court case in three or four days...a week at the most," Ben said. "I really appreciate you offering to stay with Lindy until it's finished."

Regret surged through Sarah. "I waited too late to breach the years with Mama. I don't want to make the same mistake with Lindy. Other than Jackie, she's the only family I have left."

"I understand you have an appointment with Ralph Erickson today."

Sarah heard the slight tension in Ben's voice and she suddenly realized what might be worrying him. She leaned over and touched his arm. "Ben, I'm assuming since Ralph asked to see me by myself, that means Mama left the farm to me. But you must understand if that's the case, then nothing will change. You and Lindy can continue to live there as long as you want."

Ben nodded, tension still whitening his knuckles. "Raymond Boswell, the owner of the power plant, is interested in buying the place," he observed as he pulled in behind her car at Doc Burwell's office.

"Well, he'll be disappointed. As far as I'm concerned, it's not for sale," Sarah said firmly, hoping she put Ben's worry to rest. She got out of the car. "Don't worry about Lindy," she assured him. "I'll take good care of her while you're gone."

"I'll call every evening," he promised, then, with a wave, he pulled away.

She stood for a moment, staring down Main Street. The early morning sun was kind to the old buildings, spilling down a golden light that softened the facades. It was just a little before eight o'clock and the only cars on the street were parked in front of Anna's café.

Before she realized her own intentions, her feet carried her down the block and to the café. Just a quick cup of coffee, she promised herself. Jackie would probably sleep for at least another hour.

The first person she saw as she stepped inside was Reese, sitting at the counter with a cup before him. At the sound of the door closing behind her, he turned and saw her. For a brief moment his features were unguarded and a genuine smile of pleasure curved his lips as he gazed at her. The warmth of his smile caused an answering flutter in the pit of Sarah's stomach.

Had she known that he would be here? Was that what had pulled her in? The desire, the very need to see Reese? Ridiculous, she scoffed. Why would she want to see him when she still had a bad taste in her mouth from the last conversation she'd had with him?

Still, she couldn't deny the unexpected surge of happiness that swept over her as he got up from his stool and approached her, his smile as potent as a caress. Maybe he was right. The past was over, but something between Reese and her had yet to be finished.

"How are you feeling?" he asked, standing in front of her, bringing with him the clean male scent that stirred a latent desire deep within her.

"Fine…better…" She fought against the ache his closeness aroused.

He reached up and touched the bandage on her head, his fingers as soft and tender as they had been when they'd touched her the night before. "I planned on coming out to the farm later this afternoon." He placed a hand on her elbow and led her to a booth. "Here, sit down and have some coffee with me. I want to talk to you about the shooting." He motioned for Anna to bring his coffee from the counter.

She relaxed somewhat, realizing he wasn't going to

rehash the more intimate discussion they'd had the night before.

"Hey, sweetie, Reese told me about somebody using you for target practice," Anna said, setting Reese's cup before him and adding one for Sarah.

"I guess somebody mistook me for a deer," Sarah replied as Anna filled her cup.

"Damned hunters. It would be nice if they had at least as much brain as the guns." She patted Sarah's shoulder sympathetically. "I'll send Suzanna over to take your order. I've got pies baking I need to check on." She gestured to the waitress, who was serving a couple at a booth in the back.

"Don't send her over on my account," Sarah protested. "Coffee is all I want."

"And I'm fine, too." Reese directed his attention back to Sarah as Anna nodded and hurried off. "Did you sleep okay?"

"Like the dead. That pill Doc Burwell gave me really did the trick." She sipped from her cup, wishing he wouldn't look at her so intently. She realized she couldn't hang on to her anger where he was concerned and she needed her anger desperately to obliterate the memory of the passion they'd once shared.

She wondered if his lips would still burn hers with a fevered heat, if his caresses still had the power to drive her mindless with hunger? Had the frenzied desire that had once existed between them been the passion of youth? Had their love been real, or had it merely been a matter of circumstance? These were questions that had plagued her for the last six years, questions that had haunted her in the quiet dark hours of night.

"Sarah?" His gaze didn't quite meet hers. "I'm planning on coming out this afternoon and taking another look around where you and Jackie were when you were shot, but to be honest, I doubt we'll ever find who did it.''

"What's the point of looking around again? You didn't find anything last night. I'm sure it was just some crazy mistake,'' she said faintly, too conscious of him.

"I just thank God you weren't hurt worse. It could have been a real tragedy.'' His voice was gruff and she knew the anger she'd seen in his eyes the night before wasn't gone.

She nodded and groped for conversation—anything to distill the tension that existed between them. ''I still find it difficult to believe you're now the sheriff. When I left here you were Sheriff Taylor's nemesis and now you're both on the same side of the law. How did that happen?''

Reese leaned back against the booth and smiled reflectively. "It's a long story. I was on the verge of self-destruction when Jim Taylor took me by the ears and offered me a chance to turn my life around.''

"As I recall, you always seemed to be on the verge of self-destruction,'' Sarah observed wryly. "I remember the night you tried to break the speed record for going around that hairpin curve by Miller's pond." She was instantly sorry she'd mentioned their old parking place.

The smile on his face faded and his eyes burned into her intently. "I didn't realize how much you were a part of my sanity until you left. I went a little crazy after that.''

Sarah's heart trembled in her chest as old, unwanted emotions swept through her. She'd never considered him when she'd left. She'd been so wrapped up in her own drama, her own pain. She'd never thought of what her leaving town might do to him. "You were always more than a little crazy," she teased, uncomfortable with the turn of the conversation.

He grinned, a wicked upturn of his sensual lips that merely increased his magnetism. "The only difference is that back then I was a little crazy and I was one of the bad guys. Now I'm a little crazy and I'm one of the good guys."

Sarah laughed, the laughter fading abruptly as his hand reached for hers and his eyes lighted up like fiery chunks of charcoal. "I want you, Sarah," he said in a low near whisper. "It's crazy, it's insane. I'm angry as hell with you, but that doesn't seem to matter. I want you now with the same mindless intensity I did six years ago."

"Reese…" She pulled her hand from his, a hot blush working its way up her neck. She fought against the liquid heat that swirled inside her. Oh, it would be so easy to forget the past and fall back into the magic of his arms.

"Hi, Sarah." Suzanna appeared next to them, her presence effectively breaking the moment. "Reese told us all about what happened." She peered intently at Sarah's head. "Whew, looks like it was some close call."

"Much too close for comfort," Sarah replied.

"You picking me up at seven?" Suzanna turned her attention to Reese.

"Yeah, sure," he answered absently.

Sarah looked at her watch and stood. "It's getting late. I've got to get back home." She pulled a dollar from her purse and set it on the table. "I'll see you two later."

As she drove back to the farm, her thoughts were in turmoil. She couldn't deny that there was still a powerful attraction between her and Reese. He'd spoken it aloud, and she'd felt an answering affirmation in herself. Deep inside she wanted him as much as he apparently wanted her.

But where could it possibly lead? She was only going to be in town another couple of days, and from what Suzanna had said, she and Reese were dating. Falling back into any kind of a relationship with Reese would only serve to make them both more miserable than ever. Besides, he'd made it clear he didn't want to be a father to Jackie, and therefore he could have no permanent place in Sarah's life.

And yet she couldn't deny the appeal of making love with him. The last time they had made love she hadn't known she was leaving town, hadn't realized she would never again lie in his arms and feel the wonder of him deep inside her. She felt a need to make love to him one last time…and know with a certainty it was the final chapter in their book of love.

She winced against the pounding that had begun in the side of her head. The only thing clear at the moment was the knowledge that trying to sort out her feelings for Reese gave her a headache.

"Come on in and I'll put some coffee on," Suzanna said as she unlocked the door to her apartment. The door across the hall opened a crack and two dark eyes peered out. "Hello, Mrs. Jackson," Suzanna said sweetly, laughing as the door slammed shut. "She wouldn't have a life at all if she didn't have mine to spy on," she said as she opened the door and gestured Reese inside.

Reese hesitated. The whole evening had been a mistake. He should have canceled the date rather than come when his mind was otherwise occupied. He'd barely paid attention to the movie they'd seen, although he'd been grateful that the film had made conversation unnecessary. Still, it wasn't fair to Suzanna for him to be here spending time with her when his mind, his thoughts and his heart were all filled with Sarah.

"I probably should call it a night," he finally said hesitantly.

"Ah, come on, Reese. Just one quick cup. I've got some new gourmet stuff that I've been dying to try." Suzanna's eyes pleaded silently.

"Okay, but just one," he agreed, relenting. He stepped inside so she could close the door behind him. There was a part of him that recognized Suzanna's quiet desperation, the need to fill at least an hour or two of a lonely night. He'd felt it often himself over the last couple of years.

He settled himself on the love seat, rearranging the loose pillows across the back to create a comfortable spot. Suzanna disappeared into the kitchen. A large orange long-haired cat jumped up beside him. "Hey, Tiger." He scratched the huge tomcat behind his ears, smiling as the cat rolled over on his back to give Reese's fingers access to his belly.

Over the years he'd spent many evenings on this love seat petting Tiger while Suzanna puttered around in the kitchen. He and the cat had a lot in common; both were strays that Suzanna took in on cold, lonely nights.

He and Suzanna had dated off and on since high school and had managed to settle into a comfortable relationship of companionship without commitment. It had worked fine, had been enough...until Sarah's reappearance. Now Reese realized how superficial, how pointless, his relationship with Suzanna truly was.

"Here we are," Suzanna said brightly as she carried in a tray with two cups of coffee. She plopped down next to him, pushing Tiger off and brushing at the orange hairs that clung to the material of the sofa.

"Hmm, it smells wonderful," he said, enjoying the almond, chocolate and rich coffee aroma. He took a sip, then smiled appreciatively. "This is great. Where'd you get it?"

"A friend brought it back from a little specialty shop in Kansas City. It's good, isn't it?" She took a sip, then set the cup on the table in front of them. "What's the matter, Reese? You've been quiet and distracted all night." She moved closer to him, her heavy perfume overly sweet and cloying.

He immediately thought of Sarah's perfume, a light floral scent that invited closeness rather than suffocated. He shoved the comparison out of his mind. Why couldn't he get her out of his brain? "I've got a lot on my mind," he answered.

"Sarah?" She smiled innocently as he looked at her, startled by his own transparency. She laughed. "I know you, Reese. You're a good sheriff and I know the shooting has to be eating at you."

He nodded, instantly relieved. At least he wasn't as transparent as he'd thought. "Sure it bothers me. If it was a hunter, then he needs to be found and face charges of negligence. We can't have people indiscriminately firing guns at anything that moves." He finished his coffee and stood up. "And on that note, I'd better call it a night. I'm on duty early in the morning."

Suzanna pulled at his arm. "You've had to be on duty early before and I don't remember it bothering you." She stood and pressed herself against the length of his body. "Stay a little longer, Reese." She twined her arms around his neck, pressing her full breasts against his chest. "I promise you I'll be most entertaining." Her lips moved softly against the lobe of his ear. "I can think of lots of things more fun than getting a good night sleep," she whispered.

Despite his unease, Reese laughed. Gently he pulled her arms from around his neck, "Ah, Suzanna, you make an offer difficult to resist."

"Then don't resist," she returned, seductively unbuttoning the top button of her blouse.

"Suzanna." Reese reached out and caught her hands in his. "I've really got to get home."

She frowned and walked with him to the door. "Thanks for the movie and dinner," she said, looking up at him expectantly.

He knew she was waiting for him to mention another date, another time, but he couldn't. The words simply wouldn't come. Instantly he knew this would be his last date with Suzanna. "Good night, Suzanna," he said.

"Wait." She grabbed him by the arm once again. "When am I going to see you again?"

He hesitated. "I'll call you," he finally said. However, as he walked out into the night air, he knew he wouldn't be calling her for a date again. He didn't want to hurt her, but it wasn't fair for him to see her again. He couldn't move ahead, couldn't fall in love with anyone, until he somehow reclaimed his heart from Sarah. He just hoped that in the process, he didn't lose his heart forever.

Sarah paced her room, unable to sleep with the tremendous amount of noise coming from the kitchen. Thank goodness Jackie was a heavy sleeper, and rarely woke in the middle of the night.

Lindy had been working in a frenzy all day. She'd managed to get all the old wallpaper off the walls and had been cleaning out cabinets when Sarah had come home from her afternoon appointment with the lawyer. Lindy had refused to even sit down to supper and instead had put new shelf paper in all the cabinets while Sarah and Jackie ate.

Sarah looked at her clock. Nearly midnight. How long could Lindy keep up her frantic pace? How long did these periods of manic energy last?

Walking to the bedroom window, she pressed the tip of her nose against the cool glass and peered out onto the moon-painted farmland. Her heart swelled and tightened in her chest. Her appointment that afternoon with Ralph Erickson had confirmed that she was her mother's sole beneficiary. The farmhouse and the surrounding eighty acres were hers, along with a letter from her mother detailing her wishes.

The letter explained Margaret's worry about Lindy and her concern that Ben wasn't in for the long haul.

That's why I'm leaving the farm to you. Because I fear that Ben isn't strong enough to survive Lindy's illness and I don't want the farm divided in the event that Lindy and Ben divorce. I'm certain of your strength, Sarah, and know that you'll do what needs to be done to keep Lindy safe here. The farm is our home, our roots. It and you two girls have my heart.

The letter had been a final piece of her mother and had brought tears to Sarah's eyes. Written in her mother's no-nonsense fashion, it had stressed Margaret's wish that the farm remain Lindy's home for as long as she wanted. Her mother had also written of her pride in Sarah's resilience and independence, and her wish that

Sarah finally find the strength to leave New York and come back home to Clay Creek.

Sarah had no problems granting her mother her first wish. She had no desire to sell the farm, and Lindy and Ben belonged here. But there was no way she could consider granting her mother her final wish.

She sighed and focused back out the window. The moonlight gave the landscape a kind of fairy-tale appearance. The trees were silver silhouettes against the dark horizon and there was an ethereal glow to the land. Yes, a fairy tale. And the only thing missing was her Prince Charming. She'd thought she had found him once, but he'd only been a mirage. A man who didn't want children couldn't be a prince. He could only be a lonely, unhappy man.

She jumped as she heard a muted bang from downstairs. Grabbing her robe, she pulled it on, then left her bedroom. She went to the room next door and checked on Jackie, who hadn't moved since Sarah had tucked her in. Sarah leaned over and kissed her gently on the cheek, then went downstairs to see what Lindy was doing.

Lindy squatted in front of the cabinet that held the pots and pans. She picked up first one saucepan, then another, tossing each one aside with a grunt of disgust. Sarah cleared her throat and Lindy turned, squealing in surprise. "Oh, you scared me to death," she exclaimed.

"What are you doing?" Sarah asked. Lindy's cheeks were flushed with color and her eyes were fevered with an unnatural intensity.

Lindy turned back around to the cabinet. "I'm looking for that big pot Mama always used to make soups—ah, here it is." She withdrew the large aluminum pot and stood up. "I'm going to make a huge pot of homemade vegetable soup. Ben loves my vegetable soup."

"Surely it can wait until morning," Sarah protested. "Lindy, it's after midnight. Go to bed. Get some rest."

"Rest? I can't rest. Who could rest at a time like this?" She moved like a marionette to the stove and slammed the pot down on the top of one of the burners. "I've got to make vegetable soup. That way everything will be all right again. That way Ben will love me again. He won't leave me."

"Honey, Ben isn't going to leave you." Sarah walked over and tried to put her arms around her sister, but Lindy shrugged away from her.

"What do you know about it? What do you know about anything?" Lindy yelled. "You haven't been around. You ran out on me. You don't know anything about me or my life!"

Sarah stepped back from her, shocked by the vehemence Lindy displayed, the irrational anger that blazed in her eyes. "Please don't shout, you'll wake up Jackie," she said with forced calmness.

Lindy stalked over to the pantry and began to pull out canned vegetables and stack them on the countertop. She moved like a cartoon character in fast motion, stacking the cans higher and higher until they teetered precariously.

"Lindy, you're tired. Do you really think this needs to be done now?"

"Yes," she hissed. She turned to face Sarah once again, the same irrational anger twisting her features into a mask of hatred. "I have to do it now…before Ben leaves me for good."

"Lindy, Ben loves you. He's not leaving you," Sarah protested.

"Shut up." Lindy slammed the palms of her hands against her ears. "I don't want to listen to you. You don't know what's happening around here. How could you? You've been gone. You left me, just like everyone else.'' Tears sprang to her eyes as she glared at Sarah. ''First Daddy left, then you, then Mama. Everyone leaves me. I hate all of you. I hate you for leaving me.''

Again Sarah moved forward, wanting to put her arms around Lindy, hold her close and chase away the fears, the anger, the very illness that ate at her. But Lindy shoved her away and swiped angrily at the tears that glittered in her eyes. ''When we were little and I was scared, you'd cuddle with me and tell me that you'd always be here for me. But you lied. You lied and you left me and now I hate you. I hate you!'' The last of her words rose on a high pitch of fury and she picked up one of the cans and threw it at the wall. The can hit the wall with enough force to dent the Sheetrock, then fell to the floor and rolled under the table.

Sarah stared at Lindy, astonished at the level of anger she'd displayed. Lindy's entire body trembled, as if she were on the verge of shaking herself apart. ''Go back to bed, Sarah.'' She began to pace, her arms flailing frantically around her. ''Go on, get out of here and leave me to do what needs to be done.'' She turned and began opening the cans.

Sarah watched her for a long moment, still stunned by her unexpected rage. With a worried frown, she started back up the stairs to her bedroom. There was no point in trying to talk rationally with her, she thought. At the moment Lindy was completely irrational. Her mother had often called, detailing Lindy's manic phases—the frenzied energy, the shift from reality into paranoia.

As she ascended the stairs she contemplated Lindy's anger. She'd had no idea that her sister was so bitter about her leaving, that Lindy saw it as Sarah abandoning her. Surely Lindy understood the circumstances that had forced Sarah from Clay Creek.

It's the illness, Sarah reminded herself. The illness caused her irrationality, her fits of anger. The illness colored everything in Lindy's perceptions.

She needs to see her doctor, Sarah thought in frustration. Lindy seemed to be deteriorating day by day. This fury, this unprovoked rage frightened Sarah. She needed to press Ben about getting an appointment for Lindy as soon as possible. And if he couldn't—or *wouldn't*—do that, then Sarah was going to have to be forced to take matters into her own hands and find another doctor. She hated to do that, hated to upset Lindy by taking her to a stranger, but she couldn't allow Lindy to plunge deeper and deeper into her illness. Something had to be done.

Apparently there was a lot of healing that needed to go on. She didn't want to leave for New York without attempting to restore some of the closeness she and Lindy had once shared.

She went directly to Jackie's room, breathing a sigh of relief that the little girl hadn't awakened and been frightened.

Pausing in the doorway of her own bedroom, she reached up to touch the bandage on the side of her head. She shivered as she remembered the sound of bullets whizzing by her, the vague impression she'd had that the shots had come from the direction of the house.

She shivered again as she thought of the force that had been behind the thrown can of vegetables. Indeed, there was a rage deep inside Lindy, a rage that had gotten the best of her for a moment. She was sick and the sickness created the rage. But could the same illness that created the anger also make Lindy dangerous?

Sarah crossed her bedroom and got into bed, suddenly icy cold. *It's ridiculous to think that Lindy had anything to do with the gunshots,* she thought as she pulled the comforter tightly around her neck. Lindy would never do anything to hurt her. But as much as Sarah tried to reassure herself, it still took her a very long time to fall asleep.

Chapter 6

"Sarah, somebody's here to see you." Lindy's voice drifted up the stairs at the same time that Sarah became conscious of the dogs barking hysterically.

She pushed the papers she'd been studying aside and stood up, stretching her arms over her head to alleviate the kinks from sitting too long. She'd been in her mother's office for the past couple of hours, going over financial papers and the farm accounts.

She ran a hand through her hair and smoothed her blouse, wondering who could be here, then ran lightly down the stairs and into the living room.

Sitting on the sofa was the man Sarah had seen Ben speaking to at Margaret's funeral. He stood as she walked into the room, his overgenerous mouth creasing into a smile. "Ah, Miss Calhoun, I'm Raymond Boswell." He held out his hand to her. "I'm the owner of the Boswell Power Plant."

His big hand engulfed hers, and as he released her,

she motioned for him to sit back down. "Yes, Mr. Boswell, what can I do for you?"

"The real question is not what you can do for me, but what I can do for you." He sat down and settled back against the cushions of the sofa, dwarfing the piece of furniture with his large size. He smiled at her expectantly.

"I'm afraid I don't understand," Sarah replied.

He leaned forward and smiled once again, exposing an overbite that, along with his long hooked nose, gave him a predatory appearance. "I understand that you're from New York City." She nodded, wondering why he was here. "Wonderful city, full of life. I'm sure you're anxious to get back there."

Sarah shrugged. "I'm not in any hurry," she said perversely. "There are still lots of things I need to take care of here."

"And that's where I can be of help to you. I'd like to buy this place."

Sarah immediately shook her head. "I'm afraid you're wasting your time here, Mr. Boswell. This farm is not for sale."

Raymond Boswell laughed with an amused condescension that rankled Sarah. "My dear, everything is for sale...it's just a matter of settling on the right price." He straightened his tie, then leaned forward once again, eyeing her intently. "I'm willing to make you an offer that will assure that your family lives in ease for the rest of their natural lives."

Sarah stood up. "Perhaps you didn't understand me the first time, Mr. Boswell," she replied coolly. "This is our home. It isn't for sale." She moved toward the door, indicating to him that as far as she was concerned they had nothing left to discuss.

He didn't move. Instead he settled back into the sofa once again and chuckled. "There's no doubt that you are your mother's daughter. She was stubborn as a mule, as well. Before her accident I spoke to her a dozen times and she finally verbally agreed that the best thing would be to sell out."

"I don't believe you," Sarah exclaimed, sitting back down to face him. "My mother would never have agreed to sell this place."

Raymond shrugged. "Believe what you want, but it's true. Look around you, Miss Calhoun. This place is falling apart. Your mother saw it, your brother-in-law sees it. I've had several conversations with Ben and I certainly don't think he would be adverse to cash in his pocket and a chance at a new start." He paused a moment, as if to allow his words to sink in. "Why don't you sell the property to me and go back to your life in New York City financially more comfortable."

She stood and walked to the door, this time opening it and looking at him pointedly. "I told you before, you're wasting your time here, Mr. Boswell."

He eased himself up from the sofa, shaking his head ruefully. "I'd really hoped you'd be willing to listen to reason. Personally I think you're making a terrible mistake."

"It's my mistake and I'll live with it," Sarah replied.

He walked to the door and pulled a business card from his pocket. "If you change your mind, please don't hesitate to call me."

Sarah tucked the card into her pocket and watched as he headed for the gleaming luxury car that awaited him. She leaned against the doorjamb, waiting until the dust from his car had disappeared on the wind. She then closed the door and rubbed the center of her forehead, where a dull ache had started.

"What did he want?"

She turned around to see Lindy sitting on the bottom stair step. "He wants to buy the farm."

Lindy nodded. "He tried to get Mama to sell, too." She grinned. "Mama told him to go to hell."

Sarah smiled. "I did, too, although not in those exact words." She stepped back to the door and stared outside. The first purple shadows of dusk were just beginning to paint the western sky. "I think I'll take a little walk before Jackie gets home."

"Okay, but be careful," Lindy said worriedly, her gaze lingering on the bandage on Sarah's head.

Sarah grinned and touched the gauze. "Don't worry, lightning doesn't strike twice in the same place." With a reassuring smile, she stepped outside into the cool, pre-twilight air.

Jackie was spending the evening at Gladys Prather's house. Gladys had invited several of her grandchildren over to meet and play with Jackie and it would be close to bedtime before Gladys drove them all home. Sarah smiled, thinking of her daughter's excitement at the prospect of meeting new friends.

She leaned against the porch supports and breathed deeply of the crisp air, enjoying the quiet that claimed the surrounding farmland. The golden hue of twilight mingling with the sounds of insects buzzing their final song of the day had a tranquilizing effect.

It had been a difficult day. She'd been tense, uncertain of Lindy's mood in light of the explosion the night before. When Sarah had gotten up it had been obvious to her that Lindy had stayed up all night. She was dressed in the same clothes and her eyes were red-rimmed from lack of sleep. Still, despite Sarah's unease, Lindy had been in high spirits for most of the day. Only the dent in the wall was mute testimony to the rage that had erupted in her the night before.

Sarah sighed again and lifted her face to the cool evening breeze. Her gaze automatically sought out the brown posts of the grape arbor in the distance. Ah, that had once been a place of magic. She shifted position against the porch support, her heart yearning for the ability to go back in time...to believe in magic once more... to believe in love.

She had a sudden impulse, a need to go to that place where the magic of love had once been so strong. It had been a place where she'd believed, no matter what she'd been told by others, that Reese loved her more than he loved himself.

She'd been so young, so idealistic, so very much in love. She suddenly realized she needed to go back there and confirm to herself that it was only a grape arbor with no magic at all.

She set her coffee cup on the porch railing and stepped down onto the grass. As she walked, the long weeds reached up beneath the hem of her jeans to tickled her ankles. She moved briskly, breathing deeply of the sweet-scented air, thoughts of Reese still intruding into her mind.

They had often met beneath the grape arbor in the early morning hours before she went to school and he went to work at the garage. She could remember running across the grass as the morning sun chased the night away. No matter how early she came, Reese was always there waiting for her, his arms opened wide and his eyes burning with fires that took her breath away. How many nights had they met here for a last goodbye embrace before they went into their own homes and spent miserable long nights apart?

Sarah had wondered often if her mom knew what prompted her to leave the house early for school. She had a feeling her mother suspected those early morning trysts, but Margaret was one of the few people in town who'd believed in Reese's heart. "All that boy needs is somebody to believe in him," she'd often said.

"I guess he fooled us both, Mama," Sarah said softly, shoving her memories aside as the arbor came into full view. She stopped a moment, wondering if coming here had been such a good idea. Instead of banishing the past, dispelling the magic, it seemed to have pulled her, wrapping her once again in its spell.

The last of the evening sunlight painted the arbor and surrounding brush with its lush golden light, but still she was reluctant to take the dozen steps that would carry her beneath the wire mesh laden with twisted, gnarled vines. She imagined she could smell Reese in the air, that clean, masculine scent that always stirred her to distraction.

For just a brief moment she wished she could go back, experience the overwhelming act of making love with him one last time.

She took a step forward, surprised to hear her foot echo hollowly. She looked down and realized she'd stepped on the sheet of thick wood that covered the old well. She'd forgotten about it. Before she could move, she heard an ominous crack and her stomach shot up to her throat as she felt the wood beneath her feet split and she plunged downward.

There was no time for thought, no time to scream. As she fell, her feet scrambled for a foothold and her hands clawed for something to hang on to. She sobbed in relief as her fingers gripped a large root, effectively stopping her descent and making her feel as if her arms had been pulled out of her shoulder sockets.

She gasped for breath, trying to orient herself, still the frantic beating of her heart. She had fallen only about two feet below the ground level, but as she looked up, she realized she might as well have fallen twenty feet.

She closed her eyes for a moment, adrenaline pumping through her, making it difficult to think. Oh God, she had to do something. But what? She was afraid to move, afraid to fall. She suddenly became aware of the noxious odor of stagnant water and rotting vegetation. It wafted upward, like air from a grave, and she clung more tightly to the root, trying to stop the trembling that possessed her body.

The root she hung on to crackled and gave a fraction of an inch. Sarah screamed, her feet working to find something, anything, that would ease the deadweight of her body. She gasped in relief as her foot found what felt like a dislodged brick. She placed her toes on it and was relieved to feel some of the strain on her arms dissipate.

Minutes passed while she fought off panic. "Lindy!" she screamed, shivering as her only answer was an echo from the bottom of the well. Above her, half of the board that had broken still covered a portion of the hole, allowing only a sliver of pale twilight to reach within.

How on earth would Lindy know where she was? How long would she have to hang here waiting for somebody to come looking for her? Despite the coolness of the air, she felt perspiration popping across her forehead. Her arms trembled with the effort of hanging on, and her hands ached with the intensity of her grip on the root. Night would fall before long and she'd be hanging here in the dark. She fought off a shiver of horror at the very thought.

How long could she hang here? How long before her hands cramped or her arms weakened and she fell?

"Lindy!" she screamed once more. Again there was no answer, no indication that anyone heard her. Her cry echoed eerily around her. Somewhere in a nearby tree a bird chirped, and in the distance she could hear the barking of a dog.

The dogs. Surely Lindy would come outside to feed the dogs their evening meal. And if she came outside, then she would hear Sarah's cries for help.

She yelled until she was afraid her voice would go hoarse, fighting back tears of frustration and fear.

What would happen to Jackie if Sarah fell...if she died? Would Lindy and Ben raise her? Could Ben take on the responsibility of a child along with the responsibility of Lindy? What would Reese do? Would he finally take Jackie? Learn to love her? Be a father?

A bubble of hysterical laughter caught in her throat at this thought. It seemed a little drastic to have to die in order for a man to become a dad. The laughter turned into a choking sob.

She strained her shaking arms, wondering if she could pull herself up enough to grab on to the ground above. She pressed her toes into the roughened sides of the well. She squeezed her right hand around the root and cautiously removed her left one, stretching up. But the ground was simply too far for her to reach.

Sarah closed her eyes as her grasping hand dislodged tiny pebbles and dirt clods. They rained down on her head, bouncing off her body, and it was several long seconds later that they finally plopped into the dank water beneath her.

Grabbing the root firmly with both hands once again, she cautiously looked below her. She saw nothing, only a dark yawn of blackness that filled her with terror. She moved her feet once again, seeking a better brick to stand on. Finding nothing, she returned to the small brick, the little bit of leverage easing slightly the strain on her arms.

Her arms were beginning to tremble with weariness and her fingers cramped painfully. She closed her eyes once again, her mind filled with visions of Jackie, of Lindy...of Reese. She wasn't afraid to die, but she would leave so much unfinished business behind. Jackie wasn't grown up yet, Lindy wasn't well, and Reese...she wasn't sure how she felt about him, but she knew they had unfinished business between them, too.

Dear God, she was going to die here. It didn't seem fair. But she knew more than anyone that nothing was ever fair. If life had been fair, she and Reese would have gotten married and lived happily ever after. Jackie would now have a loving father as part of her life.

"Sarah?"

The cry was faint, questioning, and Sarah responded, screaming her sister's name over and over again. A shadow fell across the opening of the well and Lindy's face appeared, her expression mirroring the horror Sarah knew was on her own face. "Oh, Sarah, what should I do?"

In an instant, Sarah knew Lindy couldn't help—at least not by herself. Lindy wasn't physically strong enough to reach down and pull Sarah up, and Sarah didn't have the strength left to assist in her own rescue. "Lindy, go back to the house and call Reese. Hurry, Lindy!"

Lindy nodded and disappeared, leaving Sarah alone

once again. "Hurry, Reese. Dear God, please hurry." She said the words over and over again, like a mantra to ward off death.

It seemed as if hours passed, but finally she heard the distant wail of an approaching siren and knew Reese was on his way. It was only then that she allowed the first tears to fall.

"Sarah?"

"Reese!" His name came out with a sob as she looked up and saw him peering down at her.

"It's all right, sweetheart, I'm here now." His voice was soothing and calm despite the concern she saw in his eyes. "Are you hurt?" He shoved the remaining piece of wood out of his way.

"No, but, Reese, please help me. I can't hold on any longer, and this root is about to pull out. I'm going to fall." Her arms trembled violently beneath the physical strain of holding herself up.

"You're not going to fall," Reese exclaimed forcefully. He leaned over the hole, stretching his arm down to her. "Grab hold of my wrist, Sarah," he commanded.

"I—I can't." She was afraid to release the root, afraid to reach out for his wrist with her fingers cramped and exhausted.

"Yes you can." His eyes blazed and his voice was as hard and demanding as she'd ever heard it. "Grab my wrist, Sarah."

She took a deep breath, reaching inside for the last strength she had left. With a cry of terror, she released the root and grabbed onto him. His hand immediately clamped tightly around her wrist. He grunted beneath the strain and she could hear him shifting his body to get better leverage. "Don't let go," she whispered fervently.

"I'm not going to let you go."

She looked up, somehow knowing from his tone of voice that he was talking about more than this moment, more than their clasped hands. And then she had no more time for thought as she was being pulled up... toward Reese...toward life.

They both collapsed onto the grass, Reese breathing harshly from his exertions and tears of relief brimming in her eyes.

He stood and helped her up, drawing her into his arms, where his strength absorbed the trembling that still overwhelmed her body. Her legs barely held her up and she leaned weakly against him. She was vaguely conscious of Lindy in the distance, standing in the glow of the porch light. As Sarah watched, Lindy turned and went back into the house.

Sarah knew she should push herself away from him, be strong. But she couldn't be strong. Not now. Instead she closed her eyes and gave herself over to the sensation of being held, safe and warm, in Reese's arms.

She shuddered, remembering the yawn of darkness beneath her, the dank air that had reached up to her, as if wanting to swallow her.

"Come on, come sit down for a minute."

She didn't protest when he led her beneath the grape arbor. She needed some time to calm herself before she went inside and saw Lindy, needed to settle her nerves before Jackie came home.

She allowed him to pull her down beside him in the cool shadows beneath the barren, twisted vines. The darkness of the approaching night combined with the thickness of the vines overhead and surrounding them created a natural cocoon of privacy.

He pulled her into his arms and she went, needing his

warmth to chase away the lingering fear, wanting his very aliveness to confirm her own. He rubbed her back, tangling one hand in her hair as he murmured words meant to calm, to soothe. Sarah kept her hands clenched into fists at his back, knowing that to open them, to spread them out and caress the broad plane of his back, was to invite the insanity back into her soul.

Still, she didn't have the strength, either physically or emotionally, to pull away from him. Instead she burrowed her head against his firm chest, enjoying the clean scent of his cotton shirt and the other, more subtle masculine smell that belonged innately to Reese. She could remember nights after she'd left town, lying in the single bed in her aunt's old brownstone, when suddenly the memory of his scent would come back to her, fill her with an aching loneliness and cause tears to spring to her eyes.

"Sarah." He whispered her name softly, bidding her to look up at him.

The caresses meant to soothe had subtly changed. His hands moved more slowly and seemed to have gotten warmer. A gasp caught in her throat as one of his hands found the bare skin between the bottom of her sweatshirt and the waistband of her jeans. His fingers stroked her flesh softly, his touch creating a spark of desire deep inside her. Against her will, she tipped her head back and looked at him, his eyes consuming her in flames of want.

Before she could protest, his lips descended, claiming hers in a hungry kiss that shattered what few defenses she had. Without thought, she opened her mouth to him, allowing his tongue to touch her bottom lip, then delve inside. With a small groan, Sarah unclenched her hands and spread them across his back, reveling in the play of muscle beneath his cotton shirt. He was a memory she'd not been able to forget, and each teasing dance of his tongue, each stroke of his hands, sharpened the desire she'd thought had gone with the passing of years.

But the past fell away in a frantic heartbeat. He pulled her closer and she felt her breasts swelling, growing fuller to press against his chest. With a sigh, she welcomed his hands as they moved beneath her sweatshirt, stroking the skin of her back with tendrils of heat.

How many nights had she slept in her lonely bed, dreaming of being back in his arms? How many times had she remembered his touch, his kiss, and wondered if the passing of time had made it more than it had been? Now she knew that her memories hadn't deceived her, that it was every bit as magical, as wondrous, as she'd remembered.

His mouth moved from hers, kissing her neck. Sarah closed her eyes, shivering as his hot breath tickled her ear, stirred against her neck. She was caught in a maelstrom of emotion, where there was no past, no future, only this moment in time. As his mouth captured hers again, she felt drugged, mindless beneath his onslaught. His hands moved from her back to cup her breasts, his fingertips finding her erect nipples through the thin material of her bra.

She pulled his shirt out of his waistband, needing to feel the warmth of his skin. Her hands swept across his chest, reveling in the familiar contours. She paused, puzzled as her fingertips lingered over a ridge of scarred tissue. It hadn't been there before, and the feel of it beneath her fingers brought reality thundering back.

What was she doing? The past was gone, dead beneath a myriad of broken dreams and shattered hopes. She couldn't go back, couldn't rewrite their past, couldn't reclaim the innocence that had once been so much a part of her love for Reese.

She pushed against him, breaking their embrace. "I—I need to get back to the house." She stood, not meeting his gaze.

"Sarah." His voice was soft, eliciting an involuntary, lingering spark of desire in her. He stood, moving so close to her she could feel the heat from his body. "Sarah, look at me."

Reluctantly she looked up, seeing the fires of passion that still flamed in his dark gray eyes. He reached out and touched her chin, then lightly stroked down her jawline. "I told you yesterday that I want you, and I know you want me, too."

She flushed, wishing she could lie, wishing she could tell him he was wrong. But she knew he'd see through any lie she might tell. Her response to him had already spoken for her. "Wanting and needing are two different things," she replied with a weary sigh. "We always had a powerful physical thing between us, Reese. I can't deny that it still exists. But we've both been down this road before, and we know it leads to nowhere. I need more than you're willing to give. I always have." She also knew that his desire couldn't sustain itself beneath the weight of his anger—an anger she felt directed at her whenever they were together. It seethed just beneath the surface, ready to explode at any moment.

She stepped away from him. "I've got to get inside. Jackie will be home soon." She turned to leave but hesitated as he called after her.

He took a step toward her, opening his mouth as if to say something, then closing it again. "I—I need to find something to cover that well," he finally said.

"You can probably find something in the barn," she answered, then started walking toward the house.

Reese watched her go, the unconscious, overtly feminine movement of her hips heating his blood once again. He tore his gaze from her and headed for the barn, still able to feel the pumping of his desire in his veins.

God, no other woman had ever managed to affect him the way Sarah did. She was an addictive elixir to his spirit, a powerful aphrodisiac that made his head spin.

When they'd been young, he hadn't been able to get enough of her. He'd awakened each morning wanting her and gone to bed each night in the same condition. But he wasn't twenty years old anymore, and she wasn't seventeen. Time had passed and there was one very important difference now.

He opened the barn door and stepped inside. He knocked aside a cobweb that hung down from one of the ceiling beams and went to the back of the barn, where scraps of lumber and old plywood were stored. As he picked through the pile, he thought of how his heart had stopped when he'd looked down in that dank hole and seen Sarah hanging on for dear life.

When he'd been younger he'd played chicken with his car at a hundred miles an hour. He'd stared down the barrel of a gun and felt terror in his gut, but nothing he'd ever experienced, past or present, even began to compare with the soul-wrenching horror he'd felt when he'd seen Sarah down in that well.

And nothing had prepared him for the glory of holding her once again in his arms, tasting the sweetness of her lips and wanting her with an intensity that had stolen all other thought from his head. In those moments of holding her, kissing her, he'd forgotten all about his anger, her betrayal, the decision she'd made that had taken her out of his life without giving him any choice.

He frowned. "Jackie will be home soon," she had said just before she'd left. She'd spoken her daughter's name emphatically, letting him know that the child would forever be between them, a bridge to the past but a barrier to any future together.

He found a large, thick sheet of plywood and carried it back toward the well. He removed the broken piece that remained over the well and replaced it with the plywood, carefully centering it over the hole. He'd have to talk to Sarah about getting the old well filled in. It should have been done years ago.

Satisfied that for the moment the hole wouldn't be a danger to anyone else, he picked up the piece of wood that had broken beneath Sarah's weight.

He looked at it, shock riveting him as he stared at the edge. The wood hadn't splintered and broken apart. It had been sawed to a fraction of an inch of being cut into. He ran a thumb down the broken edge, feeling the unmistakable smoothness of sawed wood, then the minute layer that had broken beneath Sarah's weight.

Why would somebody saw the board practically in two, then carefully lay it back over the opening of the well? It didn't make any sense.

His frown deepened as he rolled the implications around in his head. Had somebody wanted Sarah to fall down that well? What if Jackie had decided to walk out here by herself? His heart turned to stone at the very thought.

He carried the piece to his car, noting the scent of fresh-cut wood that told him it had been sawed very recently. He opened his trunk and placed the piece inside. He would take the wood to Jim and see what the old man's thoughts were.

He considered the gunshot that had nearly taken off Sarah's head. Two near tragic accidents. Somehow his gut told him it was more than mere coincidence. Somebody was trying to hurt Sarah. Now all he had to figure out was why…and who?

Chapter 7

Reese sat patiently while Jim studied the piece of wood, his bifocals resting where they had slipped down on the end of his broad nose. "Yup, I'd say this was cut recently...within the last couple of days." He set the wood aside and studied the chessboard that was on the table between him and Reese.

No matter what time of the day or night, whenever Reese stopped by Jim's old house, the chessboard was ready for a game. Jim had taught Reese to play when he'd brought Reese home from the hospital to recuperate from his gunshot wound. Every life-changing conversation Reese had had with the old man had taken place over the game board.

"I'd say the first thing you need to do is think about motive. Why would anyone want to hurt Sarah Calhoun? Who profits if she dies?" Jim moved a castle and settled back in his chair.

Reese frowned, absently studying the placement of the

chess pieces. "How would anyone know that Sarah was going to be the one to walk over that well?" He moved a pawn up a space, his mind far removed from the game at hand. "Why not Lindy...or Jackie, for that matter?"

"I'd say the odds are good that somebody expected Sarah to go across the well. The arbor was always one of her favorite spots." Jim grinned. "Hell, everyone in town knew years ago that you two were meeting out in that grape arbor." Reese looked at him in surprise and Jim laughed once again. "You two were so wrapped up in each other you didn't know the whole town was buzzing about you. I'd say it would be a fair guess that Sarah would go back out there while home visiting." Jim made his next move.

"But who would want to hurt Sarah?" Frustration gnawed at Reese's insides. "She hasn't been in town long enough to make anyone mad enough to want to kill her," Reese observed, then added dryly, "except maybe me." He made his move, then looked back at Jim expectantly.

"Motive, look for motive and you'll figure it out."

"It could just be coincidence," Reese added. "The shooting and now this...it could just be coincidental."

Jim plucked at his bushy gray eyebrow. "I never did put much stock in the odds of coincidence." He grinned. "Checkmate."

Reese stared at the board in dismay, then grinned back at Jim. "You old coot. One of these days I'll beat you." He stood up and grabbed his hat. "I think I need to have a talk with Sarah. She needs to know about the well cover, about what I suspect."

Jim walked with him to the door and clapped him on the back. "You'll figure it out. You've got a good head on your shoulders and you're a hell of a sheriff." He looked at Reese soberly. "If there's anything I can do to help, you know I'm here for you."

Reese nodded gratefully. "Thanks Jim."

Reese got back into his car and sat for a moment, thinking, assessing the recent events. Like Jim, he was beginning to doubt the odds of it all being coincidence.

A ball of apprehension grew in his chest as he remembered how Sarah had looked dangling down in that well. What if she hadn't managed to grab on to anything? What if she hadn't stopped her downward plunge? What if that dried old root had snapped?

He felt the blood leave his face and his hands tightened around the steering wheel. He couldn't let anything happen to her. Even though he hadn't known where she was for the past six years, there had been times when he'd taken comfort in the knowledge that the same moonlight that shone in his bedroom window at night also peeked into hers wherever she was. He'd been somehow at peace knowing the same sun warmed her shoulders, the same stars winked down on her at night.

"You're a hell of a sheriff." Jim's parting words flowed over him. Reese hoped the old man was right. If what they suspected was true, somebody had tried to hurt Sarah twice. What Reese had to do was figure out who and why, so that there wouldn't be a third attempt. Sarah's very life might depend on him…and that scared the hell out of him.

Jackie vacuumed up the last of her soda into her straw. Sarah frowned at the resulting slurping noise. "Can I have another one?" Jackie asked, carefully pushing her empty glass away from the edge of the table.

"You know the rules—one soda. How about a glass of milk instead?" Sarah offered.

"Oh, let her have another one," Lindy interjected. "This is a special occasion. It's not every night that we're all together eating out." She motioned for Anna, who immediately left the counter and approached the booth where the three sat.

"Anna, would you bring my favorite niece another soda, and I'd love a piece of that cherry pie," Lindy said.

Anna nodded, then smiled at Sarah. "What about you, honey? I've got some pecan pie back there."

"No, thanks. I'm stuffed." She looked at her watch, wondering what was keeping Reese. He'd called first thing that morning and said it was important that he talk to her. They'd agreed to meet here at the café at six o'clock this evening. It was now almost six-thirty and there was no sign of him.

Anticipation winged through her each time the café door swung open. She was concerned about how eager she was to see him again. It both worried her and frightened her.

She thought of those moments in the grape arbor the evening before. His caresses had successfully chased away the taste of death that had lingered in her mouth. But he'd also managed to chase away every ounce of good sense she possessed. And those brief moments of insanity had been heavenly. That's what scared her. It was ridiculous to think about getting involved with him once again, and yet it was impossible not to dream of being in his arms, making love with him.

"Here we are." Anna returned to the table, interrupting Sarah's thoughts and the conversation Lindy and Jackie had been having about dogs. "You okay, honey?" Anna asked. "You've been awfully quiet this evening."

"Mama fell down in the well last night," Jackie explained.

Anna gasped. "What?" She stared at Sarah. "What well?"

"The old one out by the grape arbor. I forgot all about it, walked over it and the wooden cover must have been rotten," Sarah explained, wishing her daughter had never brought up the subject.

"My soul," Anna replied. "How on earth did you manage to get out?"

"The sheriff man pulled her out. He saved her," Jackie said.

"Lindy called Reese and he came and got me out," Sarah explained. "I was lucky enough to manage to grab hold of a big root and break my fall."

"You poor dear." Anna clucked sympathetically. "I'll bet you're starting to feel like everyone is out to get you. First you get shot at, then you fall down a well!"

Sarah laughed. "No, I'm just feeling very unlucky."

"How's your head?" Anna asked.

"Much better." Sarah reached up and touched the tender area self-consciously. She'd stopped wearing the bandage and the wound was healing nicely. Her hair was even starting to grow back over the closely cropped area.

"Hey, ladies," Suzanna greeted them, approaching their table with fresh coffee.

"Hi, Suzanna," Lindy greeted her with a friendly smile. "Where have you been keeping yourself lately?"

Suzanna pointed a thumb at Anna. "The slave driver has been keeping me busy."

"Humph…that will be the day," Anna snorted.

"What's this I heard about a fall down a well?" she asked, looking at Sarah curiously.

"It was nothing…just an accident," Sarah replied, simply wanting to put the frightening experience behind her.

"Mr. Sheriff saved her," Jackie said.

"Well, isn't that lucky," Suzanna said, her eyes narrowing slightly as she looked again at Sarah. "It seems you're keeping our sheriff mighty busy these days. Reese hardly has time for the rest of us." For a brief moment her lips formed a pout of displeasure, then she smiled again. "Oh well, I suppose that's what a good sheriff does, takes care of those in need, right?"

Sarah nodded, somehow relieved when the blonde turned her gaze toward Lindy.

"How are you doing, hon?" Suzanna asked Lindy, touching her arm lightly in a gesture of friendliness.

"Okay, but the dogs have missed your visits," Lindy said.

Suzanna laughed. "They miss the bones I bring them."

"And I miss the days when waitresses worked instead of standing around and chatting with the customers," Anna remarked pointedly.

Suzanna rolled her eyes and headed off to refill the coffee cups of other customers.

"I didn't know you and Suzanna were friends," Sarah observed.

"When Mama got the flu last year, Suzanna came out to the farm just about every night to bring stuff that Anna had cooked," Lindy explained.

"I never seen anyone who had the flu so bad. Margaret couldn't keep anything down except my chicken-and-rice soup," Anna said. They all fell silent for a moment and Sarah knew both Lindy and Anna were thinking of Margaret.

"Ah, here comes our hero now," Anna exclaimed brightly as Reese walked through the door.

As usual, at the sight of him a burst of warmth flooded through Sarah. He was out of uniform, clad instead in a pair of worn jeans and a heavy denim shirt that emphasized the broadness of his chest, the slimness of his hips.

"I'm sorry I'm late," he said, his gaze lingering on Sarah, then moving to encompass the rest of the group. "There was an accident out on route five and I had to make a report."

"I hope nobody was hurt," Anna said.

He shook his head. "It was just a fender bender. One of Benson's cows got out of the pasture and decided to stand in the middle of the road. Mrs. Jordon was coming home from the library and in trying to dodge the cow hit a fence post."

"Mr. Sheriff?" Jackie stood up on the booth and tugged at Reese's shirtsleeve. "Mama told us that you saved her and pulled her out of the well yesterday. Thank you for saving my mama." She reached out and placed a hand on either side of his face, then kissed him on the cheek.

She immediately released him and he stepped back, his expression unreadable and his cheeks slightly colored. *I'll be damned,* Sarah thought. In all the years she'd known Reese, she'd never seen him blush. But that's definitely what he appeared to be doing at the moment.

"You're welcome," he murmured, finally offering the little girl a self-conscious half smile. He looked back at Sarah. "I need to talk to you—alone."

"We can move to a booth in the back," Sarah offered.

He frowned, obviously finding the busy diner too public for whatever he had to discuss with her. "Would you take a walk with me?"

She hesitated a moment before answering. Lindy and Jackie were just about finished with their meals. She hated to make them sit and wait for her.

"Why don't I take Lindy and Jackie on back to the farm," Anna suggested. "Suzanna can close up. I was going to leave early tonight anyway." She looked at Sarah. "I'll sit and visit with Lindy and Jackie until you get back home."

"Oh, that would be wonderful," Lindy said, smiling at Anna affectionately. "It's been months since you've been out to our place. I can show you the pattern of the new wallpaper I want to buy for the kitchen and tell you my plans for the living room."

"Great," Reese said before Sarah could protest.

"Are you sure you don't mind?" Sarah asked Anna.

"Positive. I've been meaning to get out there and this is a perfect opportunity for me to spend some time with this little peanut." She touched Jackie on the end of her nose, causing the little girl to giggle.

Sarah gave her daughter a quick kiss on the cheek. "You be good for Anna and Lindy, and I'll be home in a while."

"Reese, could I speak with you for a minute?" Suzanna called to him from across the room.

With an apologetic glance at Sarah, he walked across the room to where Suzanna stood. The blonde spoke to him quickly and placed a hand on his arm. He shook his head, said something back to her, then shook his head once again. Suzanna turned on her heels and disappeared into the kitchen.

"Sorry," Reese said as he approached where Sarah stood by the front door.

"Problem?" she asked.

"Nothing I can't handle," he replied curtly.

Moments later, she and Reese walked out into the cool night air. Although it was just after six-thirty, already Main Street looked deserted. Clay Creek was a town where evening was family time and families still ate together, talked together, shared together. There was no rush-hour traffic, no honking horns and swearing drivers. There was simply the aura of a town at rest, the light wind's sigh signaling day's end.

"So, what did you want to talk to me about? You made it sound very important when you called earlier." She broke the silence that momentarily surrounded them.

"Let's walk for just a few minutes. I need to gather my thoughts," he replied.

She nodded, finding the night, the quiet of the streets comfortable. It was as if her hometown embraced her, wrapped her in the loving arms she had missed since leaving so many years before. But what chased the comfort away was the knowledge that the welcoming warmth of Clay Creek was temporary and the town would never again be her home.

"Lindy tells me you're dating Suzanna," she said, suddenly needing to remember that she had no place here, with him.

"We were dating, but it wasn't anything serious. We aren't dating at all anymore." He grinned at her, a mocking little smile. "Why? Jealous?"

"Don't be ridiculous," she scoffed, heat washing over her face. "I was just curious."

They walked for a few minutes in silence.

"It's nice to know you can still walk the streets of this town after dark and not be afraid," she observed. She looked up at Reese, noting the proprietary gaze he cast around him. Somehow in the passing of time, he'd claimed the town as his own…or the town had finally claimed him.

She was happy for him. Happy that he seemed to have found some sort of inner peace, had learned to take pride in his roots. She wondered what had caused him to change from a rebellious, angry boy into the man he had become. Suddenly she thought of something. "Reese, that scar on your chest. How did you get it?" Her fingers tingled and she felt a blush warm her cheeks as she remembered the feel of the puckered skin along with the feel of his heated flesh and the smooth expanse of muscle. As she felt her blush deepen, she was grateful for the twilight shadows that surrounded them.

"I call it my coming-of-age wound," he said, his hand moving to touch his chest.

"What do you mean? What happened?"

He slowed their pace, his features thoughtful. "I told you I went a little bit crazy after you left. Well, to be more precise, I was on a direct road to destruction. I started drinking, getting into fights. One night I drove out to that liquor store on route ten. I didn't realize it was near closing time and the place had been robbed twice before by somebody driving a car resembling mine. I walked in, swaggering and belligerent as I was most of the time, and the clerk assumed it was a robbery. He pulled out a pistol and shot me."

"My God," Sarah gasped. Involuntarily she reached out and grabbed his arm, as if to reassure herself of his safety. They stopped walking and stood beneath the harsh glare of the streetlight. The lamplight emphasized the lean, dangerous beauty of his face, the features that had haunted her for six years. Quickly she pulled her hand away from the warmth of his arm.

"They say in those moments before death, your entire life flashes before your eyes. Death opened its mouth in my face, ready to swallow me up, and you know what scared me more than anything?" His eyes glittered darkly and his features grew taut. "Nothing flashed before my eyes. It was the bleakest, most empty feeling I've ever known, because I realized that was my life—bleak and empty. When I woke up in the hospital, Jim Taylor was there."

"And he offered you a job?"

Reese nodded. "He told me life had dealt me a crappy hand—a mother who left and a drunk for a father. He made me see that I had a choice. I could either stay angry and eventually end up in the morgue, or I could decide to do something with my life, fill up that emptiness with positive images." He gave her a jaunty grin. "I may have been wild, but I wasn't completely stupid. I knew it was time to make some changes."

He started walking once again and Sarah hurried to catch up with him. "I spent a lot of time hating this town. I blamed it for my mother leaving, for my dad's drinking. I figured if we'd lived any other place in the world, things would have been different. While I was recuperating, I did a lot of thinking and realized the problem wasn't Clay Creek, it was me. It was time to stop trying to run away from this town and learn to live in it."

"I'm glad for you, Reese." And she was. Despite her own disappointments and disillusionment, despite the fact that he couldn't change the circumstances that had forced her to leave Clay Creek or offer her any hope for the future, she was glad that he had found his own personal sense of peace. It seemed only fair that at least one of them find a modicum of happiness.

She paused as he turned to go up the sidewalk that led to a two-story clapboard house. "Where...where are we going?" she asked.

"This is my place," he replied, pulling a set of keys from his pocket. "We can talk here."

Sarah's footsteps dragged. "I thought we were just taking a walk."

"Sarah, I really need to talk to you about something important and it needs to be in private." He seemed to sense her hesitancy. "Please, just give me a few minutes."

"Okay," she relented, admitting to herself that, if nothing else, she was curious to see where Reese now lived. When she'd left Clay Creek, he'd lived with his father in a tiny shanty on the edge of town. The yard had been filled with old car parts and weeds. The screen door had hung askew and the paint had weathered to a dull gray. She'd since heard that his father had died and that old shanty had been torn down.

This place was much different. The yard was neatly tended and the shutters looked as if they had recently received a fresh coat of paint. It was obvious that a man who took pride in his home resided here.

The house smelled of him. She noticed it the moment she stepped through the door and into the living room. It smelled of cool night air mingling with the more subtle odors of shaving cream, soap and cologne—a wonderful blend of wildness and domesticity.

"Have a seat." He motioned her toward the sofa. "How about something to drink? I'm afraid your choices are rather limited—coffee or a soft drink?"

She shook her head. "Nothing for me."

"I'll just grab a soda. Be right back."

When he disappeared, Sarah looked around the room.

It was simply furnished with an overstuffed sofa in black and gray and a matching recliner chair. An entertainment center held a stereo, the television and several mystery novels.

For the first time she allowed herself to wonder why he'd brought her here, what he wanted to discuss. She was too smart to entertain the notion that he was going to profess eternal love for her and Jackie, that he was going to take her in his arms and tell her he wanted to live the rest of his life with the two of them. She still sensed an anger in him, an anger directed toward her. He didn't want Jackie but was angry for the choice she made six years ago. It didn't make sense.

She felt herself tense as he came back in and sat down on the sofa next to her. The soberness of his expression let her know that whatever he wanted to discuss with her wasn't going to be particularly pleasant.

Reese took a deep swallow of his soda, then placed the can on the coffee table and turned to look at her. She looked at him curiously, with those beautiful Calhoun eyes, and he regretted the fact that he was about to tell her something that would place fear in their blue depths. "Sarah, there's no easy way to say this. I think somebody is trying to harm you."

"What?" She looked at him incredulously. "What on earth are you talking about?"

He jumped up from the sofa and went to the coat closet. Reaching inside, he withdrew the portion of the wood that had covered the well and given way beneath her the night before. "I took this over to Jim this morning. I wanted him to look at it and see if he came up with the same conclusion I did."

"And what conclusion is that?" Sarah asked, her voice slightly impatient.

"Somebody sawed nearly through this wood. On the surface, it looked strong and safe, but it would have cracked under any weight at all. It was intended for you to walk over it, and for it to break and you to fall down that well."

"But that's crazy," she whispered, her eyes darkening in bewilderment. "There must be some mistake…you must be wrong."

"I wish I was." He moved the piece of the wood closer to her, then took her hand and guided it over the area where it had broken. "Feel the smoothness—you can see the cut marks. And smell it. There's no doubt about it, it was cut in the past couple of days."

"But—but why? Why would somebody do something like this?" She pulled her hand from his and wrapped her arms around herself, as if feeling a sudden draft.

"That's what I was hoping you could help me figure out." He put the wood back into the closet, then rejoined her on the sofa.

"Surely we're just overreacting to an isolated incident," she protested.

He nodded, understanding her reaction. "That's what I thought at first. But it's not an isolated incident. You were also shot," he reminded her. "The shooting by itself could be construed as an accident, but this…" He let his voice trail off for a moment, then continued. "I think we have to face the possibility that somebody is trying to intentionally harm you."

"But the gunshot was probably just a hunter…"

He could see by the emotions in her eyes that she was struggling to make sense of the senseless. "Sarah, we haven't had a hunting accident around here in years. Most of the men who hunt are responsible gun owners who practice safety first. Everyone knows your place. Why would anyone hunt on your property?''

She ran a hand through her hair, obviously trying to absorb everything he'd said. Once again she wrapped her arms around herself and he felt the shiver that swept over her. He fought the impulse to gather her in his arms, hold her close, keep the darkness and uncertainty at bay.

"We need to figure out why all this is happening. Is there anything you can think of, any reason why somebody would want to harm you?"

She shook her head, her shivering now uncontrollable. "You're frightening me," she said softly. This time he gave in to his impulse. He pulled her into his arms, surrounding her with his warmth and strength.

"You aren't in this alone," he murmured into the sweet fragrance of her hair. "I'll do everything in my power to keep you safe." And he would have sold his soul to the very devil to be able to go on holding her, but all too soon she pulled herself out of his arms and stood.

"Well, there has to be a reason…" she said, pacing the area in front of the sofa.

"There's all the classic motives—revenge, greed, passion." He eyed her curiously. "You didn't anger some jealous boyfriend before you left New York, did you?"

"Sure, and he followed me here and is now randomly firing guns at me and sawing through well covers," she said sarcastically, then sighed. "There are no jealous boyfriends," she informed him with a short, humorless burst of laughter. "There are no boyfriends at all. I don't have time for men."

He nodded, not knowing what else to say and unwilling to admit that what he felt was a sudden burst of satisfaction at her confession. "Can you think of any reason for somebody to want to hurt you?"

She shrugged helplessly. "I can't imagine. No jealous boyfriends, nobody who would want revenge, and I don't own anything that would bring out someone's greed." She frowned. "Unless…?"

"Unless?" he prompted.

"What do you know about Raymond Boswell?" she asked suddenly.

He looked at her in surprise. "Not much. What does he have to do with any of this?"

She shook her head. "Oh, never mind. It's probably crazy."

"Tell me and let me be the judge of crazy."

She frowned a moment and toyed with a strand of her hair. "He came out to the farm earlier today and offered to buy us out. He indicated that Ben wouldn't be adverse to selling the place." She stared at Reese, the blueness of her eyes muddied with speculation. "If he knew that Ben was willing to sell, and that if something happens to me the farm will eventually go to Jackie and Ben and Lindy…" She let her voice trail off and her eyes widened slightly. "And if he knew that Mama wouldn't sell, but that if she died the farm would go to a daughter who lived in New York…" She gasped, trembling once again. "Reese, was there anything suspicious about Mama's death?" Tears pooled in her eyes, causing them to shimmer.

"No, of course not," he answered swiftly, although she'd made him start to think. Margaret had fallen down a flight of stairs, but there was no way to tell if she was helped in that fall.

Raymond Boswell and his company had bought a number of farms in the area, and even though there had been no whispers or rumors of strong-arm tactics, maybe it was time Reese looked a little closer at the man.

Sarah collapsed onto the sofa, looking exhausted by the entire conversation.

"You okay?" he asked softly. She nodded. "I'm sorry I had to tell you all this, but you need to know. You need to be careful."

Again she nodded and sighed. Reese studied her features, a longing building up inside him. A longing to hold her, taste her, make love to her until she moaned his name over and over again. She'd said there was no man currently in her life, but had there been other men in the last six years? Certainly in the passing years there had been other women for him, but they had merely sated his physical lust. None of them had managed to quench the thirst of his soul the way Sarah had once done.

Without conscious thought, he reached out and touched the softness of her hair, ran his finger along the curve of her jaw. She looked up at him, and in the depths of her eyes he saw a like hunger, a need as tremendous as his own. With a groan, he captured her mouth with his.

He didn't kiss her gently. He kissed her urgently, savagely, unable to restrain the intense desire that she evoked. And she kissed him back, hot and wild as she tangled her hands in his hair.

He moved his hands up beneath her blouse, caressing the smooth, warm skin of her back. She moaned into his mouth, a deep moan of pleasure and abandon that further fanned the flames of his want.

He lifted his lips from hers, his breathing ragged and harsh. "Sarah?" His unspoken question hung in the air and he tensed, waiting for her to answer it.

Her eyes were hazy, glossed with passion's touch. She tightened her arms around his neck, pulling him back to her. "Yes," she whispered softly. "Make love to me, Reese." This time it was her lips that sought his.

Somewhere deep inside, he knew it was a mistake. He knew this was probably one of the most unwise things he would ever do. But he didn't want to think about that. He didn't want to examine wrong or right. He knew he should be strong for both of them, stop this before it went any further. But he couldn't be strong. He only wanted to dwell in the depths of her eyes, lose himself in the satiny sweetness of her skin, bask in the moment of passion.

In one swift movement he stood and swept her into his arms and carried her up the stairs toward his bedroom, accepting that he was weak, so very weak where she was concerned.

Chapter 8

Moonlight danced in through the window, swaying across the bed. Reese didn't turn on the light, and Sarah was grateful. She needed the semidarkness of the room to hold on to the thick fog that obscured reason from her mind. She didn't want reason, she didn't want thought. She wanted sensation, she wanted passion...she wanted Reese.

He deposited her gently on the bed then stepped back, his eyes glittering boldly as they lingered on her. He unbuttoned his shirt and took it off, the cotton material whispering against his skin before it slid to the floor. The sound of his belt being unbuckled, the hiss of his zipper, sent a shudder of wild anticipation through Sarah. Oh God, it had been so long.

His jeans fell to the floor, exposing the beauty of his masculine body covered only by his white briefs. The moonlight caressed the planes and muscles of his body, emphasizing the width of his shoulders and the leanness of his hips. The cotton material couldn't hide his blatant, magnificent arousal.

Sarah felt her breath catch in her throat as she saw the evidence of his desire, knowing she was responsible for it. The thought only added to her own arousal and she felt her blood thicken, heat with sensual stirrings.

He joined her on the bed, and she lifted her mouth to meet his, reveling in the feel of his warm body pressed tightly against her side. As his lips plied hers, his fingers fumbled at the buttons of her blouse, freeing each one until he could part the material and move his hands over the wispy silk of her bra. His hands were warm, radiating through the soft fabric and bidding her nipples to harden in response.

His mouth moved down her jawline, into the hollow of her neck, then over her collarbone. At the same time, his hands worked to unfasten her jeans. She lifted her hips, aiding him in removing the barrier of clothing, wanting to feel skin against skin, heat against heat.

She moaned as his lips captured the tip of one breast through the filmy bra. Her nipple immediately hardened and swelled, as if reaching for the source of the erotic heat. Her moan turned to a gasp as his mouth continued to blaze a trail of fire, moving down the flat of her stomach, his tongue lingering and teasing along the band of her bikini panties.

Sarah's head reeled beneath the sensual assault. It had been so long, so very long since she'd felt a man's arms around her, experienced the heady sensation of a masculine hand stroking fire into her veins. There had been no other men in her life since she'd left Clay Creek, only her memories of what she had once shared with Reese. And she now realized how weak, how pitiful her memories were compared to the reality of being here in his arms. It was more, so much more than her memory could have ever recreated.

He moved back up to reclaim her lips with his, his tongue battling hers in a dance of exquisite pleasure. Sarah gripped his shoulders, then moved her hands across the expanse of his back, memorizing the feel of sinewy muscle beneath fevered flesh.

He seemed to be in no hurry, and neither was she. She wanted each second to last for minutes, each minute for hours. She wanted this moment in time to last through eternity.

Reaching behind her, he unsnapped her bra and plucked it from her. His mouth immediately brushed against a turgid nipple. He flicked his tongue against it, then sucked the rosy tip into his mouth, creating a responding pull deep in the pit of her stomach. With his hand, he tugged down her panties, his fingers caressing softly, teasingly, at the core of her feminine heat.

"Sweet Sarah," he muttered against the swell of her breast. "You taste so good. You feel so good. It's been so long…so very long." He raised himself up and looked into her eyes; at the same time his fingers entered her moist heat. She gasped her pleasure at his intimate possession. "Touch me, love. Feel what you do to me," he urged in a hot whisper.

She reached down and tentatively touched his thigh, then moved to stroke his rigidity through the cotton briefs. She whimpered impatiently, pulling at the waistband of the last barrier that remained between them. Within a heartbeat, the briefs joined their other clothing in a pile on the floor and Sarah closed her hand around his hot, thick maleness. She heard his swift intake of breath, a hiss of intense pleasure that merely served to heighten the fires that burned inside her.

The combination of his fingers deep inside her and the silky hotness of his pulsating erection in her hand rocketed her toward the peak of pleasure. She panted for breath, unable to control the shivers that racked her.

She was vaguely aware of him whispering encouragement, murmuring his own pleasure as he pushed her closer and closer to the edge of the pinnacle. As she tumbled over, she clung to him, gasping his name as wave after wave of drowning pleasure swept over her.

Floating, momentarily sated, Sarah lay limp and exhausted in his arms. "God, you're so beautiful," he said, stroking the hair away from her face, then running a finger across the fullness of her bottom lip. With his other hand he began to caress her breast, capturing her rigid nipple between his thumb and forefinger.

Surprised, Sarah felt an immediate response, a need that went beyond the physical craving he had just satisfied. She gasped again, felt the renewed curl of heat melting her insides. He kissed her, moving his body between her thighs as he pressed hot and urgently against her center. "Yes," she whispered, emboldened by the savage hunger he stirred once again in her. "Reese, I want you inside me."

His eyes flared and he moaned as he pressed forward, entering her wetness, gloving himself deep inside her heat. For a long moment he didn't move, as if afraid that any movement at all would send him over the edge.

Tears welled up in Sarah's eyes as long-suppressed emotions exploded inside her. She'd forgotten how well they fit, how right it had always been with him. Someplace deep inside her, she knew it would never be that way with anyone else. She wrapped her legs around his hips, drawing him more deeply into her. She could feel his heartbeat against her breasts, pounding a wild, erratic rhythm that matched his ragged breathing.

Tentatively he moved, withdrawing slightly only to thrust forward and fill her once again. She moved with him, matching him thrust for thrust, needing the total fulfillment he promised with each soul-searing caress, every breathtaking stroke.

Reese struggled to maintain control, unwilling to reach the summit without her. Not yet, he told himself, wanting the sensations, the pleasure, to last forever. But as he felt her muscles convulsing, surrounding his hardness, the last of his control slipped away. He cried out hoarsely as his body stiffened and wave after wave of pleasure swept over him. He was vaguely aware of her cries and whimpers echoing his own, and his own elation was merely intensified by the fact that they had found fulfillment together.

For a long moment neither of them moved. Reese remained inside her, sated but unwilling to break the intimacy of their physical union. He could feel their heartbeats comingling, slowing to a more natural pace.

He'd forgotten the ultimate pleasure of making love to somebody who was a part of his heart. He now realized how deeply he'd cheated himself and the few women he had made love to since Sarah had left town. With them he'd sated a physical need. With Sarah he satisfied a need that went much deeper, to his very soul.

He cared about Sarah, and he didn't know what to do about it. There was a part of him that couldn't forgive her, and he didn't know what to do about that, either. She'd made the decision to take his child and begin a new life in a distant city. She hadn't believed in him and that's what he couldn't forgive.

And then there was Jackie.... He stirred against Sarah's warmth, unwilling to follow his thoughts any further. He raised himself up on his elbows and looked down at her. Tears sparkled in her beautiful eyes, and as one silvery drop slipped down the curve of her cheek, he caught it with his fingertip. "Tears?"

A sob mingled with a little laugh of embarrassment and she closed her eyes for a brief moment. "I can't help it," she whispered softly.

"You never could," he said with a smile. "It always was beautiful between us," he added, understanding that it was the depth of intensity that had brought the tears to her eyes.

She nodded and looked at him once again, her eyes filled with a torturous pain. "Yes, this part of us was always good. But it isn't enough."

He held her gaze for a long moment and suddenly realized the extent of their mistake.

She needed a husband, a man who would be a father to Jackie. She needed someone who believed in himself, his own worth. And she'd already decided that he would not be that man.

She'd decided well, he thought with a touch of sadness. Despite the biological reality, he wasn't able to play the role of father. He couldn't. He simply didn't know how.

Reluctantly he lifted himself off her and reached for his underwear.

For a moment she remained unmoving, an air of expectancy surrounding her. Reese studiously kept his gaze directed away from her. Her expectation grew heavy in the air. Then her tremulous sigh filled the room, and silently she slipped out of the bed, grabbed her clothes and disappeared into the bathroom.

"Damn it," Reese muttered as he reached for his

pants and shirt. He'd wanted to make love to her. Some-place inside him, he'd hoped he would discover that there was nothing left of the burning passion, the wondrous joy that had marked their youthful relationship. Some small piece of him had hoped that he would make love to her again and finally be able to put her firmly in his past.

But it hadn't worked. Loving Sarah again had only managed to tie his heart into a knot, one he might never untangle again. "Damn it," he repeated, sitting on the edge of the bed to put on his socks and shoes.

She came out of the bathroom fully dressed, with no trace of tears remaining. "Would you take me back to the café, back to my car?" There was a tight edge to her voice, an edge that spoke of control so taut it threatened to shatter. She nearly vibrated with the intensity of emotions suppressed.

She looked so damned vulnerable that Reese wished he could do something, say something that would make everything all right. But he knew the one thing she demanded of him wasn't in him to give.

"Sarah—" He took a step toward her.

She held up a hand. "Please, Reese, don't say anything. There's nothing left to say. This was an enormous mistake." She stiffened her shoulders and looked away. "Consider it a momentary lapse back into the past…a sort of last goodbye between the two of us. I'll be gone in a few days and I think it best that we not see each other unless absolutely necessary. Now please, just take me to my car."

He hesitated another moment, then nodded. She was right. There was nothing left to say. It had been wonderful, it had been fantastic…and it had been an enormous mistake.

They drove back to the café in silence, a silence that weighed heavily on Reese. Six years ago she'd been the one good thing in his miserable life and fate had intervened to ruin it. There was no point in going back to try to pick up the pieces. Everything had changed and now she needed too much of him.

He pulled into the café lot and parked next to her car. He shut off the engine and turned to face her, needing to say something…wanting to somehow ease the pain that caused a furrow between her brows. "Sarah, I did love you more than I've ever loved anyone in my life."

She closed her eyes for a moment. She opened them and reached out a finger to touch his cheek, a smile of deep sadness on her face. "I know. That's what makes it hurt so much." She dropped her hand and got out of his car. "Goodbye, Reese." There was an empty finality to her words.

He watched her drive away, his heart aching with a peculiar kind of emptiness he hadn't felt in years. It felt like losing her all over again, only this time he didn't have the luxury of his youthful anger to mask the pain.

Sarah drove slowly, her vision blurred by an endless stream of tears. The tears surprised her. She thought she had cried out all the Reese tears six years ago. She thought she'd gotten past the crying where he was concerned.

She'd known it would be a mistake to make love with him again. But the moment his lips had touched hers, she'd realized that they were destined to make love one last time. What she hadn't expected was the enormous ache that echoed inside her, the ache of incredible loss.

In the best of worlds, she should be able to have both Reese and Jackie as part of her life. But she wasn't living in the best of worlds. And there were times when life was rotten and choices painful.

Yet there was no choice for her to make. Jackie was as much a part of her world as the very air she breathed, the sun that warmed her on a summer day. Jackie was her heart, her soul, and she was better off with no father at all than a reluctant one.

She and Reese had loved each other once, loved with the innocence of youth, the passion of their hearts, and that love had created a miracle named Jackie. How sad that Reese chose to turn his back and never know the true miracle he'd been a part of; how tragic that he was afraid to be a father to a little girl whose innocent heart held only the purest of love and acceptance.

Sarah realized that perhaps in this one area, she identified too closely with her daughter. Sarah knew what it was like to grow up without a father. Her father had left them when Sarah was seven, and although Margaret had been a loving, supportive mother, there had been a void in Sarah's life that no amount of "mother" could fill.

But just as Margaret had been unable to hold on to her husband when he'd decided to leave, Sarah couldn't force Reese to be something he didn't want to be.

She swiped her tears away with the back of one hand, irritated by their very existence. Enough tears had been shed over the likes of Reese Walker. He wasn't worth any more.

Suddenly she couldn't wait for Ben to get home so that she could leave Clay Creek and Reese far behind. There was nothing left for her here, nothing but heartache.

When she got back to the farm she found Anna and Jackie at the kitchen table playing a game of Go Fish and Lindy sound asleep on the sofa.

"Mama!" Jackie greeted her happily, then immediately refocused her attention on the cards in her hand. "Hmm, do you have any fives?" she asked Anna.

Anna grinned. "Go fish, you little minnow."

"I'm afraid it's time for this little minnow to jump into her pajamas and head for bed," Sarah exclaimed.

"Oh, please, just a few minutes longer," Jackie protested, looking pleadingly at her mother.

"Sorry, pumpkin, but it's well past your bedtime." Sarah took the cards out of her daughter's hand. "Your Aunt Lindy is already sound asleep and it's time for all little girls to be in bed. Now jump upstairs."

"All right." Jackie sighed. "But someday I'll be big enough to stay up all night if I want to."

"And when you're finally big enough, you'll be too tired to stay up all night," Anna replied with a laugh.

"Call me when you're ready to get tucked in," Sarah called after her pouting daughter.

"She's a real pip," Anna said, a chuckle shaking her shoulders. "She's got your spunk and her daddy's stubbornness."

Again the hollow emptiness echoed inside Sarah. "She's a great kid," she agreed. She sat down at the table and pulled Anna's wrinkled hands into her own.

"You okay?" Anna asked, eyeing her suspiciously.

"Fine." Sarah shook her head for emphasis. "Thanks for bringing Lindy and Jackie home and staying here." She lowered her voice. "I just don't feel comfortable leaving Jackie alone with Lindy right now."

Anna nodded, a frown furrowing her brow. "Your mama used to hate it when she got into one of these crazy phases. I think Margaret could handle the down moods better than the up ones. At least when Lindy's down, she just stays in bed. When she's up, there's no guessing what she might do.''

"She's been going at a frantic pace for the last couple of days. I don't know how her body can tolerate it. Ben is supposed to talk to her doctor in Kansas City about getting her in and changing her medication. It's obvious what she's taking now isn't working.''

"She'd been doing real well until this past year. Poor thing. I think your mother's death threw her off as much as anything.''

Sarah sighed and rubbed her forehead tiredly. Everything seemed to be a confusing muddle. Her feelings for Reese, her worry about her sister, her concern that somebody might want to harm her all eddied in her head, creating a dull, pounding headache.

"Mama, I'm ready to be tucked in.'' Jackie's voice floated down from upstairs.

"I'll go on and get out of your hair,'' Anna said, rising from the table and pausing only long enough to give Sarah a resounding kiss on the cheek. "It's past this old woman's bedtime, too.''

"Thanks again, Anna.'' Sarah walked the older woman to the door. She watched from the doorway until Anna had gotten into her car and driven down the lane, then she turned away from the door.

Sarah went into the living room and covered up her sister with an afghan. Lindy lay sprawled on her back, a dust cloth in her hand. It was as if her body had simply given out on her and she hadn't realized sleep was approaching. If Ben couldn't get Lindy in to see her usual doctor, Sarah vowed she would find another doctor for Lindy. There had to be something somebody could do to help her.

"Mama!'' Jackie's voice sounded once again.

Turning away from Lindy, Sarah went up three stairs, then paused and went back down to the front door. In all the years she had lived in Clay Creek she could never remember a time when anyone had worried about whether the front door was locked or unlocked. But now, the conversation with Reese still whirling around in her head she knew she couldn't rest easy unless all the doors and windows were secured.

"Mama," Jackie cried plaintively.

"Coming." Sarah ran up the stairs and into the bedroom, where Jackie sat on the edge of the bed, her eyes drooping with sleepiness. "Okay, in you go." Sarah pulled down the blankets and helped the little girl into bed.

Once Jackie was snug beneath the blankets, Sarah sat on the edge of the bed, smoothing her baby-soft hair away from her face, breathing in the sweet little-girl scent that permeated the air. For a moment her love for her daughter pressed tightly against her chest, making it difficult to draw a deep breath.

"Tell me a story," Jackie said, her eyes heavy.

"Okay, just a short one." Sarah told her a story about a magical willow tree. It had been one of Lindy's favorites, and as she told it, Sarah's heart ached for her sister, who had lost herself in a world of mental illness. Again she vowed that she would do whatever she could to see that Lindy got some help.

When she was finished with the story, Jackie smiled sleepily. "I love you, Mama."

"I love you, too, sweetheart," Sarah whispered, and she felt all the tension, all the worries of the day, ebbing away. She stretched out next to Jackie and put her arms around the little girl. Jackie immediately snuggled against her and Sarah felt tears once again burn in her eyes...tears not for herself but for Reese, who would never know the love of his little girl.

Chapter 9

"Thank you, Mrs. Johnson, I appreciate your time." Reese hung up the phone and covered his face with his hands. He heaved a sigh of frustration. In the last two days he and two of his deputies had contacted most of the farmers Raymond Boswell had bought out, and none of them had been forced off their property by any unusual tactics. Money was the only tactic he'd used, and Raymond Boswell had plenty of that particular commodity.

Shuffling papers, Reese picked up the assortment of documents he'd managed to obtain on Boswell and his company. Financial statements, tax papers, credit reports—everything pointed to a multimillion-dollar industry. Raymond Boswell was apparently a smart man, a ruthless businessman, but that didn't necessarily make him a criminal.

Still, the man was the best suspect Reese had. Hell, he was the *only* suspect Reese had. Raymond Boswell had a motive, and he had opportunity. He'd been in town on the day of the shooting and he'd been at the farm the morning of the day that Sarah fell into the well. He could have messed with that board either before or after speaking to Sarah.

Reese had tried several times in the last couple of days to contact Boswell, wanting to confirm his exact whereabouts on the night that Sarah had been shot. But according to his secretary, he was now on a business trip to St. Louis and she wasn't sure when he'd return.

Reese swept a hand through his hair and leaned back in his chair, his mind still racing with suspicions. All the displaced farmers he'd contacted had succumbed to the lure of Boswell's money. What would have happened if they hadn't?

Margaret Calhoun had been a proud, stubborn woman. If she had decided she definitely wasn't going to sell the farm to Boswell, then no amount of money he offered would have changed her mind. Had Boswell then taken matters into his own hands? Had he played a long shot, hoping the estranged daughter from New York would be more agreeable to selling the property? And what would happen if Sarah continued to tell the man she wasn't going to sell?

He released a long, almost dizzying sigh as thoughts of Sarah filled his mind. A dozen times in the past two days he'd picked up the phone to call her—just to hear her voice—only to slam the receiver back down before he'd punched in the last digit of the Calhoun phone number. He knew she was right when she'd said they shouldn't see each other anymore. She was right that they had no shared future.

Still, the fact that he couldn't get her out of his mind irritated him. Before she'd arrived, he'd finally managed to find some sense of peace in his life. Now he found that sense of peace disrupted by her mere presence back in town.

And then there was Jackie. In her little face he could see so much of himself. The evidence of his paternity was stamped all over her. Physically she was all his, and yet emotionally she was so different from him. Had there ever been a child so open, so loving as Jackie? She had a smile for everyone, a giggle on her lips at all times. She had yet to learn the pain of being abandoned, the ache of being unloved. He shook his head, as if to shake these very thoughts out of his head. Jackie and Sarah, they had definitely disrupted his fragile peace of mind.

He got up from his desk and paced the small confines of his office. Who the hell was he kidding? It wasn't just their presence that had shattered his peace. It was the memory of making love with Sarah again. It was the desire to see her eyes go smoky from the heat of his caresses. It was the need to make love to her over and over again.

A perverse anger swept through him at this thought. Need. He didn't need Sarah. He didn't need anyone. He'd stopped needing the day his mother walked out on him, leaving him with a bitter alcoholic father who'd made his life miserable. On the day his mother left, he'd sworn to himself that he would never need anyone in his life again. There was only one person he could depend on, one person he completely trusted, and that was himself.

Disgusted with his own thoughts, he grabbed his hat, opened his office door and went out into the tiny reception area of the Clay Creek Police Station. "I'm going for a walk," he said to Ida Cook, who manned the phone and dispatched calls. She raised a hand to acknowledge

that she'd heard him but didn't look up from the romance novel she read.

It was one of those days that couldn't decide if it was
summer or fall. There was a slight nip to the air, but the
sun was unusually warm. A fall day pretending to be
summer.

He slapped his hat on, then began walking down Main
Street, looking for lawbreakers to take his thoughts off
more personal agonies. He stopped in front of the bank
and leaned against the brick building, observing the
town—his town—around him. The need to escape from
this place had left him long ago. He liked Clay Creek,
had made his peace with the people here. He sighed. So
what was wrong with him?

He watched an old woman slowly making her way
across the street. He could give Mrs. Tildenbaum a ticket
for jaywalking. But there wasn't any traffic and she'd
assail him with a list of her present physical complaints.
Mrs. Tildenbaum was Clay Creek's resident hypochon-
driac and was always on the lookout for a sympathetic
ear.

For the first time since becoming sheriff, Reese felt a
nagging sense of dissatisfaction with his life. Ten years
from now, would he still be leaning against this same
building, trying to decide if he should give Mrs. Tildenbaum a ticket for jaywalking?

He shoved himself away from the brick bank building
and took off walking once again. He had no direction in
mind, no final destination, just a need to keep moving…stop thinking.

And then he saw them, the three of them all walking
down the sidewalk toward him. The Calhoun women—
Sarah, Lindy and Jackie. They were all laughing, and as
his gaze lingered on Sarah, he felt a peculiar pang in his

heart. He used to be able to make her laugh. At times he'd played the fool just to bring that sparkle to her eyes and the husky laughter to her lips. Her face loved laughter, her features embraced the emotion and glowed with inner mirth.

As they got closer and Sarah caught sight of him, the smile on her lips dropped away and her footsteps faltered slightly. The only one who looked the least bit pleased at seeing him was Jackie, who released her mother's hand and raced toward him.

"Hi, Mr. Sheriff," she greeted him brightly. "Mama bought me a new baby." She held out a doll that still had cellophane wrapped around its bright gold hair.

"You better get that plastic off her head, otherwise she won't be able to breathe," Reese observed.

Jackie giggled. "She's not a real baby," she explained with childish patience. "I wanted a real baby—a little brother—but Mama says maybe when I'm older."

Reese nodded, refocusing his gaze on Sarah. God, she looked so beautiful with the sun shining in her hair and the afternoon light caressing her features. She appeared to glow with an inner incandescence. She looked warm and radiant and he wanted to capture her radiance, hold it inside forever.

She seemed to sense his thoughts. A pink blush rose up her neck and suffused her face, and she looked away.

"So, what brings you ladies out this afternoon?" he asked in an attempt to diffuse some of the tension that crackled in the air.

"We've been shopping for wallpaper," Lindy explained. "I stripped all the old out of the kitchen and Sarah helped me pick out the new."

Sarah smiled at her sister. "Of course Lindy wanted to buy new paper for every room in the house, but I talked her into doing one room at a time." She looked back at Reese. "Have you found out anything...about what we discussed the other day?"

Reese knew she was talking about Raymond Boswell and he shook his head, his frustration coming back to gnaw at him. "Nothing."

"You'll let me know if you discover anything?"

"Of course," he replied. "When's Ben getting back into town?"

"He called last night and said it would probably be another week. By that time I should have all the farm business pretty well taken care of," Sarah said, her gaze once again skittering away from his.

And she'll be leaving Clay Creek again, he thought, fighting off another deep wave of irritation, mingling with dissatisfaction.

"We'd better get going," Lindy said impatiently, shifting her shopping bag from one arm to the other. "I'd like to get this paper up tonight."

Reese nodded and stepped aside, fighting his desire to grab Sarah by the arm, watch her eyes widen, get a reaction of any kind from her—anything but her cool distance.

"Bye, Mr. Sheriff," Jackie said as they moved past him and down the sidewalk. He nodded to her then watched until they disappeared around the corner.

Another week and she'd be gone and he wouldn't have to worry about running into her on the street or bumping into her at the café. And he hoped out of sight would prove to be out of mind for good.

He continued his walk down the street, nodding to the people he passed, fighting off another wave of deep inexplicable depression.

In another week Sarah would go back to her life in

New York. Eventually she would meet and marry a man who would love her, a man who would be a father to Jackie. And probably, eventually, they would give Jackie a little brother or sister. It was all for the best. It was the way it should be.

So why did it make him feel so bad?

"Lindy, why don't you wait until morning to finish this up," Sarah suggested, watching as Lindy struggled with a piece of the wallpaper. She'd offered her help several times, but Lindy had insisted she wanted to do it all herself. She'd managed to get the paper up on one wall but was having problems with the rest of it.

"How about if I make us a cup of tea and you take a little break," Sarah suggested, knowing her sister had to be exhausted. She'd been keeping a frantic pace for the past four days. Sooner or later she was going to crash, and Sarah dreaded the time when that happened.

"I don't want a cup of tea and I don't want to take a break," Lindy replied, her voice cutting with a sharp edge. She slammed the tape measure down on the table and picked up the roll of paper and a pair of scissors.

Sarah, sensing one of her sister's irrational bursts of anger, went into the living room, where Jackie was sprawled on the floor. "What are you doing, pumpkin?" she asked, sitting down on the sofa near her daughter.

"I'm drawing a picture," Jackie replied, not looking up from her artistic efforts.

"What kind of a picture?" Sarah asked, leaning forward to peek at the masterpiece.

Jackie giggled and covered it up with one hand. "It's a surprise."

Sarah settled back into the sofa and smiled. "I like

surprises.'' She leaned her head back and closed her
eyes, realizing she was tired. It had been a full day.

She'd spent the morning in her mother's bedroom,
packing up clothes and shoes to give to the church, box-
ing up personal items that wouldn't be given away. It
had been a difficult task, one that had caused a ball of
emotions to press fully against her heart. It had been like
the final goodbye to her mother.

After lunch she'd spent the remainder of the afternoon
with the lawyer, signing papers that would allow the
lawyer to oversee the financial end of things on her be-
half. Within another week she should be able to tie up
all the loose ends that would permit Ben and Lindy to
work the farm and receive the proceeds without Sarah's
presence in Clay Creek.

Over the past two days she'd had plenty of time to
reflect on the two accidents that had nearly taken her
life, and she had come to the conclusion that she and
Reese had overreacted. There was a logical explanation
for the stray gunshots, and although there wasn't such
an easy explanation for the sawed-through well cover,
she didn't want to believe it had been intentionally
weakened with the design of causing her harm.

Much more harmful than the two accidents had been
making love to Reese once again. It had been a stupid,
foolish mistake. She'd known better but had been unable
to control the passion that had exploded between them.
It had been like a raging wildfire, out of control before
she even knew it existed.

It would have been nice if she could have come back
here and found some sort of peace where he was concerned. If, despite their past relationship and the presence of Jackie, she could have left here in friendship
with Reese. But she knew in her heart a friendship with

him was impossible. Their emotions were still too intense—he still clung to his feelings of unworthiness and sense of betrayal and she couldn't let go of her own hurt.

"Mama, I'm all done with my picture." Jackie crawled up on the sofa next to Sarah and held out her latest creation. "It's all the people I like," she explained. "Here's you and Aunt Lindy." She pointed to each figure. "And this is Anna and Mr. Sheriff."

Mr. Sheriff. He seemed to take up an enormous portion of the page. Jackie had gotten his dark hair color right, and his broad shoulders were in proportion to his long legs.

What would Jackie say if she knew he was her father? What was Sarah eventually going to tell the little girl about Reese?

"Do you like it?" Jackie asked eagerly.

"It's a wonderful picture," Sarah answered softly, shoving aside the painful truths she would one day have to share with the little girl. "And now it's bedtime."

A yawn stifled Jackie's protest. "I am sort of tired," she admitted.

"You run on upstairs and I'll be up to kiss you goodnight in just a few minutes." Together mother and daughter got up from the sofa. "I want to put your picture with the others on the fridge door."

Jackie nodded and ran up the stairs and Sarah went back into the kitchen, where Lindy was still struggling to finish papering one wall. "How's it coming?" she asked as she placed Jackie's picture under a colorful magnet on the refrigerator door.

"It's not," Lindy said flatly. With a muttered curse she ripped off one of the pieces she'd just put up. In a fury she wadded it and tore it into pieces. "I can't do this...I can't do anything." Her voice rose hysterically.

"I'm just stupid...stupid!" She threw the paper aside and with a strangled cry ran out of the room and thundered up the stairs. Sarah sighed as she heard the distant sound of Lindy's bedroom door being slammed. It worried her, these outbursts of anger that seemed to explode from nowhere.

She took a few minutes and cleaned up the mess Lindy had made, hoping Lindy's blowup had exhausted her enough so she would sleep for the rest of the night.

Suddenly exhausted herself, Sarah turned out the kitchen light and headed up the stairs to kiss Jackie good-night, then go to bed herself.

She found Jackie in bed, a frown furrowing her little forehead. "Is Aunt Lindy mad at us?" she asked worriedly.

Sarah realized her daughter must have heard Lindy storming into her room. She sat down on the bed next to Jackie and smiled at her reassuringly. "No, honey, she's not mad at us. Aunt Lindy just gets overexcited sometimes." Sarah frowned, wondering how much a five-year-old could understand about Lindy's condition. "Sometimes she gets real sad, and sometimes she gets really happy, and sometimes she just gets upset."

Jackie plucked her bottom lip thoughtfully. "Kind of like Mrs. Rosellini?"

Sarah laughed. Mrs. Rosellini was the Italian woman who lived in the apartment next to theirs back in New York. "Kind of," Sarah admitted. "Although it's not quite the same." She pulled the blanket up around Jackie's shoulders and kissed her on the forehead.

She started to stand but hesitated as Jackie called to her. "What, sweetie?" she asked.

"I like it here," Jackie said softly. "Better than in New York."

"It is nice, isn't it?"

"Can't we just stay here and never go back?"

"Honey, we can't do that. I have a job. I have to work."

"You could work for Anna." Jackie's eyelids drooped sleepily. "She says you're the best damned waitress she ever had."

Sarah started to reprimand the little girl for her language, then paused, realizing she had fallen asleep. Placing another tender kiss on Jackie's cheek, Sarah then turned off the light and softly closed the bedroom door behind her.

As she went past Lindy's bedroom she didn't hear any noises from behind the closed door and hoped Lindy had fallen asleep. The ringing of the telephone split the silence and Sarah hurried into her mother's bedroom and answered the phone by the side of the bed.

"Sarah?"

"Oh Ben, I'm so glad you called. I was going to try to get in touch with you later."

"Why? Is something wrong? How's Lindy?"

Sarah sat down on the edge of the bed and rubbed her forehead tiredly. "She's not good, Ben. Have you managed to get her an appointment yet?"

"Not yet. Dr. Manning has been out of town for the last couple of days. His secretary has promised that he'll call the moment he gets in."

"I don't think we should wait," Sarah replied.

"I hate to force her to see somebody else." Ben's voice deepened. "She has such a good rapport with Dr. Manning. I expect to hear from him tomorrow, the next day at the latest. Can't it wait another day or two?"

Sarah sighed heavily, unsure what to do. "I don't know, Ben," she finally answered truthfully.

"I just know Lindy hates any break in her normal routine and I hate to negate all the good that Dr. Manning has done with her in the past."

Sarah sighed again. "Okay, I suppose we can give him another day or two."

They spoke for a few minutes longer, most of the conversation Sarah answering questions about Lindy, then they hung up. Sarah went directly to the bathroom where she drew a tub of hot water. Minutes later she sank into the relaxing warmth.

Ah, she could stay here forever, she thought, feeling tight muscles relaxing and a drowsy languor overtaking her. Unfortunately, the languor wasn't numbing enough to completely erase thoughts of Jackie's bedtime plea.

Jackie wanted to stay in Clay Creek, and Sarah understood that desire. Jackie was in the process of developing friendships with Gladys Prather's grandchildren. For the first time in her life, she was living in a house instead of an apartment, enjoying the freedom of playing in a yard instead of a city park. Yes, Sarah certainly understood her daughter's desire to remain here.

But we can't, Sarah protested inwardly. Moving back here now would open up a whole new set of hurts and problems. Reese had made no move to develop any kind of a relationship with his daughter since they had been in town. Eventually Jackie would grow old enough to hear gossip, sense the secrets surrounding her paternity. Eventually she would start asking questions and demanding answers.

Sarah sank lower in the water, feeling her neck muscles tightening with tension once again. How would Jackie handle the knowledge that Reese was her father biologically but was uninterested in being her father emotionally?

Would things have been different had she stayed years ago when she'd discovered that she was pregnant? Would Reese and her relationship have survived had she told him she was going to have his baby? Had she made the correct decision by leaving? She didn't know anymore. And in any case, it didn't matter.

She realized she was fooling herself. Whereas in the past she wouldn't have considered making her home here because of the pain it might cause Jackie, she now knew there was another reason why she couldn't move back. She didn't think she herself was strong enough to see Reese every day, share the community life with him and know he would never be able to offer her what she really needed—love for Jackie and love for herself. She now realized she couldn't move back because of her own emotional weakness where Reese was concerned.

She sat up suddenly, aware the water had turned tepid around her. Besides, she was indulging in a useless form of torture by thinking about Reese and what would never be.

As she dried off, she paused a moment, cocking her head. She thought she heard a noise drifting up from downstairs. She wrapped the towel around herself and opened the bathroom door, listening intently. Nothing. No light radiated up from the darkness downstairs and she heard nothing else.

Water gurgling down the pipes, ducts expanding from the heat of the furnace—the house was always full of night sounds, she thought as she put on her robe and belted it around her waist. Before going into her own bedroom, she checked on Jackie, then Lindy, relieved to find them both sound asleep.

It took Sarah only minutes to change into her nightgown and crawl beneath the blankets of her bed. She smiled to herself, remembering the wintry nights when she was little and her mother would tuck her in, layering blankets on top of her that made movement difficult but kept her snug and warm. She wished her mother was here now to kiss her cheek, to reassure her that all was well. She wished her mother was here to tell her that she'd done the right thing six years before. With a sigh, Sarah closed her eyes.

The scream ripped through the silence of the night. Sarah bolted upright in bed, her heart pounding in inexplicable terror. She fumbled on the night table for the lamp and flipped the switch. A soft glow filled the room.

She stumbled out of bed and to her doorway, pausing, wondering if the scream had really happened or had been part of a dream. She couldn't remember any nightmares, but that didn't mean that whatever had awakened her hadn't been some figment of her sleep-fogged mind.

She jumped as the shriek resounded again, her heart resuming its frantic beat. This time she recognized the scream. It was Jackie.

She flew down the hallway to the little girl's room, flipping on the light switch as she entered. Jackie met her, throwing herself into Sarah's stomach, her shoulders heaving as she squealed in horror.

"Jackie, honey, what's wrong?" Sarah held the trembling child tight against her, looking around the room but seeing nothing amiss, nothing that accounted for Jackie's obvious terror.

"There was somebody in here, Mama. Somebody was in my room." Jackie didn't release her death grip on Sarah's waist.

"Honey, you must have been dreaming," Sarah soothed, stroking her daughter's hair gently.

"No, it wasn't a dream. Somebody was in here and they tried to choke me." She was crying now, her shoulders shaking with childish sobs, sobs that were punctuated by a fit of harsh coughing.

"Sweetheart, there's nobody here. You just had a really bad dream." Sarah reached down and picked Jackie up in her arms. Jackie immediately cuddled into her, hiding her face in the crook of Sarah's neck. "Bad dreams are scary because sometimes they seem real." She carried Jackie back over to the bed, rubbing her little back reassuringly, murmuring words of comfort.

She started to place Jackie back on the bed, but the child clung more tightly to her. "Please, Mama, don't go. Don't leave me in here alone. Just hold me for a little longer."

Sarah sat down on the bed with Jackie on her lap. It must have been some dream, Sarah thought as she felt Jackie's body still trembling. "My throat hurts," Jackie said softly.

"I'll go get you a glass of water, maybe that will help," Sarah replied. Jackie must be coming down with something and that was what had caused the bad dreams, she thought.

"What's going on?"

Sarah turned to see Lindy standing in the doorway, rubbing her eyes sleepily. "It's all right. Jackie had a bad dream."

"You okay, pumpkin?" Lindy asked.

"It wasn't a dream. It was real," Jackie whispered adamantly.

"Come on, sweetheart, let's get you tucked back in and I'll get you a glass of water." Sarah moved Jackie off her lap and pulled down the blankets. When Jackie got back beneath the covers, Sarah smoothed her hair away from her forehead and smiled reassuringly. "It's all right now. You're safe…" Her voice trailed off as she leaned closer to her daughter. For the first time since coming into the bedroom, she looked at her daughter's face. Jackie's cheeks were tear-streaked, her eyes slightly swollen. Her nose was running from her crying. But what caused a shiver of terror to dance up Sarah's spine was the red marks that were livid against Jackie's pale skin—red marks that encircled her neck, marks that were already beginning to turn blue.

"Lindy? Call Reese and get him out here," she said tersely.

"Why? What's wrong?"

"Somebody tried to choke Jackie. Please…just call him and tell him to get out here because somebody has been in the house."

As Lindy left to make the call, Sarah turned back to Jackie, who stared at her with huge, fear-filled eyes. "It's okay, honey," she tried to reassure her.

"Is Mr. Sheriff going to come?" Jackie asked tremulously.

Sarah nodded. "Yes, he should be here in just a few minutes."

"And he'll keep us safe?"

"Yes, he'll keep us safe," Sarah answered without hesitation. She pulled Jackie back into her arms, suddenly more frightened than she had ever been.

Somebody had been in this room. Somebody had sneaked in here in the dead of night. Somebody had placed their hands around Jackie's neck and squeezed, trying to choke the very life out of her. Thank God Jackie had managed to awaken and fight. Thank God she had managed to scream.

Sarah had been scared when she'd thought it was her

own life in danger, but that was nothing compared to the gut-wrenching terror that now swept through her veins.

Somebody had tried to hurt Jackie. Somebody had tried to kill her baby.

Chapter 10

Reese drove faster than he'd ever driven in his life, his heart thudding with concern, fear and an incredible anger that choked in his throat and twisted his stomach.

Lindy's phone call had been vague, but she'd said enough for Reese to understand that somebody had been in the Calhoun house—somebody who'd apparently tried to hurt Jackie.

His heart beat a rapid tattoo in his chest and a roar resounded in his ears as he tore down the gravel road that lead to the Calhoun farmhouse. When he pulled up in front, all the lights in the house were on, including the spotlight that illuminated most of the property at the front. The barking dogs announced his arrival and he was met at the door by Sarah, her eyes huge and luminous with fear.

"Oh, Reese, thank God you're here," she said. The distance he'd felt from her the day before was gone, swept away and replaced by the greater emotions of fear and need. For a moment he thought she was going to launch herself into his arms and he tensed expectantly. Instead she stiffened her shoulders and led him into the living room, where Lindy and Jackie sat on the sofa.

"Hi, Jackie," he said softly, relaxing slightly as he saw that she didn't appear to have suffered any physical harm.

"Hi, Mr. Sheriff," she answered wanly. He sat down next to her. He didn't know exactly what had happened, but whatever it was, it had stolen Jackie's sunny smile, and that in itself was criminal.

"Can you tell me what happened?" he asked.

"Somebody tried to get me," Jackie said soberly, her gray eyes widening. "They came into my room while I was sleeping and tried to choke me."

"Show Reese your neck, sweetheart," Sarah prompted the little girl.

Jackie tilted her head back and pulled down the collar of her nightgown, exposing her small neck to Reese's gaze. "It hurts," she said softly.

As he saw the vivid marks, the bruised, tender flesh, a red haze of rage descended on him, for a moment obscuring any other thoughts.

"Doc Burwell is on his way over. I thought he should take a look at her just to make sure she's all right," Sarah explained.

Reese nodded. "And I've got Deputy Johnson coming. He'll dust for prints and see what he can pick up." He looked back at Jackie, his blood boiling.

He'd been angry that somebody had tried to harm Sarah, but to think that someone had crept into a darkened bedroom and wrapped their hands around this innocent, helpless child's neck—his child's neck—

He fought to keep his seat next to Jackie, taking a

deep breath to steady his dizzying rage. "Did you see what the person looked like?" he asked the little girl.

Jackie shook her head. "It was too dark in the room. I was sleeping, and when they grabbed me and I opened my eyes, I couldn't see anything. I just kicked real hard and screamed real loud and they ran away."

"Her screams woke me up, and when I went into her bedroom, I just assumed she'd had a bad dream," Sarah explained.

"So you didn't see anything, either?"

Sarah shook her head, a frown of frustration creasing her brow. "Nothing."

"When they ran away, which way did they go?" Reese asked Jackie.

She frowned. "I'm not sure...but I guess out in the hallway."

"Was the window open? Any signs of entry?" He looked at Sarah.

Again she shook her head. "Since we called you I've been through every room of the house, looked in every closet, but there's no sign of anyone. Reese, what's going on?"

"I wish the hell I knew. Was the front door locked?"

"Yes. For the past couple of nights I've been paying special attention to locking everything up."

He stood and pulled a flashlight from his back pocket. "I'm going to go outside and look around the house. You all stay in here."

Sarah walked him to the front door. "Reese...be careful," she called after him as he went outside. He clicked on his flashlight as he began to walk around the perimeter of the house. He scanned for signs of an intruder—footsteps in the grass, a window screen pulled askew—but found nothing amiss.

Why would somebody go after Jackie? What could possibly be the motive for trying to kill a five-year-old girl?

One thing was certain—there was no way this could be chalked up to some strange sort of accident. It had been attempted murder and his blood chilled as he thought of what the outcome would have been had Jackie not managed to scream and waken Sarah.

Never had he felt so incredibly helpless. Even though he knew he wasn't the man to be a father to Jackie, paternal feelings he didn't know he possessed reared up at the thought of somebody harming her.

Frustration still gnawing at his insides, he went back into the house. Jackie was curled up on the sofa, sound asleep. She looked so tiny, so helpless in her little pink nightgown and matching fuzzy slippers.

He looked away. The sight of the vulnerable little girl caused strange emotions to flood through him, emotions he didn't know what to do with. He frowned, shoving them away, not wanting to deal with what he felt.

Lindy sat at the opposite end of the sofa. The energy that had radiated from her the last time he saw her was gone, as if sucked out by the confusing events of the night. Was she somehow a part of this? There was no rational reason to think so, but much of what Lindy did was irrational. Had her illness progressed to the point where she could be a threat to Sarah and Jackie? He didn't want to think so for Sarah's sake.

"Did you find anything?" Sarah asked, rising from the chair where she had been sitting. The furrow still deepened her brow.

"No. There doesn't appear to be any sign of forced entry. None of the brush and grass next to any of the windows appears disturbed."

"How about a cup of coffee?" Sarah asked, her expression telling him she wanted to speak to him in the kitchen. He nodded. "Lindy, would you mind staying in here with Jackie? I don't want her to awaken and be frightened again," Sarah said.

Lindy nodded and together Reese and Sarah left the living room and went into the kitchen. While Sarah fixed the coffee, he watched her, trying not to notice how her robe gaped open at the throat to expose her delicate collarbone, how the short robe displayed the shapely length of her legs.

Who could want to hurt Sarah? The first two attempts had been subtle. Had either worked, it was possible he might not have realized it was murder. Both the shooting or a fall down the well could have been deemed accidental death. But this attack on Jackie tonight was different. There had been no subterfuge. It had been a blatant attempt of murder. What worried Reese was the fact that the attack on Jackie spoke of desperation, of a killer not even trying to hide the crime. It spoke of a killer on the verge of losing control.

"Thanks," he said much later as Sarah placed a mug in front of him.

The doctor had left, proclaiming Jackie fine, and Reese's deputies had gone after dusting everything in the little girl's room for fingerprints and finding nothing but smears and blurs and prints that matched Jackie, Sarah and Lindy. Whoever had been in the house had left nothing behind.

She joined him at the table and wrapped her hands around her own cup, as if seeking warmth. "Reese, I can't find Mama's gun."

He looked at her sharply, a renewed burst of frustration zinging through him like an electrical current. "What gun?"

"Mama had a shotgun she kept in the coat closet in the living room. It's been there for as long as I can remember, and I know it was here when we first arrived because I saw it when I hung our coats up."

"When did you notice it missing?" Reese leaned forward. Was it possible that had been the gun that had shot her?

"I noticed it tonight, when we were checking through the house, but I have no idea how long it's been missing." He saw her hands tighten around the coffee cup, her knuckles turning white beneath the pressure.

He reached out and gently pried the cup loose from her grip. "You're gonna shatter that if you hold it any tighter," he admonished gently. He took her hands in his. Despite the warmth of the cup, they were icy cold. "If you need to hold tight to something, hold on to me," he added softly.

He squeezed her hands, felt her hesitation, then an answering pressure. "Sarah, I wish I could tell you what's going on. I wish I could tell you who's doing this and why."

Again rage swept through him, a white-hot fury and a sense of utter helplessness. He was the sheriff, he was supposed to solve crimes, keep the people of Clay Creek safe, but how could he safeguard against an unknown enemy?

"Reese..." she protested softly, making him realize he squeezed her hands too tightly.

He released his grip and stood up. He swept his hand through his hair and leaned against the counter. "I keep coming back to the fact that somehow this is all related to the farm. It's the only thing that makes any kind of sense.''

''But why Jackie? Why on earth would somebody want to hurt her?'' Sarah's eyes were huge, containing a haunting that he guessed only a mother would feel when her child was threatened. He almost envied her that...the power of a love for a child that was so intense, so undiluted and pure that it swept away personal fear, turned cowards into heroes, sacrificed everything for the child's well-being.

Would he have felt the same way had he been there from the beginning of Sarah's pregnancy? Would he have bonded with Jackie had he been there to feel her kick, hear her heartbeat, watch her birth?

He shoved these disturbing questions aside. He couldn't afford the energy to analyze them. At the moment he had far more troubling things to worry about.

''But why Jackie?'' she repeated.

He pushed a hand through his hair once again and frowned thoughtfully. ''The way things stand now, if something happens to you, the farm would go to Jackie...unless you've made out a will with other arrangements.''

''I haven't,'' she replied.

''So if Raymond Boswell was willing to do anything to get the farm into Ben's hands so he could buy it, it makes sense that he'd not only have to get rid of you but your daughter as well.'' Reese straightened as a new thought struck him. ''How well do you know your brother-in-law?''

''Ben? Not very well, why?'' She stared at him for a long moment, then realized where his question led. ''Oh, Reese, you can't honestly believe that Ben has anything to do with this?''

"Honey, I honestly don't know what to believe. All I know is somebody wants you and your daughter dead, and the only people who profit from that happening are Lindy, Ben and ultimately Raymond Boswell."

"But Ben couldn't have anything to do with it. He's been in Kansas City," Sarah protested.

"And Raymond Boswell is supposed to be in St. Louis for business," Reese said. "However, I intend to find out exactly where both of them are tonight—and they better have damned good alibis."

He walked back to where she sat and placed a hand on her shoulder. He wanted to take her in his arms, hold her tight, assure her that he would never let anything happen to either her or Jackie. But he knew she wouldn't welcome his arms encircling her and he knew he couldn't promise to keep her safe, no matter how badly he wanted to.

"In the meantime, I don't like the idea of you staying here on the farm. Why don't you all pack a bag and come into town and stay with me?" he finally suggested.

She shook her head almost vehemently. "That's not necessary." She frowned and rubbed her forehead tiredly. "I'm sure we'll be fine at least for tonight. Whoever it was surely won't come back." She sighed. "I don't know...maybe I did forget to lock the front door tonight."

Reese watched her a moment, knowing what he was about to say would anger her. But he had to say it, he had to explore all possibilities. "Or maybe the person who tried to choke Jackie was already in the house."

She stared at him. "Already in the house? What are you talking about?"

He hesitated a moment, then said in a low voice, "Lindy."

She gasped. "That's ridiculous," she shot back, her face turning a shade paler than it had been. "Lindy would never hurt me, and she certainly wouldn't hurt Jackie." Sarah stood up, her eyes more haunted than ever.

"Think about it." He stepped closer to her, smelling the sweet scent of her, fighting the impulse to wrap his arms around her, take her someplace where she would be safe. "Are you sure, Sarah?" He placed his hands on her shoulders. "You've been gone from here a long time. How well do you really know your sister? How ill is she?"

She flushed and shrugged away from his touch. "Well enough to know she would never do anything to hurt us. Lindy might have some problems, but she isn't homicidal." She glared at him, anger momentarily usurping the fear. "I can't believe you'd even think such a thing."

"Sarah, at this point you'd be a damn fool to discount anyone. You can't trust anyone, except me." He hesitated a moment, then added, "But I guess you never were very good at doing that, were you?" He hadn't meant to say it, and he didn't wait for her reply. "If I can't talk you into leaving with me tonight, then there's nothing more I can do here."

She nodded and followed him out of the kitchen. Lindy and Jackie were both asleep, each sprawled on opposite ends of the sofa. He walked to the front door and turned back to Sarah. "Does your bedroom door have a lock on it?" he whispered.

"Yes."

"Put Jackie in with you and lock your door for the rest of the night. Sarah, I could very well be wrong about Lindy. But I'd rather we err on the side of caution," he said. "And make sure you lock up after me."

"I will." She met his gaze and looked as if she wanted to say something. She colored slightly and glanced away. "Thanks for coming out."

He smiled and touched her cheek lightly. "I can't have criminals running amok in Clay Creek." He turned and went back out to his patrol car.

He started the engine and waited until she'd closed the door, then he pulled down the lane. Instead of going out onto the main road, he drove into a grove of trees at the end of the driveway. He parked and turned out the lights. From this vantage point he knew he was hidden from the house and from the road, but he had a perfect view of both and would be able to see if anyone approached from any direction.

If the danger came from an outside source, he would be right here to see it coming. However, if the danger came from within, well, Sarah would have to depend on her own resources. The thought made his blood run cold. Despite the chill of the night, he rolled down his car window, hoping that he would be able to hear if Sarah or Jackie screamed for help.

He didn't want to believe that Lindy had anything to do with all this, but he wasn't willing to discount her. She'd had opportunity. Of the three suspects, Raymond, Ben and Lindy, she was the only one who had been present at all three incidents. As far as motive…who knew what thoughts drifted through Lindy's mind when she was in one of her mania periods.

He'd heard the various stories that circled the town about her—Lindy cooking day and night because she thought it was her mission to end world hunger, Lindy accusing Gladys Prather of spying on her and trying to steal Ben away. The stories went on and on. For the most part, Lindy's delusions had been relatively harmless, but everyone knew that over the past several months she'd been getting worse, and who knew what effect Margaret's death was having on her? Was she angry with Sarah for not being here in town when Margaret fell down the stairs? Was all of this a form of revenge that made sense only in Lindy's deluded mind?

Reese rubbed his forehead tiredly, not taking his eyes off the old farmhouse. He was the sheriff, he was supposed to have all the answers. It was his job to keep everyone safe. And of all the people he wanted to keep safe, Sarah and Jackie...

He slumped down in the seat, trying to find a more comfortable position. It was going to be a long night. He wished he had asked Sarah for an extra cup of the coffee she'd made.

Sarah. He sighed, trying to forget the enticing scent of her, the warmth that had emanated from her, the way her robe had hugged her curves. God, would he ever get her out of his mind? Years from now would he still remember that scent of hers, the way her eyes deepened in color when she was lost in thought?

It was useless to be obsessed with her, a waste of energy to want her. They'd had their chance years ago. She'd made her decision then, just as she had the other night after they'd made love. Years ago she hadn't trusted him enough to do the right thing. There was no reason to believe that she would trust him now. And in truth he couldn't blame her. Where she was concerned, he simply didn't trust himself.

Sarah checked the front door three different times to make sure it was locked before she went back into the kitchen and dumped the remainder of the coffee she'd made. As she washed out the carafe, unwelcome thoughts whirled in her head.

Was Reese right? Was it possible that Lindy was part of this madness? Her gaze drifted to the dent in the wall. Lindy's rages had been vicious, especially in the past couple of days. Were they also more insidious?

Even though Sarah had told Reese she wasn't sure she had locked the front door before going to bed earlier in the evening, in truth she was almost positive she had. And if she had, how had the intruder gotten in? There had been no signs of forced entry, no evidence of anything being disturbed. Without a key, it seemed impossible that somebody could have gotten inside…unless they had already been inside.

Earlier when she'd stepped out of the bathtub, she'd thought she'd heard something. Had it been Lindy sneaking out of bed and down the hallway, or had it been an unknown intruder? When Sarah had checked on Lindy, had she only been feigning sleep? The thought made a cold rush of horror shiver up Sarah's spine.

She dried the glass carafe and placed it back on the coffeemaker, then started to leave the kitchen. At the doorway she hesitated, then crossed the room once again. She opened one of the cabinet drawers and stared at the silverware inside.

Before she could argue with herself, allow reason to overcome instinct, she drew out a razor-sharp paring knife and tucked it into the pocket of her robe.

What are you going to do with that? a little voice niggled in the back of her mind. You couldn't stab anyone if your life depended on it, the voice taunted. But as Sarah thought of the livid bruises around her daughter's neck, she knew the voice was wrong. She could and would do whatever it took to protect Jackie.

She went into the living room, where she roused
Lindy by gently shaking her shoulder. Lindy opened her
eyes and looked around, obviously disoriented. "Lindy,
you can go on back up to bed."

"Is everything all right?" she asked, standing up.

"As right as it can be," Sarah answered. "I think the
excitement is over...at least for tonight."

Lindy nodded and Sarah watched as she stumbled up
the stairs and disappeared into her room. "Jackie,
honey." Sarah leaned over and scooped her daughter up
in her arms.

Jackie immediately wrapped her arms around Sarah's
neck. "Mommy, can I sleep with you?"

"I think that sounds like a wonderful idea," Sarah
agreed, holding Jackie more tightly against her. She
couldn't think about how close she'd come to losing her
daughter. She couldn't contemplate what might have
happened had Jackie been unable to scream and waken
her. If Sarah dwelled on these thoughts, she knew she
would lose her mind. Instead she focused on the reality
of holding Jackie close, smelling the baby-sweet scent
of her hair, feeling her little body molded against hers.

Once in her bedroom, Sarah tucked Jackie into the
bed, relieved when the little girl immediately went back
to sleep. Although she was exhausted herself, sleep was
the furthest thing from Sarah's mind. She locked the
bedroom door, then as an extra precautionary measure
she wedged the top of a chair beneath the knob. Certain
that nobody would be able to sneak in, she went back
over to the bed. Taking the knife out of her robe pocket,
she slid it beneath her pillow.

Wrapping the robe more closely around her, she
moved over to the window and stared out into the darkness of the night. God, things were such a mess. She

was a prisoner in her own room, with a knife beneath the pillow, haunted by a man who disturbed her almost as much as the attempts on her life. She shoved thoughts of Reese aside, focusing instead on the mystery of the attacks on her and Jackie.

Who was responsible? Was it possible that the attacks had nothing to do with the farm? Then what? Lindy had spoken of how angry she had been when Sarah left so many years before. Had that anger never really gone away but instead festered until it had reached the point of explosion?

Dear God, she didn't want to believe that Lindy was in any way responsible, but she realized Reese was right. She couldn't afford to take chances. She couldn't afford to discount anyone.

She frowned as she suddenly realized that she didn't remember hearing the dogs barking. At no time during the night had she heard the dogs. If an intruder had crept into the yard, headed for the house, Lindy's dogs would have gone crazy. However, other than when Reese had arrived, the dogs had been quiet. Somehow this only made the evidence more damning for Lindy.

She'd hoped that within the next couple of days Ben would return home and she and Jackie could leave and go back to New York. Now she realized she couldn't just leave here without knowing who was after her and why. She refused to go back to New York having to look over her shoulder, wondering if somebody was after her or her daughter.

She sighed and turned away from the window, realizing the darkness of the night was a perfect reflection of the darkness in her mind. She shrugged out of her robe and crawled into bed next to her sleeping daughter. Reaching over to turn out the lamp, she then threw one arm around Jackie. The other she moved beneath the pillow so that her fingers curled around the handle of the knife. It was going to be a very long night.

Chapter 11

"Pancakes," Jackie announced. "I want pancakes for breakfast."

"How about some oatmeal instead?" Sarah countered, too tired to face the mess that pancakes always created.

"Yuck." Jackie's facial expression mirrored the verbal one.

"I'll throw in some brown sugar and cinnamon," Sarah offered.

"And some apple, too?" Jackie asked.

Sarah hesitated, then nodded. It would have been easier to make pancakes, she thought with an inward groan. She got out all the ingredients and put the water on to boil, trying to ignore the numbing exhaustion that pulled at her.

She'd been awake most of the night, jumping at every noise, clutching the knife each time the furnace kicked on or the house creaked and groaned. Tormenting thoughts rolled through her head…thoughts of Reese, of Lindy, of Ben.

She'd finally gotten out of bed at dawn and had stood at the window, staring out over the farmland she loved. She'd been surprised when she saw Reese's patrol car pull out of the grove of trees at the far end of the driveway and head toward town. Had he spent the night watching the house, protecting them against evil in the dark? The fact that he'd found that necessary filled her with renewed anxiety. The fact that he'd done it suffused her with a reassuring warmth.

"Mama, is Mr. Sheriff gonna find the bad person who came into my bedroom last night?" Jackie's voice interrupted Sarah's thoughts.

Sarah turned away from the stove and looked at Jackie. The little girl rubbed her neck, a worried expression on her face. Sarah sat down at the table and took Jackie's hands in hers, recognizing the fear that still lingered in her daughter's gray eyes. "I don't know if Reese will be able to catch the person or not. But I can tell you this, he'll do everything in his power to make certain that the bad person doesn't hurt you again."

Jackie touched her neck once more. "But maybe it was a monster that came to get me."

"Reese isn't afraid of monsters," Sarah replied.

"But monsters are big and strong." Jackie obviously needed lots of reassurance.

Sarah smiled. "Reese is big and strong. Remember, he pulled me out of the well, and that took somebody really, really strong."

Jackie's wrinkled forehead relaxed and a smile curved her lips. "I like Mr. Sheriff."

Sarah nodded and stood up, her heart wrapping itself in knots at Jackie's words. As she cut up an apple, she

wondered if it was possible that somehow, in some neb-
ulous way, Jackie felt a bond with Reese.

Jackie had never been a child who took easily to men.
The only males in her life were Sarah's boss at the restaurant and a neighbor in the apartment complex where
they lived. Jackie kept herself curiously aloof from both
despite their friendly efforts with her.

Sarah had just set the bowl of oatmeal in front of
Jackie when the phone rang. It was Reese. "Did you get
any sleep at all?" he asked.

"Not much," she admitted. "What about you?"

He hesitated a moment. "It was a long night," he
finally said, although he didn't mention the fact that he'd
spent the night in his car hidden in a grove of trees. "Are
you going to be around there all day?"

"I guess. We don't have any definite plans."

"Good. I'd prefer you all stick around there so I know
where you are. I'm going to do a little investigative work
today. I want to call around and see if I can discover
exactly where Raymond Boswell and Ben were around
midnight last night."

"Then you'll call me and let me know what you find
out?" Sarah asked, her anxiety back. She had to know
if Ben was a part of this, and despite the fact her heart
cried out in denial, she had to know if Lindy was responsible.

"I'll let you know the minute I know anything," he
promised. "How's Lindy this morning?" he asked, as if
able to read her mind.

"I don't know. She hasn't been down from her room
yet," Sarah said in a low voice. "Reese, I just can't
believe—"

"I know," he interrupted. "You never want to believe
betrayal is possible with somebody you love."

The words hung in the air between them for a long moment, words that held a volume of emotion, words that filled Sarah with an unexpected pang of guilt. Was that what he thought she'd done? Did he see her leaving so long ago as a form of betrayal?

"I'll call you later," he said before she could reply. Then he was gone, leaving the dial tone buzzing in her ear. She slowly hung up the phone. Had the statement been a jibe at her or had she taken it too personally? Had he merely been commenting on her own pain in suspecting Lindy, or had it been a pointed reminder of their past relationship?

She was too tired to pick through the muck of the past, too tired to defend or justify her decision to leave Clay Creek. Besides, it was too late to change anything, too late to make things different.

She and Jackie had been in town for a week, and although Reese had been kind to Jackie, he certainly hadn't attempted to form a lasting relationship with her. He hadn't tried to be a father, and this, more than anything, told her there was no way she and Reese could ever share a future together.

"Good morning," Lindy said as she stumbled sleepily into the kitchen. She was still clad in her pajamas and looked as if she'd just rolled out of bed and straight down the stairs.

"You want some oatmeal?" Sarah offered.

"It's got cinnamon and sugar and apples in it," Jackie added.

"No thanks, I'm not hungry," Lindy replied, sinking down into a chair at the table. "I guess I could drink a cup of coffee," she said, starting to get up.

"Sit still. I'll get it," Sarah said, pouring herself and her sister a cup, then joining Lindy and Jackie at the table. "So what are you going to do today?" she asked her sister. "Are you going to work on finishing up the paper in here?"

Lindy frowned and looked around. "I don't think so. I really don't feel very well this morning."

"It was a disruptive night," Sarah said softly, wishing she could crawl into her sister's mind, see what was going on in there, confirm that Lindy harbored no threat to Jackie or herself.

"Can I go watch cartoons?" Jackie asked when her cereal was gone.

Sarah nodded. "Put your bowl in the sink." After Jackie had done as she was told and left the room, Sarah turned back to her sister. "Lindy? Is Ben happy here... on the farm?"

"I...I don't know. I guess. Why?" A flicker of curiosity darkened her eyes.

"Has he ever mentioned to you that he wants to sell out to Raymond Boswell, perhaps take the money and make a new start someplace else?"

Lindy's eyes widened. "Did Ben say something to make you think he wants to do that?" Her fingers worried the coffee mug she held. "He's going to leave me, I just know it."

"No, Lindy, he didn't say anything like that to me," Sarah hurriedly assured her. "I was just wondering if Ben had mentioned that, if he could, he'd be interested in selling the farm to Boswell."

Lindy ran a hand over her face in confusion. "He's never said anything about it. We both knew that Raymond had made offers to buy the farm from Mama, but Ben never told Mama what he thought she should do." A ghost of a smile curved Lindy's lips upward. "Of

course, Ben knew Mama would never listen to him anyway.''

"How did Mama and Ben get along?" Sarah asked,
needing answers, wishing she'd been here to see all the
family dynamics at work.

Lindy shrugged. "All right, I guess." She tilted her
head and frowned. "I don't think Mama really trusted
Ben. It didn't have to do with anything Ben said or did.
Mama didn't trust him because of me.''

"What do you mean?"

Lindy's frown deepened. "Mama didn't think Ben
was in our marriage for the long haul—because of my
illness. Sometimes I'm really hard to live with, Sarah."
She sighed in frustration. "I know when I'm acting
crazy but I can't stop. I can't control what I do all the
time. I think Mama was afraid that Ben would get tired
of living with me and eventually leave. She was probably right." She got up from the table. "I've got to feed
my dogs," she said, letting Sarah know that, as far as
she was concerned, the conversation was finished.

Sarah watched as her sister got out the large pot that
she used to take food to the dogs in the pen. With the
expertise of habit, Lindy opened several cans and emptied them into the pot, then she got into the refrigerator
and pulled out several covered dishes. "Are you going
to eat any more of this casserole?" she asked Sarah.

Sarah shook her head. "No, you might as well give
the rest of it to the dogs.''

As Lindy emptied several dishes of leftovers into the
pot with the dog food, Sarah got herself another cup of
coffee, once again feeling the deep exhaustion weighing
heavily on her body and spirit.

"I'll be right back," Lindy said as she headed out the

back door. Sarah nodded and sank back down at the kitchen table.

She felt as if she needed to sleep for twenty-four hours straight to make up for all the sleepless nights she'd suffered in the past week. Since she'd come back home, her nights had been interrupted by Lindy's outbursts, disturbing thoughts of Reese, intruders in the dark. And even when she did manage to sleep, she experienced haunting dreams of Reese and his passion, and vivid nightmares in which she was running for her life.

She took a sip of her coffee, then rubbed her eyes tiredly. She felt as if she'd been plunged into a nightmare from which she couldn't wake up. And the nightmare was one where all her loved ones wore masks, making it impossible to discern who she could trust and who she couldn't.

She thought again of what Reese had said the night before, about her not being very good at trusting him. His words had spoken of the bitterness he still felt toward her and her decision to cut him out of her life.

Didn't he realize she'd made her decision based on the man she thought he was, the values and beliefs he'd professed at the time? He'd done and said everything in his power to let her know he wasn't a family kind of man and now, years later, was blaming her for making the only choice she could have made.

A scream interrupted Sarah's thoughts, a scream of such magnitude that the hairs on the back of her neck rose in fear. Lindy. It had been Lindy who'd screamed. Sarah jumped out of the chair, sending it crashing to the floor, and exploded out the back door.

Lindy stood by the dog pen, her body vibrating as another scream of horror emanated from her. As Sarah got closer to the pen, she realized what was causing

Lindy's screams. The German shepherd was writhing on the floor of the pen, convulsing as he foamed at the mouth. The other two dogs were cowering in the corners of the pen, whining their displeasure at the German shepherd's unusual actions.

"Lindy, go call the vet," Sarah commanded. "Jackie, stay in the house," she yelled to the little girl, who'd started out the back door.

"Mama, what's happening?" Jackie asked worriedly.

"One of the dogs is sick," Sarah answered her daughter, then turned back to Lindy. Grabbing Lindy's trembling shoulders, Sarah shook her. "Lindy, you have to go call the vet."

"Yes…yes…the vet…" She stumbled off toward the house and Sarah turned back to the pen. The dog appeared to be in bad shape. His breathing was labored and his eyes had rolled back in his head. She knelt down by the animal.

"It's okay," she murmured softly, stroking his furry, heaving side. She looked up as Lindy came running back out.

"Dr. Sutherland is on his way," she said, then shoved a fist into her mouth to stifle a sob. "Oh, Sarah, what's wrong with him? He was fine when I first came outside."

"I don't know what's wrong with him." Sarah stood up and Lindy took her place next to the dog, tears streaming down her face. "Tell me exactly what happened," Sarah said softly.

"They all seemed fine when I came out. I put the food in the dish and Peanuts here gobbled some of it down. He always eats first, the others wait until he's done." Lindy's face blanched and another sob caught in her throat. Sarah kicked the food dish out of the pen, staring at it in horror.

"Something I fed him did this to him. Oh God, it's all my fault," Lindy wailed.

Sarah stared at the food left in the bowl, able to see the remains of the casserole Lindy had added to the canned dog food. They'd eaten the hamburger dish the night before and there was no way it could have gone bad so quickly. Besides, bad meat wouldn't cause such a violent reaction.

Within fifteen minutes Dr. Sutherland arrived. He did a cursory examination of the dog and quickly placed it in his van. "It looks like this animal might have been poisoned," he explained. "If he's going to make it I need to get him back to my office where I can treat him." He picked up the pan of food containing what the dog had eaten. "I'll check this out and see if we can identify exactly what we're dealing with." He frowned, staring for a moment at the pen. "Are you sure this dog couldn't have gotten into some rat poison or something stored in the barn or one of the other outbuildings?"

Lindy shook her head. "They haven't been out of the pen all week."

"Dr. Sutherland, would you please let me know as soon as you identify whatever made the dog so ill?" Sarah asked.

"I'll have to send a sample to my toxicologist and we should have some answers by this afternoon." With a curt nod, he got back into his van and took off.

It was early afternoon when he called to tell them the lab had sent him the results of the tests. He told Sarah lethal levels of rat poison had been found in the casserole fed to the dogs.

"I had the lab test for rat poison and some of the other more accessible poisons. Bingo on the rat killer."

"I'm afraid I don't understand, Dr. Sutherland," Sarah replied. "How would rat poison get into that casserole?"

"Sarah, I can only tell you what's in it, not how it got there." He went on to tell her that the German shepherd hadn't made it. The amount of poison in his body had simply been too much. Sarah hung up, knowing the worst task was yet to come. She had to tell Lindy.

Jackie was asleep on the sofa, obviously exhausted from the disruptive night. Sarah found Lindy sitting in their mother's bedroom. "Lindy, the vet called."

"Peanuts died, didn't he?" Her voice was flat and curiously devoid of emotion.

"Yes." Sarah sat down next to her sister and placed a comforting arm around her shoulder. Tears began to fall down Lindy's face.

"The lab discovered rat poisoning in the casserole." For the first time Sarah realized the full implication of what Dr. Sutherland had told her, and she shivered in disbelief.

Lindy's shoulders began to shake with suppressed sobs. "Why? Why would somebody want to poison my dogs?"

"I don't think the poison was intended for the dogs," Sarah said softly. "It was in the casserole. Someone intended for us to eat it."

Lindy looked at Sarah, her eyes wide. "Oh my God," she gasped. "Why? Sarah, what's going on around here?"

"I don't know," Sarah answered. But she knew now that Lindy wasn't responsible for any of this. There was no way Lindy would have poisoned the casserole, then fed it to her dogs. She loved those dogs as if they were her children.

"Whoever was in the house last night must have put the poison in the food," Sarah said, thinking aloud. Her chest constricted, squeezing her heart as she thought of making breakfast that morning for Jackie.

What if Jackie had decided she'd wanted some of the casserole for breakfast? What if they'd decided to warm it up for lunch? What else might be poisoned in the refrigerator? In the cabinets? "We can't stay here. It isn't safe here any longer."

"What do you mean? Where can we go?" Lindy asked fearfully.

"Reese said we could stay with him, and I think that's a good idea. We'll be safe at his house." Although Sarah was reluctant to spend any time at all with Reese, Jackie's safety far outweighed any reservations she had.

"Sarah, I don't want to stay with Reese. I don't know him that well and I'd feel better staying with Anna. I'll call her. I've stayed with her lots of times. I'd much rather go to her place."

Sarah stood up, suddenly unable to wait another minute to be out of this place. "Pack a bag and we'll talk about it as we drive into town."

It took Sarah only a few minutes to throw some clothes for herself and Jackie into a suitcase. Thank goodness she'd overpacked for this trip and she and Jackie had plenty of clothes with them. She was also glad that Jackie hadn't started school yet so their extended stay here didn't disrupt any classes.

Jackie. She had to get her baby someplace safe. As she packed, her mind whirled with horrifying visions of Jackie lying on the floor. Who could possibly be responsible for such a vicious attack? Who was devious enough to sneak into the house and poison food to make people die?

She didn't begin to relax again until they were all in the car and driving toward town. Only then did her breathing return to a more normal pace and her heart stop its frantic, fearful pounding.

"I called Anna. She said I was welcome to stay with her for a while," Lindy said. "So you can just drop me off at the café."

"Are you sure you don't want to stay with us at Reese's?" Sarah asked, reluctant for the three of them to separate. Who knew to what extent Lindy's own life was in danger? It was possible that for some reason somebody might be after all the Calhouns.

"I'll be much more comfortable with Anna," Lindy replied. "And I'll be safe there, too."

Sarah nodded, only wanting Lindy someplace where she'd feel safe and secure.

It was nearly four o'clock when Sarah finally parked in front of Reese's house. She'd dropped Lindy at the café, where she and Jackie had grabbed a late lunch, then learned from the secretary at the police station that Reese had already gone home for the day.

Sarah had driven directly to Reese's house. Now, sitting out in the driveway, she felt a curious dread mingling with the anticipation of safety. It was going to be difficult to share living space with Reese and not feel anything for the man himself. But she was more than willing to sacrifice her own peace of mind for Jackie's well-being. And of one thing she was certain. Even though Reese didn't want to be a real father to Jackie, he would never, ever allow anyone to harm her.

"Does Mr. Sheriff know we're going to stay here?" Jackie asked as they got out of the car.

"He'll know in a minute," Sarah observed, getting their suitcase from the trunk. Together mother and daughter walked up to the front door.

Reese answered on the first knock, his eyes lighting from within then darkening with questions as he looked first at Sarah, then at the suitcase she clutched tightly in her hand. "I hope you were serious last night about our staying here," Sarah said lightly.

"What happened?" he asked.

Sarah looked pointedly at Jackie. "We just decided it would be fun to stay here with you for a few days."

"Mama says you have a VCR," Jackie exclaimed.

"That's right, I do." Reese opened the door and let them in, his brow still creased with questions. For a moment the three of them stood awkwardly in the living room.

"So, where are we gonna sleep?" Jackie asked, breaking the tension.

"Come on up and I'll show you," Reese said, gesturing for them to follow him up the stairs. As Sarah walked behind him, she felt her face flush with heat as she remembered that the last time she'd been here he'd carried her up the stairs and to his bedroom. When he got to the top of the stairs he turned and looked at her, and in the smoldering depths of his eyes she saw that he entertained the same memory.

"Uh, I've got two spare rooms. You can have one and Jackie the other," he said.

Jackie grabbed hold of her mother's hand. "I want to sleep with you," she said in a loud whisper. Anger resounded throughout Sarah as she nodded affirmatively. Jackie had always been wonderfully independent, but the events of the last couple of days had stolen some of that independence from her. And for that reason alone Sarah hated the person responsible.

"We can both stay in the same room," Sarah told Reese. She smiled reassuringly at Jackie. "We like bunking together, right?" Jackie nodded with a smile.

He led them into a sparsely furnished room with a beige spread on the bed and matching curtains at the window. The bed and a double dresser were the only pieces of furniture in the room. "It's not much," he said.

"It's okay," Jackie quipped. "You just sleep in a bedroom."

"Jackie, I'm sure Reese wouldn't mind if you went downstairs and turned on the television. It's just about time for your favorite cartoons."

Jackie looked at Reese for permission. When he nodded, she scampered back down the stairs. "So, tell me what's going on," Reese said the minute she was gone.

Sarah quickly told him about the poisoned casserole and the death of the dog. "If Lindy hadn't given that food to the dogs, we probably would have eaten it. Reese, I couldn't stay out there, not knowing what else might be poisoned, what else could happen."

"You did the right thing coming here," he agreed. "I have a little bit of news to tell you. Raymond Boswell was in St. Louis last night. There's no way possible that he was the intruder. I spoke to the bellman and the desk clerk at the hotel where he's staying. There's no doubt about him being there."

"What about Ben?" Sarah asked hesitantly.

Reese frowned, his eyes darkening to a shade of midnight. "Ben is another matter. According to the desk clerk at the hotel where he's staying, he retired about nine o'clock last night and asked that he not be disturbed. He didn't order room service and apparently nobody saw him between nine last night and eight this morning. Between those hours it would have been possible for him to drive here, get into the house and get back to Kansas City.''

"I can't believe it. I mean I don't want to believe it," Sarah said softly. "Poor Lindy. If it's true, it will break her heart."

"We don't know that it's true," Reese replied. "Just because he doesn't have an airtight alibi doesn't mean he's the culprit. But at the moment he's definitely at the top of my suspect list."

"At least I know now for certain that Lindy isn't in any way responsible. There's no way she would poison one of her own dogs."

Reese nodded. "Where is she?"

"She went to stay at Anna's. She's always felt very close to Anna and will be more comfortable there." She hesitated a moment. "I hope you don't mind us coming here."

He touched her arm, a light touch that still evoked an immediate response in Sarah. "I'm glad you're here. You'll be safe and that's the most important thing in the world to me." His gaze held hers for a long moment until she finally broke the contact and looked away.

"I've decided not to return to New York until we find out who's doing all this. I don't want to go back home and take my fear with me. I want all this settled before we leave."

"I think you're smart," he agreed. Again a moment of awkward silence fell between them. "Well, I guess I'll get out of here and let you get unpacked. Are you hungry?"

She shook her head. "We ate at Anna's when we dropped off Lindy."

"Let me know if you need anything." He hesitated a moment longer, then turned and walked down the stairs.

Sarah expelled a breath she hadn't realized she'd been holding. This was going to be far more difficult than she'd realized. Even now she could feel his presence surrounding her, the scent of him lingering in the air. She'd come here seeking safety, but she suddenly didn't feel safe at all.

Reese sat alone at the kitchen table. The floorboards squeaked overhead as Sarah moved around in the bedroom, and Jackie's giggles mingled with the sounds of the television, drifting in from the living room. The house had never been so filled with life.

His blood ran cold as he thought of the poisoned dog…poison intended for the Calhoun women. Dear God, how long could Sarah's luck hold out? Somebody was trying every means possible to see her dead. Who in the hell could it be? He hadn't lied when he told Sarah that Ben was at the top of his suspect list, but he wasn't fool enough to jump to conclusions.

One thing he had learned in this lifetime was that things weren't always as black and white as they seemed. And besides, he didn't have enough concrete evidence to prove anything. He had his men checking out every possibility, pursuing anything that made sense and much that didn't. Somehow, someway they had to get a break.

The best he could do was wait…wait for the guilty party to tip a hand, get careless, make a mistake. In the meantime he knew it would take all his willpower, all his energy, to maintain a pleasant, platonic relationship with Sarah.

There was an old saying that familiarity breeds contempt. A part of him hoped it was true. Perhaps the enforced closeness of their living condition would prove to Sarah once and for all that he wasn't—and could never be—father material.

He loved Sarah, had probably never stopped loving her. And there was a part of him that loved Jackie. He loved them both enough to let them go on with their lives and find a man who could be everything and all to them. He loved them both enough to know that he wasn't the right man.

He was vaguely aware of the sudden silence in the living room and the sounds of Jackie's footsteps climbing the stairs. A moment later he heard the same pattering feet coming back down the stairs.

Jackie entered the kitchen and sat down across from him at the table. "Mama's asleep," she announced, staring at him in the unselfconscious fashion of her age. She giggled. "She was making little snoring sounds."

"She must be exhausted," Reese said, feeling a need to fidget beneath the little girl's direct gaze.

Jackie leaned back in the chair and crossed her legs exactly the same way Reese's legs were crossed. "Mr. Sheriff, I guess if Mama's asleep, that means you're baby-sitting me until she wakes up." She smiled, a sweet smile of complete acceptance. "So, what do you want to do?" she asked.

Reese stared at her. He'd faced down a drug-crazed teenager with a gun, he'd been cornered by a rabid dog for an hour, he'd done a million dumb, dangerous things. But never had he felt the gut-twisting kind of fear that now blossomed inside him as he realized that, until Sarah awakened, he was in charge of entertaining his own daughter.

Chapter 12

Sarah stretched languidly and kept her eyes firmly closed, reluctant to leave her sleep behind. Ah, she'd slept so deeply. There had been no disturbing nightmares, no confusing dreams, only a dark, peaceful oblivion. It had been wonderful.

She stretched again, this time knowing that she was awake to stay. She opened her eyes and looked around the darkened bedroom, for a moment tense and disoriented as she viewed the unfamiliar surroundings.

As the events of the day flooded back to her she relaxed once again. Of course, they were safe…in Reese's house. She looked around again, wondering how long she had been asleep. She hadn't meant to actually take a nap, had only intended to stretch out for a few minutes. She squinted and looked at her wristwatch, shocked to see it was almost nine o'clock. She'd been asleep for more than four hours.

Jackie. Where was Jackie? She jumped out of bed, her

heart pounding in her chest. My God, what had Jackie been doing for the last four hours? How could she have fallen so sound asleep and left her daughter to her own devices?

As she walked down the first two steps of the staircase she heard Reese and Jackie's voices coming out of the living room. She paused and sat down in the stairwell, then peeked into the room below.

Reese and Jackie lay on their stomachs facing each other, both holding cards for the game in progress. "Okay, what do you have?" Reese asked the little girl.

Sarah watched as Jackie showed him her hand. "I've got three sixes," she said.

"And I've got two pairs. That means your hand beats mine, little squirrel. You get the pot." The pot consisted of a small pile of toothpicks.

Poker? He was teaching her little girl how to play poker? Sarah frowned, trying to decide how she felt about her five-year-old learning to play poker. Somehow it didn't matter what he was teaching her to play. What mattered was the smile on her daughter's face and the reflection of that smile curving Reese's lips.

"Let's play again," Jackie urged.

"Again? You've already beat me a dozen times," Reese protested. Jackie giggled and the sound touched the soft core of Sarah's heart. "You want another piece of pizza?" Reese asked her.

"No, my tummy is too stuffed," Jackie replied, then grinned. "But we made it good, didn't we?"

"We sure did," he agreed.

They'd made pizza? Surely they had just ordered one and warmed it up, she thought. She watched a few more minutes, feeling like a spy but unable to tear herself away from the vision of father and daughter playing cards, laughing, obviously enjoying each other's company. It made her ache inside with a curious mixture of pleasure and pain.

She closed her eyes, allowing the pain to momentarily usurp the pleasure. It was a false picture, she told herself. Reese was entertaining a houseguest for the evening, nothing more, nothing less. It was one thing to be kind to a little girl and play games with her, quite another to make the kind of emotional commitment a father would make.

Standing up, she went down the remaining stairs, smiling at the two people who held her heart. "Hi, Mama. You sure took a good nap," Jackie greeted her. "Mr. Sheriff teached me how to play poker."

Reese sat up with a sheepish grin. "We got tired of Go Fish." He stood up and raked a hand through his hair, looking more relaxed and boyish than Sarah had ever seen him. "You hungry?"

"We made pizza, just the two of us," Jackie said. "It was pretty yummy, right, Mr. Sheriff?"

"Right," Reese agreed. "You know, Jackie, you can call me Reese."

She studied him for a long moment. "Nah, I like Mr. Sheriff better."

Reese shrugged. "Suit yourself," he said, then looked back at Sarah. "So, how about some pizza?"

Sarah nodded, realizing she was hungry. "Jackie, why don't you go on up and put your pajamas on. It's already past your bedtime."

Jackie sidled over to Sarah and leaned into her. "Come with me, okay? I don't want to go by myself."

Sarah looked down at her daughter and realized the events of the previous night had made a deeper scar than the bruises around her neck. "I'll tell you what. How about we go upstairs and get your pj's on, then you can stay down here on the sofa until I'm ready to go to sleep.''

Jackie hesitated a moment, then nodded. "We'll be right back," Sarah said, smiling apologetically to Reese.

"No problem," he assured her. "I'll just warm up the pizza in the oven."

As they went up the stairs, Reese went back into the kitchen, where he placed the remaining pizza in the oven, then sat down at the table. His thoughts were in a jumble. And what kept coming to the foreground was utter, complete amazement.

He'd never dreamed a kid of his would be so smart. He'd only had to show Jackie something once and she immediately caught on. Hell, he'd known grown men who'd caught on to the rudimentary rules of poker slower than she had. Amazing. She must have gotten that particular attribute from Sarah.

And she was witty, too. She'd made him laugh a dozen times with humorous quips that displayed a quick mind. He warmed inside. That had to be his genes knocking around inside her.

She'd talked a lot, sharing with him some of the details of their life in New York. She spoke at length about the preschool she attended, whispering that her teacher, Mrs. Cannon, was often cranky. She'd told him about her trips to the city park to play with her friend Regina. She'd explained to him that their neighbor, Mrs. Rosellini, brought them a pot of homemade spaghetti every Sunday and occasionally baby-sat her when Sarah was at work. Finally she'd told him she liked it here in Clay Creek and wanted to stay.

That particular statement had caused a myriad of warring emotions inside him. There was a part of him that would have loved to have them here, loved to have the opportunity to continue to be a part of their lives. But there was another part of him that didn't want them around. It scared him. He knew eventually he'd make the same kind of mistakes his father had made, and he couldn't stand it if Jackie came to hate him. Besides, how would she feel if she discovered her father had been nothing but a juvenile delinquent who, without a miracle, would have ended up in jail instead of upholding the law? No, it would never work. She would eventually come to be ashamed of him.

Jackie flew through the kitchen door, bringing an end to his thoughts. "Come tuck me in," she said, grabbing his hand and pulling him up from his chair.

Reese allowed himself to be dragged into the living room, where Sarah had placed a pillow on the sofa and was now unfolding the afghan that had been draped across the back of the couch. "In you go, young lady," Sarah exclaimed.

"Mr. Sheriff is gonna tuck me in," Jackie said.

Sarah handed him the afghan as Jackie scampered up on the sofa. Reese placed the blanket around her, then started to back away. Jackie caught his wrist and grinned up at him. "You gotta kiss me good night," she admonished gently.

Reese felt his chest tighten and he fought down a protest. Ridiculous to allow the thought of kissing a child good-night to bring on the symptoms of panic. He leaned over and touched his lips to her sweet, soft cheek. Before he could pull away, Jackie wrapped her arms around his neck and gave him a hug. "Good night, Mr. Sheriff," she whispered in his ear. "Thanks for being a good baby-sitter."

For a moment he couldn't speak around the lump in

his throat. "Good night, Jackie," he finally muttered softly, then stood up and went into the kitchen.

A moment later Sarah joined him, sitting down at the table while he pulled the warmed pizza out of the oven. He put the pan, a plate and silverware in front of her. "You want something to drink?"

"Just water," she answered, noting the tension that radiated from him. He looked almost angry, his motions jerky as he got a glass and filled it with ice, then added the water.

Sarah cut a piece of the pizza and placed it on her plate, wondering if he was angry with her for showing up on his doorstep then promptly falling asleep and leaving him to baby-sit a child he'd never wanted. She waited to speak until he set the glass of water down and joined her at the table.

"Reese, I really apologize," she began. "I had no idea I was so exhausted. I just meant to lie down for a few minutes. I certainly didn't intend to be asleep for so long and leave Jackie to you."

"No problem," he said tersely. "I handled it."

"But you shouldn't have had to. I know she can be demanding and it shouldn't have been left for you to entertain her."

"I said it was all right," he repeated forcefully. He got up and went to the refrigerator and grabbed a can of soda, then returned to the table. "Eat," he commanded, then smiled slightly. "I can promise you there's nothing wrong with it other than the hot dogs Jackie insisted we cut up and put on top."

"Hot dogs?" Sarah stared at the pizza. "I thought it was some kind of pepperoni."

"I asked her what kind of pizza she liked and she told me hot dog pizza, but nobody had ever made it before.

So we made hot dog pizza. I did manage to talk her out
of the mustard, which she insisted goes with hot dogs.''

Sarah laughed. It wasn't fair. It wasn't right, the two
of them sitting here sharing the comical creative efforts
of their daughter.

She focused once again on her pizza, eating with
small forced bites while her heart ached with a hunger
no amount of food would ever sate. She didn't know
what to say to him, was tired of speculating about who
was after her and felt as if the subject of Jackie was off-
limits unless he brought it up.

The silence that grew between them was not a comfortable one. She could feel his gaze on her while she
ate but she didn't look up. The tension surrounding them
grew. Had they nothing to talk about? Had they nothing
in common except a powerful physical attraction they'd
agreed wasn't enough, would never be enough?

''Are you happy, Sarah?'' His voice was quiet, as if
he, too, had been contemplating the same questions.

''Happy?'' She looked up at him in surprise. ''Most
of the time I don't think about happiness. It takes a lot
of work and energy to survive in a place like New
York.''

''Do you need money? I could send—''

She stopped him with a glare. How dare he! How dare
he offer money to compensate for his resistance to fatherhood. ''I don't need your money,'' she snapped.

''I know, I know,'' he said, looking chagrined. ''That
was a stupid thing to suggest. I just…'' He looked away
from her, then back. ''I just wish there was something I
could do to…'' He sighed. ''I don't know.''

''Let's just drop it,'' she replied. She got up and carried her plate to the sink. Her heart ached with painful
regrets, bittersweet longings for what might have been.

She felt miserable and he looked miserable. "Thanks for the pizza. I think I'll go back to bed now." She didn't give him a chance to say anything more. She fled the kitchen and roused Jackie from the sofa. Together the two of them went up the stairs and into the bedroom.

Once in bed, Sarah realized she'd been fooling herself when she'd thought she was through crying over Reese. Apparently her tears had not all been spent, for fresh ones coursed down her cheeks and she turned her head and cried silently into her pillow.

Sarah emerged from the bathroom and bumped square into Reese. "Oh...excuse me," she exclaimed, stepping aside to let him pass. Her eyes didn't meet his.

He grunted and stepped into the bathroom, slamming the door behind him. God, the past three days had been the longest of his life. Ever since Jackie and Sarah had been in the house, he felt like a time bomb ticking to detonation.

Sarah's presence disturbed him to the point of utter distraction. Jackie's laughter filled the house, brightening dark corners he hadn't known existed. He felt as if he were being punished, being offered a glimpse of heaven before he was sent straight to hell.

He never knew sexual tension could reach such a peak. Over the course of the past three days he seemed to be in a continual state of arousal. All it took was a brush of their hands when grabbing for the same butter knife, an unexpected locking of eyes, a sudden whiff of her sweet scent. Her presence was everywhere, taunting him, tormenting him.

Each night he lay in bed, thinking of her in the next room. For the most part sleep remained elusive, and when at last he did manage to fall asleep, he dreamed erotic dreams of her.

He got into the shower and turned the water on so that the hot spray hit him with an almost brutal force, hoping the fierce heat would burn thoughts of Sarah right out of his flesh. Yet somehow he knew the shower wouldn't do the trick. It wasn't enough, wasn't strong enough to battle her very essence. He was possessed by the spirit of Sarah and what he really needed was a powerful exorcism to release her hold on him.

He closed his eyes, able to envision how she had looked when she'd left the bathroom moments before. She'd been clad in a cotton nightgown that covered her from her neck to the floor, and there had been nothing provocative about the gown. And yet Reese thought she'd looked as sexy as he'd ever seen her. Her hair had been pulled up and fastened clumsily with a barrette, leaving damp tendrils clinging to her neck. She'd smelled of fragrant soap and shampoo and he'd immediately thought of the two of them in the shower together, soaping each other, caressing each other.

God… He took a deep breath and turned around and allowed the hot spray to scour his backside. He picked up the bar of soap, wondering if only moments before it had glided over the fullness of her breasts, down the length of her rib cage… Damn it! He ducked his head into the water, sputtering in frustration.

At least he didn't have to worry about a cozy family scene this evening. Only a few minutes before, Anna and Lindy had picked up Jackie. The three of them were going to eat out then catch a movie and Anna had said she'd have Jackie back by bedtime. That's when Sarah had decided to take a shower and get into her nightgown.

The only problem with Jackie being gone was that he

and Sarah would be alone together for the next couple of hours. He twisted the faucets so that the water spraying out was cold. He needed something to cool him off before he left the bathroom and faced her.

Within minutes, dried and dressed and feeling almost in control, he left the bathroom and followed his nose to the kitchen and the marvelous scent of something wonderful cooking.

"Hmm, something smells delicious," he said as he entered the kitchen. He was grateful for the fact that a long robe now covered the nightgown he'd glimpsed earlier. She was apparently intending it to be an early night. That was fine with him. If she was smart, she would go into the bedroom and lock the door against him.

She half turned from the stove, a spoon paused in mid-air. "It's just spaghetti sauce. I know we ate a late lunch but I thought you might be hungry again. I just opened some canned stuff and added some extra spices. Here, taste it." She held the wooden spoon out to him.

He moved over to where she stood, standing so close to her he didn't know if the heat he felt emanated from the stove or from her. As she raised the spoon to his lips, her mouth opened unconsciously. The sauce was sweet and tangy, but he hardly tasted it. He was focused on her mouth, the way her tongue darted out to wet her bottom lip.

"Hmm," he murmured. "Now you taste it." Before she could bring the spoon to her own mouth, he grabbed her and placed his lips on hers, sharing the lingering taste with her.

"Reese..." she said as she pulled her mouth from his. It wasn't a protest, rather it was a trembling sigh.

"Don't tell me no, Sarah." He looked into her eyes,

saw the flickering flames that lighted their violet depths. "If you do, I think we'll both explode." He captured her mouth once again.

For a brief moment she stiffened against him, then with a low moan she returned his kiss, molding her body against his in complete surrender. In that instant Reese knew that he was completely out of control, and so was she. The spoon she'd been holding clattered to the floor as her hands entwined around his neck, pulling him more tightly against her.

There was no time for thought, no opportunity for reason. Reese knew only one thing—a rapturous hunger for Sarah, a hunger he knew she felt equally for him.

He plundered her mouth, his tongue easing into the dark recesses that tasted of passion, and she responded in kind, her tongue dueling with his in a heated dance. He kissed her greedily, moving his mouth down her jaw-line to her ear, where he nibbled hungrily. She moaned, tangling her hands in his hair, crying out as his mouth nipped at the tender flesh in the hollow of her neck.

He tugged at the belt around her waist, loosening the robe and pushing it off her shoulders. It fell to the floor behind her and he pulled her closer against him, his hands caressing her back through the cotton nightgown.

Her fingers fumbled with the fastening of his jeans, her breathing rapid and shallow against his mouth. She emitted little mewling sounds that only fed his hunger, stoked his fever for her.

He pulled her nightgown up and grabbed her buttocks through the thin silk material that covered them. She gasped in pleasure as he splayed his fingers beneath the silk, and at the same time he kicked off his jeans and briefs.

There was no need for prolonged foreplay. They were

both ready to culminate what had begun a lifetime ago between them. He lifted her up and she wrapped her legs around his waist. He buried himself in her hot warmth, his knees sagging with the intensity of sensation. Her hands tangled in his hair and she moaned his name, further fevering his desire.

He carried her into the living room and together they fell on the sofa. He was still inside her, surrounded by her velvet warmth, and as he eased himself out then in again, he looked into her eyes, saw the smoky violet hues urging him harder...faster.

Her fingers clutched his shoulders as he moved in a frenzy, each of his thrusts welcomed and returned by her. He knew the moment she reached her peak, felt her tighten and convulse around him, and then he tumbled over the edge, crying out his pleasure...his love.

Silence. Minutes passed and neither of them moved. Reese kept his head buried in the sweetness of her hair, unwilling to break their embrace, unwilling to raise himself up and look into her eyes and see regret. Still, the silence spoke of regret, and Reese closed his eyes, steeling himself to face what would happen next.

"What are we doing to each other?" she finally asked. Her voice was filled with a weary defeat that tore at his heart.

He rose up on one elbow and looked at her. "I don't know," he said unsteadily.

"I swore to myself I wouldn't allow this to happen again. But I just don't seem to have any willpower where you're concerned."

"Nor I with you," he admitted.

She placed her hands on either side of his face, her eyes such a deep violet they were almost black. "I love you, Reese," she said slowly, as if the very words pained her. "God knows, I've tried not to. I don't want to. But I loved you when I was seventeen and absolutely nothing has changed since that time."

Her words caused a curling warmth to seep through him, as potent as the heated passion they'd just shared. He closed his eyes, for a moment merely basking in her words. He opened his eyes and looked at her once again. "I love you, too." The confession was torn from him and left him weak, because he knew it wasn't the beginning of anything. It was the end.

"Then why?" Her eyes beseeched him. "Why won't you let us be a part of your life? Why don't you want to be a father to your daughter?"

Reese sat up, his emotions divided. His body still tingled with the pleasant sensation of their lovemaking. His heart knew there would never be another woman he loved like Sarah. But his head wouldn't allow him to think beyond the gut-wrenching fear that had always been his closest companion.

"Sarah, I told you a long time ago that I wasn't father material. I don't know how to be a father. I never wanted a family. I never wanted children. They expect too much...need too much."

"But you are a father." Again her voice was soft, but filled with deep emotion.

"And it's because I love you both that I can't be a part of your life." Anger, sorrow and regret all pressed tightly against his chest, and to his horror he felt tears burning his eyes.

He stood up and stalked into the kitchen, where he grabbed his clothes and quickly put them on. His hands shook as he zipped his jeans and buttoned his shirt. Then, picking up her robe, he carried it back into the living room, where she hadn't moved from the sofa.

He paced back and forth before her, his insides in turmoil. "Sarah, I don't know how to be what you and Jackie need."

"Just be yourself—that's enough." She took the robe from him and slipped it on, belting it firmly around her slender waist. She stood up and approached where he stood. "Reese, you say you don't know how to be a father, but what do you think you've been doing for the last three days? You've made her breakfast and you've played games with her." She placed her hand on his arm, the touch killing him. "You listen to her when she talks and you answer her questions with thought and patience. You tuck her in at night and tell her she's safe and she believes you. That's what being a father is all about."

Suddenly she was angry. He could see it in the violet flare of her eyes, the rapid rise and fall of her chest. "Damn it, Reese, you've been angry with me ever since I came back to Clay Creek and you discovered Jackie's existence. You've been mad because I didn't tell you I was pregnant, I didn't give you a chance to do anything about it. Now I'm giving you a choice—a chance to make everything right."

Again emotions pressed tightly against his chest. "But the fact is, you didn't believe in me six years ago."

"And what did you give me to believe in? You were so angry, so filled with rage, so certain that all you wanted to do was leave Clay Creek and start over someplace else. Had I pushed you, made you do the right thing and marry me, how long would it have taken for you to grow to hate me, hate our child?"

Reese didn't answer, he couldn't. There was nothing to say. He knew the truth in her words.

She sighed. "Reese, you're like a fugitive, running

from the law, only in this case you're running from the two people who love you most.''

He moved over to the window and stared outside, his fear a living, breathing power inside him. It was greater than his fear that he wouldn't be what Sarah and Jackie needed. It was deeper than that.

He was eight years old again, bewildered by the physical abandonment of his mother, dazed by the emotional distancing of his father. The two people he'd needed most hadn't found anything redeeming in him. They hadn't needed him, hadn't wanted him.

He couldn't give his heart again, couldn't watch two more people he loved walk away from him when he screwed everything up. It was easier to be the one who walked away. He turned back to face Sarah, loving her so much, so intensely that his chest ached with it. "I can't, Sarah. You're better off without me. I can't do what you want. You were right years ago. You did the right thing in getting as far away from me as you could. I would have eventually destroyed you."

"Damn you, Reese," she cried, her voice trembling. "What are you so afraid of? You aren't your father. You could never be a father like him. You aren't that angry, bitter boy anymore. You've outgrown him. Don't let the past destroy our future. Don't turn your back on us. Let us be in your life."

Reese held his hands out to her, a gesture of helplessness. "I can't, Sarah. Don't hate me...I just can't."

Tears glistened on her lashes and there was a profound sadness on her face. Her anger was gone. Her face seemed to sag with weary resignation. "We couldn't ever hate you, Reese. You hate yourself enough for all of us.'' A tear fell onto her cheek. She swiped it away, then turned and silently went back up the stairs, leaving Reese the way he had been for most of his life...alone.

Chapter 13

The phone rang in the silence of the night. A curious dread swept through Sarah, mingling with a sense of déjà vu, as she tried to climb out of sleep to consciousness. She didn't like phone calls in the middle of the night— they always brought bad news. Middle-of-the-night phone calls brought death.

Still half-asleep, Sarah fumbled on the nightstand for the receiver, then remembered she was in Reese's spare bedroom and there was no phone there. She lay back down, her hand automatically checking to make sure that Jackie was still asleep next to her. The little girl had come home from the movie bubbling and happy and had gone right to bed.

Sarah sat up as a faint knock fell on her door. She got up and grabbed her robe from the end of the bed. Wrapping it around her, she opened the door to Reese. "What is it? What's happened?" she asked anxiously, the somber look on his face letting her know the call had not been pleasant.

"It's Lindy, Sarah." He put his hands on her shoulders as if to brace her. "She's in the hospital."

"Oh my God, what happened?" Sarah asked, her heart jumping into her throat.

"She apparently tried to commit suicide. She took some sleeping pills. They've pumped out her stomach and she's stabilized, but she's asking for you."

Sarah closed her eyes, a wave of despair washing over her. She should have seen this coming. She should have known that the death of Lindy's dog would hit her hard. Lindy had already peaked in her most recent manic phase and had been coming down. The death of Peanuts had apparently shoved her over the edge.

"Oh God, Reese," she finally gasped, and sagged against him. Their earlier fight was momentarily forgotten as she sought the strength of his arms. "I should have insisted she come here with us. I should have kept a closer eye on her. I should have never let her go to Anna's by herself."

She pushed herself away from his warmth, realizing she needed to get dressed, get to Lindy.

Once again Reese grabbed her shoulders and steadied her. "Sarah, don't blame yourself for this," he said gently. "Lindy needs your help and support, not your guilt."

She nodded, realizing he was right. "I know… I'll just get Jackie up and we'll—"

"Don't be ridiculous," Reese briskly interrupted. "There's no reason to wake Jackie. There's certainly nothing she can do. They won't allow her in the hospital rooms—she's too young. Let her sleep. I'll be here with her."

"Are you sure?" she asked hesitantly. Coming as it

did on the heels of their most recent discussion, she was reluctant to take advantage of his offer. Still, she knew he was right, and, besides Jackie would probably stay asleep while she was gone.

"I said it was fine," he assured her. "Now get dressed and get down to the hospital."

She gave him a quick smile of thanks, then went back into the bedroom. She turned on the bedside lamp, grateful Jackie didn't stir from her sleep. She grabbed a pair of jeans and a sweatshirt and pulled them on, her thoughts once again on her sister.

Pills. Where would she have gotten pills? Surely she wouldn't have swallowed a handful of her medication. Damn it, Sarah should have checked Lindy's medicine. She didn't even know what Lindy took.

She replayed Reese's words in her mind. He'd said she'd taken sleeping pills. Sarah hadn't seen any sleeping pills at the farm. Had Lindy kept them hidden somewhere, then packed them along with her clothes, planning to end her own personal agony?

One thing was certain. It was time Sarah took Lindy's medical well-being in hand. She wasn't going to wait around for Ben to get Lindy an appointment with a doctor in Kansas City. Lindy needed to see somebody immediately, at least before she was released from the hospital. Even though Clay Creek was small, surely the hospital had some sort of psychotherapist on staff for suicide attempts.

Dressed, she turned out the light and left the bedroom and went down the stairs. She found Reese sitting in the living room. He rose as she entered, a frown puckering his forehead. "I don't like the idea of you taking off and leaving to drive to the hospital alone in the middle of the night."

"I'll be fine," she assured him, despite the small niggling of fear his words created. "There's no way all this could have been orchestrated by anyone. I'll drive straight to the hospital and straight back here. I'll be fine."

He nodded, reluctant to have her go but knowing she had to. He walked with her to the door. "Park in front of the emergency entrance. There's always somebody there and the area is well lit."

"I will, and I'll try to be back before Jackie wakes up."

"Stay as long as you need to. We'll be fine here." He watched her until she got into the car and pulled out of the driveway, then he relocked the door and wandered back into the living room. He knew sleep was out of the question. He hadn't been sleeping when the phone call had come from the hospital. His earlier conversation with Sarah had pretty much chased sleep away.

He sank back on the sofa and buried his head in his hands…thinking, rehashing and, finally, regretting. He suddenly realized that at some point in the last couple of hours the bitterness he'd harbored toward Sarah about her decision to leave six years ago had disappeared. It was odd how empty he felt without that cloak of bitterness, without his shield of anger.

He now realized Sarah had made the only choice she could, given what he'd told her, how he'd acted at the time. Even then he'd been afraid to show her how important she was in his life, afraid that if he loved her too much she would eventually leave him. Had he somehow set himself up with a self-fulfilling prophecy? Having never really known happiness before, had he subconsciously shoved it away, fearing it?

He got up off the sofa, somehow afraid to delve into

his soul for answers. He'd made his decision where Sarah and Jackie were concerned. Now all he wanted to do was find out who was after them and why. Once that was settled and they were safe, they would be on their way back to New York City and their life there.

He walked up the stairs and quietly opened the door to the bedroom where Jackie slept. The light from the hallway spilled in and seemed to spotlight the sleeping child. He stood at the doorway for a long moment, wondering what in the hell he was trying to prove to himself.

Despite an inner reluctance, he stepped closer to the bed as if drawn toward her by some magical bond. He had no desire to wake her, just a wish to look at her, get his fill of her, be able to conjure her image in his mind after she was long gone.

Jackie. Sarah's child. His child. Jackie, his daughter. The words whirled around in his head. His heart swelled tightly against his rib cage. It had been so much easier when he hadn't known about her. Even knowing about her existence would be easier if he didn't know her as a person, as a tiny entity unto herself.

He wanted to get away, run, but curiously he remained. He knew he was indulging himself in a form of emotional torture and yet he needed to look at her, drink in her presence, love her.

He stood at the side of the bed watching her sleep, marveling at the way her eyelashes dusted the tops of her cherub cheeks, the way her long dark hair was an exact match to the color of his own. He thought of the sunshine her smile contained, the sweetness of her mouth pressed sloppily against his cheek, the utter trust that radiated from her eyes whenever she looked at him.

That's what got him the most—that trust. The simple assurance she had that he wouldn't hurt her, wouldn't do anything to make her sad, that he could be depended upon for whatever she needed. That's what frightened him more than anything. A child's dependence on her parents...so incredibly pure, so incredibly needy.

What if he agreed to marry Sarah, parent Jackie, and eventually the responsibility became too much? Would he run like his mother, or retreat emotionally like his father? He, more than anyone, knew the kind of pain, the sort of emotional scars those actions left on a child. He couldn't risk doing that to Jackie. He loved her, and that's why he couldn't take a chance on being a parent to her. He'd rather not parent her at all than be a bad parent.

He reached out and lightly touched the smoothness of her cheek. She remained asleep but smiled, the gesture so sweet, so pure, it caused an arrow of agony to shoot through him. He gasped beneath the pain of the emotional assault and slowly backed out of the room.

He closed the door and leaned against it wearily. Yes, he was doing the best thing for both Jackie and Sarah by not being involved with their lives. He would keep them safe from harm while they were here in Clay Creek, then he knew he had to let them go. He just hadn't expected it to hurt so damned much.

Sarah parked in one of the spaces just in front of the emergency room entrance and hurried inside. She was immediately greeted by the faint medicinal scent and hushed tones of a hospital at rest. It was almost two in the morning and nobody manned the information desk. The tiny gift shop was closed and it was obvious that the Clay Creek Hospital was not accustomed to night-time visitors. The overhead lights had been dimmed to provide only a faint illumination and the security guard slept in the corner on a chair.

Sarah hesitated in the dim foyer. Two long hallways led in opposite directions and she wondered which one to take. She had no idea where Lindy was. Reese hadn't mentioned any particular room number or section of the hospital.

At that moment she saw Anna come out of a room at the far end of the hallway to her left. She started toward the old woman. As they drew closer to each other, she could tell by Anna's red-rimmed eyes that she had been weeping.

"Oh, Sarah," Anna exclaimed, her arms opened to embrace her. "I'm so sorry…it's all my fault. I should have thrown those pills away a long time ago." Sobs overcame the older woman and Sarah wrapped her arms around her, trying to soothe her.

"Anna, I don't want you blaming yourself for this. I should have seen it coming, warned you that Lindy was on the verge of another depression." She gave Anna a final hug, then released her. "Now, tell me what happened."

Anna pulled a white lacy handkerchief from her coat pocket and dabbed at her eyes, suddenly looking every day of her sixty-eight years. "We got home from the movies and Lindy said she was going straight to bed." Anna shook her head and swiped at her eyes once again. "I should have known. She was withdrawn and quiet all evening."

Sarah nodded and led her over to several plastic chairs pushed up against the wall. They sat down and Anna continued. "Anyway, she went into the bathroom and was there for a few minutes, then told me good-night and went on to bed. I puttered around in the kitchen, then read the paper. It was probably an hour before I went into the bathroom to get ready for bed. I saw the pill bottle on the sink and knew Lindy had done something crazy.''

''What kind of pills?''

Anna frowned. ''Sleeping pills. I went through a bad bout of insomnia a year ago and Doc Burwell gave me a prescription for them. I took them a couple of nights but didn't like the way they made me feel, so I stuck them in the medicine cabinet and forgot all about them.'' Again the handkerchief shot up to her eyes and she moaned softly. ''I should have thrown them away.''

''You couldn't know that Lindy would be in an emotional condition that would make her search for those pills and take them. Don't blame yourself.'' Sarah smiled at the woman. ''It's Lindy's illness that made her do this—not the fact that you didn't throw some pills away.''

Sarah stood. ''I've got to get in there and see her. There's no reason for you to stay here. You go on home and get some rest.''

Anna nodded and also stood. ''I'm just grateful that she left the bottle out on the sink where I could see it.''

''It sounds to me like this wasn't so much a suicide attempt as a cry for help,'' Sarah said more to herself than to Anna. She gave the woman a quick hug. ''Go home and rest. And thank you for getting Lindy here so quickly. You probably saved her life.''

Anna smiled at Sarah and reached out a hand to touch her cheek. ''Ah, Sarah, you've always been so strong, so much older than your years.''

Sarah nodded, tears burning at her eyes. ''I've had to be.''

Anna dropped her hand. "And Lindy's always been so childlike. I hope she's all right."

They hugged again, then Sarah watched until the older woman disappeared down the hallway. She turned to go into Lindy's room.

Although it was a two-bed room, Lindy was alone, looking pathetically small in the hospital bed. Her head was turned toward the window, away from the doorway.

Sarah crept in silently, wondering if she was asleep. As she moved closer to the bed, Lindy turned and looked at her, her blue eyes deep wells of misery. "Oh, Sarah," she whispered painfully, tears brimming and spilling down her cheeks. "I've made such a mess of things."

Sarah sat down on the edge of the bed, wanting to cradle her sister in her arms but afraid of disturbing the IV that was connected to the back of one of her hands. "No you haven't," she replied, smoothing the dark hair off Lindy's forehead. "You've just let us all know that you need some help."

Lindy nodded, one of her hands grasping Sarah's tightly. "I do, Sarah. I need help." She closed her eyes and released a trembling sigh. "I'm so afraid. I can't keep living like this." She opened her eyes and looked at Sarah once again. "It's not so bad when I'm up and busy. But it's horrid when I get down. It's like I'm in a black hole and I can't get out. Tonight, I just decided it was all too much."

Carefully, Sarah gathered Lindy in her arms, stroking her back, her hair, soothing her the way she often soothed Jackie when she was ill or hurt. She looked up as Doc Burwell and a nurse entered the room.

"Sarah," he greeted her as Sarah untangled herself from her sister and stood. "I think the best thing for your sister right now is sleep. Karen will sit with her and see that she's comfortable.'' He gestured to the nurse, who smiled sympathetically and sat down in the chair near the bed, then motioned for Sarah to follow him out of the room.

Sarah leaned down and kissed Lindy's pale cheek. ''You get some sleep. I'll come back tomorrow to see you. Don't worry, Lindy, we're going to get you some help.''

''Why don't we go downstairs to the cafeteria,'' Doc Burwell said to Sarah as she joined him in the hallway. ''There isn't any food at this time of night, but there's always a coffeepot working.''

Minutes later they entered the cafeteria in the basement of the hospital. They got a cup of coffee, then sat down at a small round table. ''What a night,'' Doc Burwell said, running a hand through his thin gray hair. ''I need to retire. I'm getting too old.''

Sarah smiled. ''If you retired, how would you spend all your time?''

''I'd fish twelve hours and sleep the other twelve.'' He grinned, as if finding the fantasy infinitely pleasing. He took a sip of the coffee and shook his head.

''Sounds good,'' Sarah replied.

''Yeah, sounds good, but I'd probably be bored to death. Anyway…about Lindy. We pumped her stomach and she's going to be just fine. I managed to get Ben's hotel number from Lindy and called him. He said he should be here in a couple of hours. I also called in Dr. Westliner. He should be here presently.''

''Dr. Westliner?''

''He's a psychiatrist. Moved outside of town about three months ago. I know Lindy's been seeing some doctor in Kansas City, but I didn't think this could wait until he could get here from the city to see her.''

"No, I want her to see somebody right away. What do you know about this Dr. Westliner?" Sarah asked, remembering she'd heard Ben mention something about the new doctor in town.

"He seems a straight-up kind of guy. He's semi-retired, moved his family out here from Chicago. He told me he was overwhelmed at work there and wanted a slower pace." Doc Burnell offered Sarah a wry grin. "I'm not sure he'll get a slower pace here—there are days I think the maladjusted far outweigh the well adjusted here in Clay Creek."

Maladjusted... Yes, there was definitely somebody maladjusted someplace in the peaceful town of Clay Creek, somebody who had tried to kill Sarah, had choked Jackie and poisoned a casserole in hopes that the Calhouns would eat it. Maladjusted seemed too mild a term for a person capable of such madness.

"Sarah?"

She looked back at Doc Burwell. "I'm sorry, what did you say?"

"I asked how your head wound was doing. Giving you any pain?"

"No, none. It's fine." She reached up and touched the area.

"Ah, there's Dr. Westliner now." Doc Burwell stood as an older, distinguished man entered the cafeteria. "Roger, thanks for coming so promptly." Doc Burwell quickly made the introductions and it took Sarah only moments to realize she liked the doctor. He listened intently as she told him all she knew about her sister's condition. His attention didn't waver from her and his eyes radiated a warm compassion she found comforting and reassuring.

"I'll fax her doctor in Kansas City in the morning for

her records," he said when Sarah had finished. "I can't do anything for her until I see what her treatment has been to this date."

"I know she's on some kind of medication, but I don't know what it is." Sarah held her hands out in a gesture of helplessness.

"I'm going to insist that Lindy remain here for a couple of days, order a complete physical workup and then we'll decide where to go from there. The only thing you have to worry about is being your sister's friend. You leave the rest up to me."

Sarah nodded, his words causing an overwhelming sense of relief to cascade through her. It was nice to let somebody else share some of the responsibility. He stood and offered her another smile of reassurance. "And now I think I'll go in and check on your sister."

"There's nothing more you can do here," Doc Burwell said to Sarah. "You might as well go home for the night. Lindy will probably need you more tomorrow. Go home and get some sleep. I'd better catch up with Dr. Westliner. There are a few things I need to discuss with him. You okay?"

Sarah nodded. "I'll just finish my coffee and go on home. I'll be back tomorrow."

Doc Burwell gave her a quick pat on the arm, then disappeared in the same direction Dr. Westliner had gone. Sarah sipped her coffee and leaned back in the chair. The cafeteria was silent around her, the quiet and the dim lighting conducive to thinking.

Her head was filled with questions and worries, and her heart was filled with pain. She was worried about Lindy, although some of that concern had been alleviated by putting her care in Dr. Westliner's hands. She hoped he would be able to take over her treatment and find some sort of therapy or drug that would help Lindy live a more normal life.

Then there was the fear of knowing somebody was after her and the people she loved—somebody unidentified, somebody with a motive she wasn't aware of. Raymond Boswell? Ben? Who was behind the attacks on Sarah and her family? Who could possibly want them dead?

Swirling around with all the questions was the remaining pain of the last conversation she'd had with Reese. She hadn't realized how much hope she'd foolishly harbored in her heart—hope that somehow he would overcome his past and live a future with her and their daughter.

Sarah had always known that his bravado, his anger and intensity had hidden a deep core of insecurity and a feeling of unworthiness. She'd hoped he would outgrow those feelings along with his teenage rebellion. Unfortunately, he hadn't, and she knew now there was nothing more she could do or say to help him heal. It was time to truly put Reese in her past.

She drained the last of her coffee and stood. She needed to get home and get some sleep so she could be here first thing in the morning when Lindy awakened. Grabbing her purse, she left the cafeteria, her shoes echoing hollowly in the hallway that led to the elevator. She punched the up arrow and leaned against the wall. The burst of adrenaline that had flooded through her after the phone call about Lindy was gone, leaving her drained of energy.

She pushed herself off the wall and turned, frowning slightly. Had that been the sound of a footstep? She peered down the darkened hallway, noticing how the lighting created deep shadows along the outer edges of the corridor. Was somebody there...hiding in the shadows?

"Hello?" she said softly, her voice sounding abnormally loud in the silence. "Is—is somebody there?" There was no answer, no noise at all to indicate the presence of anyone else.

She turned back to the elevator and punched the button once again. *I'm tired and on edge, and my imagination is obviously playing tricks on me.* She pulled her purse close against her side, tensing as once again she thought she heard the sound of distant footsteps.

Wild thoughts jumped into her head, caution lights exploded in her brain. She should have left with Doc Burwell. She should never have allowed herself to be in such an isolated place alone when she knew somebody was after her. What better place for mayhem than a hospital basement in the middle of the night?

The footsteps came closer, sounding furtive, as if deliberately camouflaging themselves in the pounding of her heart. At that moment the door to the stairwell burst open. A scream crawled up Sarah's throat, a scream she swallowed as a young nurse came through the door, eyeing her curiously as she headed toward the cafeteria.

As the woman hurried down the hallway, casting a backward glance at Sarah, Sarah leaned against the wall once again, trying to still her racing heart.

She suddenly realized that she was an emotional wreck. She hadn't been fully aware of it until this very moment. The strain of the past several days came crashing down on her head. Dealing with a broken heart, frightened by somebody who was stalking her family, Sarah knew that if she wasn't careful, she would be the second Calhoun to end up in Dr. Westliner's care.

The elevator dinged and Sarah stepped on, fighting

back a sudden sob as the doors whooshed shut. What she really needed was strong arms to enfold her and make her feel safe. She needed a man who could make her forget the broken dreams of the past, the horrifying fear of the present, and make her look forward to the future with renewed hope and love.

She wanted her mother. And damn it, she needed Reese. Unfortunately, one was no more accessible than the other. Her mother was gone forever, and she had to face the fact that Reese was, too.

Chapter 14

For the first time since he had become sheriff of Clay Creek, Reese didn't want to go to work. He sat at the kitchen table, the morning sunshine demanding he stop lingering over his coffee and get moving. Usually he was at the office early, but he was in no hurry this morning. He hated to leave Sarah and Jackie alone for the day.

Sarah had come back from the hospital in the wee hours of the morning. She'd looked more than tired, almost as if she suffered a soul sickness. Sinking down in the chair across from the sofa, she had briefly filled him in on Lindy's condition. It wasn't until she had told him that Ben was on his way back to town that her face filled with horror. "If it's Ben who's responsible for everything, surely he wouldn't try anything in the hospital?" she'd asked worriedly.

Reese had quickly called the hospital and spoken with Doc Burwell, explaining the events of the past couple of weeks to the old man and that he wanted a nurse in Lindy's room at all times. Doc Burwell readily agreed.

Sooner or later in the day, Reese intended to talk to Ben. He was going to lean hard on the man to get some straight answers. He had to find out who was after Sarah and Jackie. He had to make certain they were safe, then send them on their way. He didn't think he could handle them living with him for too much longer.

Even last night, he'd had to fight with himself not to wrap his arms around Sarah, hold her tight against him and try to remove the hollow emptiness from her eyes. But he knew he didn't have that right.

He started as she walked into the kitchen, obviously surprised to see him still there. "Oh, I thought you had to be at work by eight," she said, self-consciously pulling the belt of her robe more tightly around her waist.

"I do. I've still got fifteen minutes." He watched silently as she moved across the kitchen to the cabinet that held the coffeemaker. He watched her covetously, trying not to notice that her hair was bewitchingly tousled, that her scent drifted in the air, surrounding him. He felt his body responding to her presence, realized his hands trembled slightly as he picked up his coffee mug.

She poured herself a cup, then hesitated, as if reluctant to join him at the table. "Reese, I think it would be best if Jackie and I stay someplace else until all this is settled."

"Where would you stay?" he asked, his voice carrying with it weary resignation. He knew she was right. It would be better for both of them if they were not living so intimately, tempting themselves to distraction. And yet the thought of her staying anyplace else unsettled him.

"I don't know…we can get a room at the Clay Creek Motel."

Reese frowned. He hated the idea of Jackie cooped up in a motel room. He also hated the thought of both of them being out of his sight, away from his protection. He had a gut feeling that whoever was after them wouldn't dare try anything as long as they were here, in his house. But if they were in the motel on the edge of town, a motel that was usually deserted…

"Sarah, give me another day or two. Stay here where I know you're safe. I plan on talking to Ben today. If he's the one who's been after you, then perhaps he'll say something that will incriminate himself."

"I just want to solve this mystery and get back to New York." There was a desperate edge to her voice and her gaze didn't meet his.

He pushed away from the table and stood. "I've got to get going. What are your plans today?"

"If I can get Anna to watch Jackie, then I'm heading back to the hospital."

He nodded. "I'd rather you not go anyplace else. Even though there haven't been any incidents since you and Jackie moved in here, that doesn't mean the danger has passed." He hesitated a moment longer. "I'll call you if we find out anything." She looked small, so damned vulnerable. He felt a tug on his heart that matched the tightness in his groin. It would be so much easier when the head made a decision, if the heart and body followed suit, he thought. "I'll talk to you later." Before he did something stupid, he left.

Hurrying down the sidewalk toward the sheriff's office, Reese felt a renewed burst of desperation seep through him. It was a desperation mixed with frustration. What kind of a sheriff was he? He couldn't even figure out who was after Sarah. Maybe he'd been kidding himself all along. Maybe he'd never been cut out to be a sheriff. Jim had made him see potential in himself for the first time in his life, but maybe they'd both been fools.

He shoved these disheartening thoughts aside as he entered the building. Nodding curtly to Ida, he went directly to his office and closed the door. He sat down at the desk and pulled out the folder that had all the facts on Sarah's case.

The gunshot had probably been fired by a shotgun...Margaret's missing gun? That implied somebody who had access to the Calhoun house. On the night that Jackie had been attacked, Sarah had mentioned that the dogs hadn't barked. That implied somebody the dogs knew.

He closed the folder and decided it was time to have a little talk with Ben. Heading toward the hospital, he tried to keep his thoughts on the subject at hand, tried to keep thoughts of Sarah from filtering in. Thinking of her only muddied his mind, and he needed to be clearheaded if he intended to trip up Ben.

It took him only minutes to reach the hospital. He found Ben at Lindy's bedside. Lindy was asleep, and Ben looked like a ghost, his face pale and gaunt as he sat unmoving in the chair next to the bed. He stood as Reese entered the room.

"How's she doing?" Reese asked, noting that Ben looked as if he'd aged a dozen years since Reese had seen him at Margaret's funeral.

"She's fine. We were lucky this time." He ran a hand over his face in a gesture of utter exhaustion. "I'm not taking any out-of-town cases anymore. I can't take a chance on something like this happening again."

"I need to talk to you, Ben. Why don't you come out in the hallway with me," Reese suggested.

Ben looked at Reese quizzically then nodded his assent. The two men stepped out into the hallway and Reese led Ben away from Lindy's doorway. "While you've been out of town, there's been some excitement going on."

"Lindy told me about the dogs being poisoned." Ben frowned in frustration. "Why didn't somebody call me immediately? If someone is trying to hurt Lindy or Sarah, why wasn't I told?"

"I told them not to tell you," Reese replied cooly.

"But why?" Ben asked incredulously. He stared at Reese in accusation and must have found his answer in Reese's expression. He blanched and stumbled backward a step. "Surely you don't think...you can't believe that I..." He leaned against the wall, his face holding such horror that Reese's gut instinct was that the man was innocent. Or a damned good actor, he thought, unwilling to be swayed by a convincing performance.

"I need to know where you were last Thursday night between the hours of 9:00 p.m. and 7:00 a.m.," Reese said. His stomach muscles tightened as he thought of Jackie being awakened by hands wrapped around her throat.

"You know where I was—in Kansas City. God, I don't believe this." There was no outrage in Ben's voice, only a stunned disbelief that made his innocence even more credible.

"Exactly where were you between those hours?" Reese pressed.

"Thursday night?" Ben's frown deepened. "I was probably in my hotel room asleep."

"Did you see anyone? Order room service? Is there

any witness that can state that you were at the hotel all night?''

"No…the trial had run long, I was exhausted. Reese, surely you can't believe that I had anything to do with what's been going on here." Ben's face held the shock and bewilderment of an innocent man, but still Reese refused to listen to what his gut told him. Ben was the only one who made any sense.

Reese felt his frustration rolling around inside him, bubbling up into an impotent rage. He stepped closer to Ben, aware that he was invading the man's personal space. "I don't know who's after Sarah and Jackie, but if something happens to them and I find out you had anything to do with it, I'll kill you." The words were said softly but with the suppressed rage that coiled inside him.

Ben's pupils dilated and he nodded. "I'd feel the same way if I was in your position, but, Reese, it's not me."

Reese stepped back. "Just remember what I said." He turned and walked down the hallway, his frustration nearly blinding him.

Who was after Sarah? Why did somebody want to hurt her? Was the motive really the farm? Was Ben not only greedy, but an exceptionally good liar as well? Or was it Boswell? Even though his alibi had checked out, was it possible the wealthy man had hired someone to do his dirty work? God, Reese had never been so frustrated, or so afraid in his life.

What if the motive wasn't the farm at all? Could it be somebody from Sarah's past? He tried to remember the boys she'd dated in high school, but there was nobody. Sarah had been his and there had never been any question about it. Everyone in town knew of their passion, their love for each other. A warmth swept through him as he thought of their innocence, the intrinsic rightness of their love.

He thudded into somebody, the collision pulling him from his thoughts as he turned to apologize to the little woman he'd nearly knocked down. "Mrs. Jackson," he greeted Suzanna's neighbor. "What brings you to the hospital? I hope you aren't ill."

"I'm here for a flu shot," she said, smiling at him slyly. "Haven't seen you around for a couple of weeks. I think maybe Suzanna has gotten tired of waiting around for you." Again the woman smiled as if enjoying being able to give him a bit of juicy gossip. "Maybe she's got a new beau. She's gotten so she comes and goes at all hours of the night."

"All hours of the night?" Reese felt a sudden wash of unease sweep through him. Suzanna? "When was the last time you saw her leave in the middle of the night?"

Mrs. Jackson cackled with glee. "I knew that would shake you up!"

Reese took her arm and held it tightly. Her laughter instantly died. "This is really important, Mrs. Jackson. When was the last time you saw Suzanna leave her apartment in the middle of the night?"

"I don't know, a couple nights ago." She pulled her arm from his grasp. "It was Friday...no, Thursday night. I remember it was Thursday because I took the trash out that night."

"Do you remember what time it was?" There was a pounding in Reese's ears, a roar of unreality.

"It was after midnight, but I'm not sure of the exact time. Reese, is something wrong? Is Suzanna in trouble?" Her forehead crinkled worriedly.

"It's not Suzanna I'm worried about," Reese said, his mind racing. He leaned down and kissed the old woman on her cheek. "Go get your flu shot and I'm going to stop a crime before it happens." Without a backward glance he raced out the door of the hospital and to his patrol car. He needed a search warrant and he knew a certain judge who owed him a favor.

As he drove, his mind whirled with images of Suzanna and visions of Sarah. Was he grasping at straws? Was Suzanna truly capable of such heinous actions? And yet even as he asked himself these questions, he knew the answers. He'd been so focused on Sarah and what could possibly cause somebody to be after her that he hadn't questioned the people in his own life.

Someplace deep inside, he'd always known Suzanna was in love with him, an obsessive kind of love that had lasted through the years despite his more casual feelings toward her. He knew Suzanna had a horrible temper, had seen it occasionally. He remembered one particular time, when he and Suzanna had gone out dancing. Sally Richards, a schoolmate of theirs, was at the bar celebrating her most recent divorce. She'd gotten tipsy and had flirted outrageously with him. Two days later, the tires on Sally's car had been slashed. At the time Reese hadn't connected the two things. But now his blood ran cold as he considered the implications.

Suzanna had often been a visitor to the Calhoun farm. It was possible she had a key. The dogs would have known her and not barked if she'd crept into the yard in the middle of the night. She had been at the Calhouns after the funeral. She could have cut that board, then placed it back over the well. All the pieces were there…but did they fit together?

He pulled up in front of Judge Melrose's house and hit the sidewalk at a run. There was a horrible sense of imminent danger whispering in his ear, a dreadful knowledge of time running out.

Within twenty minutes Reese was back in his car, heading for Suzanna's apartment. The search warrant seemed to burn through his breast pocket straight into his heart. He liked Suzanna, but if he found out that she had tried to hurt Sarah and Jackie, he would see her in prison for as long as the law would allow. Or worse.

He tightened his grip on the steering wheel, trying to get a handle on the rage that flooded through him. Nobody hurt what was his without facing his own particular brand of consequences.

When he pulled into the lot outside Suzanna's apartment building, he noted that her car was gone from the space where she usually parked. Good, she was probably at work, he thought. He didn't want a confrontation with her...not until he was absolutely sure she was guilty.

The owner of the building, Ralph Baker, let him into Suzanna's apartment. When Reese offered to show him the search warrant, he waved his hands dismissively. "If you're wanting in here, I'm sure you got a good reason," the old man said as he unlocked the apartment door. He hesitated a moment before opening the door. "Am I gonna have to find a new tenant?"

"I hope not," Reese said truthfully, "but I'm not sure."

Ralph nodded. "Just lock up when you're through."

Reese nodded absently and stepped inside. He was immediately surrounded by the pervasive scent of Suzanna's perfume. He didn't know where to begin his search, wasn't even sure what exactly he was looking for. He only knew that if Suzanna was involved in this in any way, evidence would be here someplace.

"Hey, Tiger," he said softly, greeting the big cat that

rubbed against his shins. He leaned down and scratched the cat behind an ear, his gaze focused on the room around him.

How many evenings had he spent here, filling empty hours, fighting memories of Sarah? He'd never made any promises to Suzanna, never implied a commitment of any kind. Yet he now realized that he had a certain culpability in this mess. He'd used Suzanna to attempt to fill the void that Sarah's leaving had caused.

He left the cat and began looking around, starting in the living room. He searched beneath the furniture, in the cabinets of the entertainment center, behind the curtains, in the coat closet—anyplace where a gun or any other evidence could be hidden.

He found nothing and moved into the kitchen. Again a thorough search yielded nothing. He looked at his watch, fighting against the feeling that somehow time was slipping away. Almost noon. He wondered what Sarah was doing. He wondered where Suzanna was.

A cursory inspection of the bathroom also proved fruitless. He went into the bedroom, looking around desperately. Here was Suzanna's haven. While the other two rooms had been neat and orderly, the bedroom was decorated with chaos.

He picked his way across the clothes-strewn floor to the dresser, checking each drawer, still unsure what he was looking for but certain he would find something here. If his instincts were right about Suzanna, then she had tried to kill Sarah, tried to kill Jackie. But knowing and proving were two different things, and he had to find some sort of evidence that would prove Suzanna's guilt.

In the nightstand next to the bed he found an old yearbook. Clay Creek High School. He ran his hands across the red embossed letters. The year on the cover told him it was the annual from Suzanna's senior year.

Quickly he scanned the color portraits of the senior class, finding Suzanna's and studying it for a moment. Her hair hadn't been quite as blond back then, and her face had held a confidence, an unshakable belief in her own prettiness and popularity. The face of a would-be murderer? Reese frowned, his conviction wavering momentarily. Maybe he was wrong. Maybe Suzanna's nighttime excursions were nothing more than a new boyfriend.

He started to close the book, then remembered that when Suzanna had been a senior, Sarah had been a sophomore. He flipped through the pages, needing to see her, wanting to drink in the vision that she had been when he'd first fallen in love with her.

He found the page and stared down, his blood turning cold. Sarah's picture had been destroyed beneath the point of a pen. Her face had been scribbled over with strokes that screamed of hatred. "Suzanna," he whispered aloud. The uncertainty he'd felt only moments before blew away, leaving him once again with the chilling knowledge that Suzanna was guilty.

Within minutes he'd found a container of rat poison in the closet and a shotgun beneath the bed. He pulled the shotgun out and placed it on the bright floral sheets. He ran his fingers over the initials carved into the wooden stock of the gun. MC—Margaret Calhoun. Suzanna had stolen the gun from the Calhoun farm, then tried to kill Sarah with it.

Sarah. A picture of her face exploded in his head. He dialed his own number on the phone next to Suzanna's bed. He needed to make sure Sarah and Jackie were safe. He needed to tell her what he'd found out.

"Sarah…" He expelled a sigh of relief as she answered the phone.

"Oh, Reese," she exclaimed breathlessly. "You barely caught me. I was just on my way out to the hospital."

"Anna is there with Jackie?" he asked, his gaze lingering on the gun. How close she had come…how close Suzanna had come to killing Sarah.

"No, Anna had to work at the café. Suzanna called me back from the café and said she had the afternoon off and would be glad to watch Jackie while I visit Lindy. She picked her up just a few minutes ago."

A roar filled Reese's head, causing him to stumble against the side of the bed. "Wh—where was she taking Jackie?"

"They were going out to the farm to feed the dogs, then shopping or something. Reese, what's wrong?"

He hesitated a moment, then realized she needed to know. "It's Suzanna, Sarah. It's been Suzanna all along."

"Oh, my God."

Sarah's gasp fed Reese's fear. "I'm on my way out there now. I won't let anything happen to Jackie. Sarah, it will be all right. I'll call you later." He hung up, his sense of time running out now a living, breathing demon inside him. Suzanna had Jackie. His daughter was in danger.

Chapter 15

Sarah hung up the phone slowly, feeling as if she were moving under water. She gasped. The room seemed to have been sucked clear of oxygen. She couldn't breathe. She couldn't move.

Suzanna? It had been Suzanna and she now had Jackie. Sarah had just handed her baby to a potential killer. The thought broke the paralysis that had momentarily gripped her. Grabbing her purse and car keys, she flung herself out of Reese's house and into her car. She had to find Jackie. She had to get to her before it was too late.

She drove the familiar route to the farm, her thoughts whirling around in her head. Why? Why did Suzanna hate her? Why did she hate her enough to want to kill her? Kill her daughter?

She frowned, searching her mind for an incident, a reason for Suzanna's hatred. She'd hardly seen Suzanna since she'd been back in town. Her frown deepened as she delved into memories of the past, trying to remember a slight, a wrong she might have dealt Suzanna, anything that would make sense of what was happening now.

Something whispered in her ear...the edge in Suzanna's voice when she talked about Sarah taking up all of Reese's free time. Reese? Was it possible he was the reason for all this? Of course. That had to be it. Reese might not have thought his relationship with Suzanna was serious, but Suzanna had been deadly serious about Reese. It was the only thing that made sense. She thought of the times she had felt the woman's eyes on her, those blue eyes narrowed in hatred. She thought of that moment in the café when Suzanna had taken Reese aside and spoke with him, then stomped off angrily. It all made sense now. Suzanna was angry that Reese was leaving with Sarah. Suzanna had always loved Reese and the reappearance of Sarah in Clay Creek had threatened her.

Sarah tightened her grip on the steering wheel and emitted a sharp burst of hysterical laughter. Oh, how absolutely incredible it all was. Suzanna must have believed that Sarah had Reese's affection, his love, and the only way to get it back for herself was to get rid of Sarah. What Suzanna didn't realize was that Sarah didn't have Reese. Reese belonged only to his own painful past and the burden of his fears.

She shoved aside thoughts of Reese, instead focusing on Jackie. *Oh dear God, don't make me be too late,* she prayed over and over again. Surely Suzanna wouldn't harm an innocent child. And yet as she thought of the bruises around Jackie's neck, bruises received when the little girl had been choked, Sarah knew Jackie's very life was threatened.

What if they weren't at the farm? Jackie had only been

with Suzanna about thirty minutes. What if Suzanna had never intended to take the child to the farm to feed the dogs? Sarah shook her head. She couldn't think of all the what ifs. If she did, she would surely go mad.

She pressed down on the gas pedal, gravel spewing out from beneath her tires as she turned onto the lane that led to the farm.

She nearly sobbed in relief as she pulled up in front of the farmhouse and saw Suzanna's car. Maybe Reese was wrong about Suzanna, she thought as she turned off the engine. Maybe the woman really had just wanted to baby-sit Jackie and had nothing to do with the threats, the near misses. For a moment, Sarah was unsure what to do. She rolled down her window and listened. Nothing.

"Jackie," she called as she stumbled out of the car and toward the front door.

"Mama!" Jackie's voice drifted faintly out from the inside.

"Jackie!" Sarah screamed in relief. She burst through the front door and into the living room, her relief expanding as she saw Suzanna and Jackie sitting on the sofa.

"Hi, Mama," Jackie greeted her with a cheerful smile, gesturing to the picture-book opened on her lap. "I'm reading to Suzanna."

"Ah, Sarah, I'm so glad you're here. It saves me a phone call to get you here."

"G—get me here?" Sarah looked curiously at the blond woman. A little smile curved her lips and her eyes held an unfocused, faraway expression that caused a shiver of dread to sweep through Sarah. "Jackie? Why don't you come over here with me?" Sarah said softly.

She needed her daughter beside her, where she would be safe. Suzanna looked so odd.

As Jackie started to get up to go to her mother, Suzanna moved with the speed of hummingbird wings, grasping Jackie around the neck and pulling her more closely against her.

"No, I want Jackie to stay right here with me," Suzanna protested softly, the smile not wavering from her full lips. As Sarah watched, she pulled a knife from her coat pocket, the silver blade glinting in the afternoon sunlight that danced in through the window.

"Suzanna..." Sarah's voice trembled as Suzanna slid the weapon back into her pocket, her hand remaining inside, the point of the knife obviously directed at Jackie's side. "Suzanna, what do you want?"

Jackie, hearing the tension in her mother's voice, looked at Sarah in uncertainty. Sarah saw Suzanna tighten her grip on the little girl. Jackie's eyes widened and her bottom lip began to tremble. "Mama?"

"It's all right, Jackie," she said smoothly, her arms aching with the need to gather her daughter close, make her feel safe again. She focused her attention back on Suzanna, trying to keep her fear at bay, not wanting Jackie to see the terror that churned inside her. "What do you want?" she repeated.

"I think we should all take a walk outside. It's a beautiful day. Wouldn't you like to take a walk with me, Jackie?" Suzanna stroked the top of Jackie's head. Jackie nodded hesitantly, her gaze going back to her mother.

Sarah wanted to scream. *Don't touch my baby. Get your filthy hands off my daughter.* She bit her lip to keep her outrage, her horror, inside.

Suzanna stood, her grip on Jackie not loosening as

she tugged the little girl off the sofa. "After you," she said pleasantly to Sarah, motioning to the front door with a nod of her head.

As Sarah walked out the door and down the steps to the grass, Suzanna held tight to Jackie, keeping a healthy distance between them. "Just head out toward the grape arbor," Suzanna instructed her. She pulled the knife from her pocket, keeping it trained close to Jackie's side.

"Suzanna, let Jackie go. Whatever is going on, it's between you and me. She's just a child. Let her go." Sarah hated the pleading tone of her voice, hated having to beg for her daughter's safety.

What she wanted to do was smash Suzanna in the face, take the knife and plunge it into her. The violent thoughts both shocked and satisfied her. She hadn't thought herself capable of such hatred, but as she saw the fear that wrinkled Jackie's brow and widened her eyes, she felt a flood of anger so rich, so full, it caused her head to pound.

"I can't let her go," Suzanna said, the pleasant tone of her voice as incongruous as the glint of the knife in the sun on this beautiful fall day. "I can't let her go until after the accident."

"What accident?" Sarah asked, her heart beating with dread. She felt as if she were living her worst nightmare…a nightmare that was never-ending.

"The one where you accidentally fall down the well." Suzanna shook her head regretfully. "It would have been so much easier had you just fallen in that first time. None of this would have been necessary if you'd just died when you were supposed to."

"Mama?" This time there was undisguised panic in Jackie's voice.

Sarah kept her gaze carefully focused on Suzanna,

knowing that if she looked into Jackie's eyes, saw her daughter's fear, she would do something stupid. There was nothing worse than seeing your own child's fear and not being able to do anything to soothe it. "Why, Suzanna? Just tell me why you are doing this."

The smile on Suzanna's face fell, replaced by a grimace of such hatred that Sarah unconsciously took a step backward. "He was mine," she spat. "He would have eventually been mine forever if you hadn't come back here. You changed everything. You ruined everything. I hated you years ago when you had him." Her eyes narrowed and the knife trembled in her hand. "I saw you once, you know. In the grape arbor. I followed him and I saw him make love to you. The best day in my life was when you left town...and the worst day of my life was when you came back here." She gestured toward the grape arbor. "Now walk," she demanded.

Sarah took a few more steps, then stopped and turned back to Suzanna. "We'll leave again," she insisted fervently. "We'll go back to New York and never come here again."

"Do you think I'm crazy? Don't you realize it's too late for that?" Any facade of control was gone. Suzanna's face flushed red and her voice rose with a note of hysteria. "He'll never stop thinking about you...not until you're dead. You have to be dead!"

Jackie was crying now, mute sobs shaking her body. "Suzanna, for God's sake, let Jackie go," Sarah said softly. "Please, she's just a baby."

"*His* baby," Suzanna whispered, her hand once again stroking Jackie's hair. Again a glaze seemed to descend over the blueness of Suzanna's eyes. "Don't worry, sweet Jackie. This will all be over soon." She looked back at Sarah, the glaze lifting and replaced by a look of harsh enmity. "Let's get this over with—to the well."

If only she'd let go of Jackie for a minute...a second. If only she'd allow the knife to waver an inch...a fraction of an inch. Sarah knew time was running out for her, but there was nothing she could do as long as Suzanna held Jackie. And she also knew with a fatalistic horror that she would prefer to jump to her death in the dank, dark well than see Jackie hurt.

Where the hell was Reese? Why wasn't he here? It felt as if she'd been here for hours...days. She saw the board that covered the well just ahead and she slowed her pace, her knees nearly buckling beneath the intensity of her fear.

"Shove that board off the top," Suzanna instructed.

"Mama," Jackie sobbed.

"Shh," Suzanna soothed. "It's all right. It's all going to be over very soon. Then your daddy and me and you will live happily ever after."

There was a dreamy singsong to Suzanna's voice and Sarah realized the woman had completely lost touch with reality. Did she really think she could kill Sarah and then be mother to Jackie? Did she really believe she would get away with this? That Reese wouldn't know? That Jackie wouldn't tell?

"I told you to move those boards off the well." The sharpness of Suzanna's voice jolted Sarah back to the horror of her own situation. Still she hesitated, buying time. The knife flashed closer to Jackie's face. "Don't force me to hurt her," Suzanna warned, her voice ominously quiet.

Sarah bent down and shoved the board off the well, her mind racing to figure out a way to save both Jackie and herself. If only Suzanna would move closer...if only she could kick the knife out of her hand and push Jackie out of harm's way. But she couldn't risk Jackie's safety.

The horror of the well reached up to her, and as she remembered those minutes she had hung inside, she felt her throat closing up, her body start to shiver.

She looked around frantically. Where was Reese? Dear God, where was Reese? Her gaze focused once again on Suzanna. The smile was back on her face, a soft, dreamy smile. The knife was still a mere heartbeat away from the tender skin of Jackie's neck. "Jump," Suzanna said.

"Reese!" Sarah exclaimed, her gaze darting behind Suzanna.

Suzanna turned to look, the knife point dropping for just a second. Sarah launched herself at Suzanna and Jackie, knocking all of them to the ground. She was vaguely aware of Jackie's screams as the little girl scrambled crablike away from the two adults. "Run, Jackie," Sarah yelled. "Run to Mama's favorite hiding place."

As Jackie took off running, Sarah dodged the sharp edge of the knife. Suzanna slashed at her, her face twisted with a malevolence that nearly stole Sarah's breath away. They rose to their feet at the same time, Suzanna still gripping the knife, her chest heaving.

"You always ruin things," she said, striking out with viciousness. Sarah jumped back, aware that Suzanna was backing her toward the uncovered well opening. "Reese would have fallen in love with me years ago if it hadn't been for you. And eventually I would have gotten him if you hadn't come back here." Again she struck out, causing Sarah to stumble backward another two steps.

The thick brush around them made it impossible for Sarah to contemplate running. The only way out was down the well or through Suzanna and the knife. Neither held much appeal. ''It was you who shot at me, wasn't it?'' she said, wanting to stall, hoping that Reese would arrive at any moment.

Suzanna nodded. ''I shot at you. I also cut the well cover. You've been so incredibly lucky.''

''And it was you that put the poison in the casserole.''

''Lindy gave me a key to the house last year when your mother had the flu. It was so easy to get in and put the poison in the food.'' She grimaced. ''Once I was in the house, I crept upstairs. I didn't mean to hurt Jackie. I just wanted to get you. I went into her room by accident and I lost control...it was a mistake.'' Suzanna sighed. ''I'm tired of this now. I'm tired of you. Why don't you make this easier on both of us and jump?''

''Did you kill my mother?'' Sarah asked, holding her breath for the answer. She had to know if somehow Suzanna had orchestrated Sarah's return to Clay Creek by killing Margaret.

''Your mother?'' Suzanna's face reflected her bewilderment. ''I didn't do anything to Margaret. I heard she fell down the stairs.'' Her features tightened again. ''Stop talking. I don't want to talk anymore. Just jump,'' she demanded.

''Suzanna.'' Reese's voice boomed as he stepped into the clearing behind her.

A rush of warm relief swept through Sarah at the sight of him. ''Reese,'' she whispered. But he didn't look anything like a hero come to save the day. He looked like an avenging angel, his eyes lighted with the fires of rage, his entire being seeming to expand to fill the clearing. His gun was drawn, adding to his ominous appearance.

For a moment as his gaze scanned the area, Reese's heart bucked in raging protest. No, he couldn't be too late. Where was Jackie? The uncovered well taunted him. If he'd arrived too late and something had happened to Jackie, he knew it wouldn't take another thought to kill himself.

In that instant he recognized the depth of his love for his daughter. His daughter...his love...his life. "Wh-where's Jackie?" His voice was hoarse with anger and dread.

"She's safe, Reese," Sarah answered quickly.

"She can be *our* daughter, Reese," Suzanna said, the singsong quality back in her voice.

"Drop the knife, Suzanna, it's over."

She cocked her head and looked at him quizzically. "I can't. It's not finished yet. It won't be finished until Sarah is gone for good. Then you'll love me." She took a step toward Sarah, who had no place else to go but into the well. The knife blade glittered cold and harsh in the light and Reese saw the flare of fear that darkened Sarah's eyes.

He felt a responding surge of anger—a rage so intense he felt his finger tighten on the trigger of his gun. For a moment he fought against the familiar red haze of his boyhood rage. "Suzanna, if you hurt her, I'll have to kill you."

Suzanna blinked and stared at him in confusion. "You don't understand. If she's dead, then I'll have you. You'll be mine."

"No, Suzanna," he said wearily. "Killing Sarah won't make me love you. Even in death she'd have my heart." He looked at Sarah for a moment, felt her love radiating toward him. "She and Jackie, they're my family and you've threatened them. I will never love you, Suzanna."

Suzanna stifled a moan with the back of one hand, her eyes never wavering from Reese. "But, Reese—"

"Never." There was a hard finality in his voice and with another moan Suzanna crumpled to the ground, the knife falling from her grasp. Immediately two deputies jumped out of the brush and took control of the woman, while Reese rushed toward Sarah.

He enfolded her in his arms, fighting against a sob that was caught halfway between his chest and his throat. "Oh, thank God," he finally managed to mutter into the sweet fragrance of her hair. "Thank God you're all right."

"Reese, what should we do with her?" one of the deputies asked. Reese looked up to see Suzanna, her head hanging down, her hands cuffed behind her back.

"Take her into town and book her for attempted murder. I've got a few things to clean up here." He tightened his arms around Sarah, still unwilling to let her go, realizing he was never going to let her go. "God help me but I wanted to shoot her. When I saw her threatening you, I wanted to kill her," he whispered.

"Why didn't you?" She pulled away and looked at him.

"I would have…once. I would have let my anger sweep me away to a place where I didn't worry about consequences, wasn't concerned with repercussions. But I'm not that boy anymore. And I'm not the man I was yesterday or even this morning."

She stepped completely out of his arms. "What do you mean?" she asked, her voice trembling slightly.

He looked at her, the face he loved, the woman he wanted, desired like no other. "When I stepped into the clearing and saw Suzanna threatening you, I felt just as I had years ago when that bullet entered my body and I knew my life was worth nothing. I thought since that time I'd made all kinds of strides in personal growth. I'd left behind my boyhood rebellions, become a man the town respected and admired. But when I saw Suzanna threatening you, I knew I hadn't come far enough. If I let you walk away from me again, my life would continue to be as empty, as bleak as ever. And in that instant I knew I couldn't let you walk away.''

''Oh, Reese.'' She started toward him but he held up a hand to stop her.

''Sarah, I love you and Jackie, and I want to spend the rest of my life being a husband to you and a father to Jackie.''

''Reese…'' Tears trembled on her lashes, the last tears he hoped she would ever shed because of him. He opened his arms and she came back into his embrace and he knew, finally, a peace he had never known before in his life.

''Where's Jackie?'' he asked, suddenly needing the three of them to be together. He had so much to catch up on, so many missed moments to recapture, so much future ahead to share.

''She's in a safe place.'' Sarah took him by the hand. ''Come on, let's go get her.''

''Just a minute…'' He broke away from her and carefully replaced the wooden barrier across the top of the well. ''The first thing tomorrow we need to get somebody out here to fill that in.''

Sarah nodded. He took her hand and together they left the clearing and walked around to the side of the house. ''So, Miss Calhoun, how soon do you think we can pull a wedding together?'' he asked as they walked.

''Oh, I could probably pull something together in a day…an hour…this minute.''

He stopped walking and studied her, loving the sparkle in her eyes, the faint flush of color on her cheeks. "Don't you want to do it up right? You know, the white dress and lots of flowers and a church full of friends?"

The smile she gave him took his breath away. It was the smile of the girl he had fallen in love with years before—yet it was the smile of a woman who knew exactly what she wanted. "I've got a pretty pink dress and I never cared much for flowers, and we've got a built-in witness in our daughter. Oh, Reese, I don't need a big fancy wedding. You and Jackie are all I need to be happy."

Again Reese felt a lump rise to his throat. How could he have been such a fool to allow his fears to close him off from the full intensity of loving Sarah and being loved by her?

"So, where is this little witness of ours?" he finally asked.

Sarah pointed ahead, to the tree. "Jackie?" she called out.

"Mama!" Jackie answered, her voice floating down from above.

"You can come down now, honey. It's all right. You're safe," Sarah said as she and Reese stood beneath the tree.

"I can't," Jackie whimpered. "I can't come down. I'm too scared."

Reese looked up and saw the little girl clinging to a branch over his head. "Jackie honey, Suzanna is in jail now. She can't hurt you or your mommy ever again. You're safe now."

Jackie peered over the branch. Reese could see her face...a little face with eyes like his, a little face he loved. "When we were in the car coming here, she told me…she told me that you're my daddy."

Damn her, Reese thought. Damn her for telling what Sarah and he should have told Jackie together. He looked at Sarah, knew she was thinking the same thing, then he gazed back at Jackie. "Suzanna was right, Jackie, I am your daddy." He waited, holding his breath, wondering what was going on in her marvelous little mind.

"Really?" she asked.

"Really. And if a little girl was up in a tree and couldn't get down, she could drop into her daddy's arms and he would catch her because he loves her." He held out his arms. "Jump, Jackie, jump to your daddy and I'll catch you."

She dropped. There was no hesitation, no second of distrust. And he caught her. He held her in his arms, felt her little arms surrounding his neck. "Thank you, Mr. Sheriff," she said softly, then pressed her lips against his cheek.

"Come on, let's all go home," he said, putting his arm around Sarah and drawing her close to him and Jackie. As they walked toward his patrol car, Jackie snuggled against him, fitting her head into the hollow of his neck as if that's where she belonged.

"You know I'm probably going to make mistakes," he said to Sarah, sure that she would realize what he was talking about.

"Probably," she agreed with a smile. "I know as a mother I make at least a dozen mistakes a day." Her smile widened. "But I have a feeling you're going to do just fine."

"Mr. Sheriff, does this mean we're gonna live at your house?" Jackie asked.

"Would you like to?"

"Yes. I like it there," Jackie answered.

"You know, Jackie, you could call me Reese," he suggested.

Jackie was silent for a long moment. "Nah, I think I'd rather call you daddy."

Reese's eyes misted. When he looked at Sarah he saw in her eyes the reflection of himself. He'd left behind his fears, his anger, all the baggage of his past. A different person had walked into that clearing from the one who had walked out. At some point in the past few minutes he had become a husband...a father...a man.

Epilogue

"Jackie, honey, you'd better grab a sweater before we go," Sarah yelled up the stairs to her daughter.

"Okay," Jackie called back.

Sarah squealed as strong arms grabbed her from behind. She leaned back against the firm body as masculine hands cupped her breasts and warm lips kissed the nape of her neck. "Hmm, if you want to continue in this vein, you'd better hurry. I'm expecting my husband home at any minute." She laughed as Reese growled in her ear.

She turned in his embrace, her lips finding his, as always amazed at the instant ignition of fire and passion. After six months of marriage their love, their desire for each other, had only grown stronger.

As his hands caressed down the length of her back, pressing her closer against him, she laughed and broke away from him. "Don't start something you can't finish, buster. We're supposed to be at Lindy and Ben's in half an hour."

Reese groaned. "What's more important? Going to dinner at Lindy and Ben's, or giving our daughter her wish of a little brother or sister?"

"This evening, dinner at Lindy and Ben's." She smiled and touched his cheek softly. "But later to-night..."

"I'm going to eat fast," he promised. "I'll just go change from my work clothes to my visiting clothes."

Sarah nodded, watching as he disappeared up the stairs. She smiled as she heard Jackie greet him, their voices teasing, filled with the love Sarah had once only dreamed about.

As she waited for them to finish getting ready, she drifted into the living room and sat down on the sofa, her heart filled with the kind of contentment she'd never dreamed she'd own.

Lindy was doing well under Dr. Westliner's care. He had placed her on a drug program that would never cure her illness but allowed her to live a more normal life. Lindy wanted to move to a small house in town. Ben had agreed to do whatever made Lindy happy. As a result Sarah was free to sell the farm. She and Lindy had agreed to put the money in trust for Jackie. Somehow Sarah knew Margaret Calhoun would approve. All she'd ever wanted was happiness for her two daughters.

In the past few months Sarah had gained a new respect for her brother-in-law. Ben had been by Lindy's side every step of the way and Sarah had never seen her sister looking happier or healthier.

Sarah and Reese had faced Suzanna only one more time—at the trial. She was now in a women's penitentiary, where she would be for some time to come.

Yes, the past six months had been eventful ones. Sarah stood up and wandered into the kitchen, staring out the back window to where a tire swing swayed in the spring breeze. Reese had hung the swing for Jackie.

She'd always known the potential for love that Reese had in his heart, a potential that had come to fruition in the last few months.

She turned as she heard footsteps behind her. Reese stood just inside the doorway, Jackie riding high on his shoulders. ''All set?''

''All set.'' For a moment Sarah didn't move, she just stood and smiled at the two people who held her heart.

''What?'' Reese looked at her curiously. ''Is my hair messed up or something?''

''No,'' Jackie scoffed, rubbing her hands over his hair. ''I combed it and it's perfect.''

''You're both perfect,'' Sarah said with a laugh.

''Daddy says we have to eat our supper real fast,'' Jackie said as they headed out the door. ''He says we have to eat real fast so you and Daddy can come home and talk about getting me a new baby sister or brother.''

Reese grinned at her, his eyes promising things that made Sarah shiver in delicious anticipation. ''And if we don't talk about it well enough tonight, then we'll talk about it tomorrow night…and the next night…''

''Reese.'' Sarah laughed, feeling a blush sweeping up her neck.

He grinned and captured her hand in his as they began the three-block walk toward Lindy and Ben's place. Sarah squeezed his fingers gently and felt a responding pressure from him. She looked at him and knew he shared her happiness, the utter joy of the three of them together. ''Have I told you today that I love you?'' he asked her suddenly.

''Hmm, if you have it still wouldn't hurt to hear it again.''

"I love you, Sarah Walker. Today and always."

"And I love you, Reese. Forever and always."

"Hey, are you guys making my little brother or sister right now?" Jackie asked curiously.

Reese laughed and looked at Sarah. "Not yet, little squirrel," he said. He squeezed Sarah's fingers once again and his loving gaze reached inside her and wrapped around her heart. His eyes were filled with not only the promise of the nighttime to come, but the promise of a lifetime.

* * * * *

SILHOUETTE
INTRIGUE™

AVAILABLE FROM 17TH AUGUST 2001

SAFE BY HIS SIDE Debra Webb

No-one could find special agent Jack Raine if he didn't want to be found. So how did a beautiful amnesiac end up on his doorstep with a killer close on her heels? 'Kate' couldn't remember her own name but she wanted Jack the moment she saw him—a man her flashes of memory suggested she might have been sent to capture…

THE BODYGUARD'S ASSIGNMENT Amanda Stevens

Texas Confidential

When Brady Morgan had to protect beautiful witness Grace Drummond until she testified, their passionate past came back to haunt him. Grace was desperate to avoid testifying, but could she trust Brady with the reason? With a killer on their trail and desire boiling beneath the surface, Brady would need all his expertise to keep Grace alive—and in his arms…

AMANDA'S CHILD Rebecca York

43 Light Street

Amanda Barnwell had no choice but to trust her handsome kidnapper, Matt Forester. He swore he was *saving* her from the family of the sperm-donor who had fathered her unborn child—a family who would stop at nothing to claim the baby, including eliminating Amanda. But was Matt telling the truth?

JUST ONE LOOK Mary McBride

Coming around after being attacked, the first person Sara Campbell saw was detective Joe Decker. Sara was the one living witness to a killer's face, *if only she could remember!* Which meant this rugged cop had to protect her from danger…*all day and all night!*

08

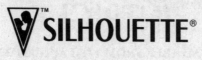

FREE!

2 Books
and a surprise gift!

We would like to take this opportunity to thank you for reading this Silhouette® book by offering you the chance to take TWO more specially selected titles from the Intrigue™ series absolutely FREE! We're also making this offer to introduce you to the benefits of the Reader Service™ —

- ★ FREE home delivery
- ★ FREE gifts and competitions
- ★ FREE monthly Newsletter
- ★ Books available before they're in the shops
- ★ Exclusive Reader Service discounts

Accepting these FREE books and gift places you under no obligation to buy; you may cancel at any time, even after receiving your free shipment. Simply complete your details below and return the entire page to the address below. *You don't even need a stamp!*

YES! Please send me 2 free Intrigue books and a surprise gift. I understand that unless you hear from me, I will receive 4 superb new titles every month for just £2.80 each, postage and packing free. I am under no obligation to purchase any books and may cancel my subscription at any time. The free books and gift will be mine to keep in any case.

I1ZEB

Ms/Mrs/Miss/Mr ....Initials...
                                                                                    BLOCK CAPITALS PLEASE

Surname ....

Address...

....

....Postcode ....

Send this whole page to:
UK: The Reader Service, FREEPOST CN81, Croydon, CR9 3WZ
EIRE: The Reader Service, PO Box 4546, Kilcock, County Kildare (stamp required)

Offer not valid to current Reader Service subscribers to this series. We reserve the right to refuse an application and applicants must be aged 18 years or over. Only one application per household. Terms and prices subject to change without notice. Offer expires 28th February 2002. As a result of this application, you may receive offers from other carefully selected companies. If you would prefer not to share in this opportunity please write to The Data Manager at the address above.

Silhouette® is a registered trademark used under license.
Sensation ™ is being used as a trademark.